MW01492187

SUCH
SHELTERED
LIVES

SUCH SHELTERED LIVES

A Novel

ALYSSA SHEINMEL

EMILY BESTLER BOOKS

ATRIA

New York   Amsterdam/Antwerp   London
Toronto   Sydney/Melbourne   New Delhi

EMILY
BESTLER
BOOKS

ATRIA

An Imprint of Simon & Schuster, LLC
1230 Avenue of the Americas
New York, NY 10020

This book is a work of fiction. Any references to historical events, real people, or real places are used fictitiously. Other names, characters, places, and events are products of the author's imagination, and any resemblance to actual events or places or persons, living or dead, is entirely coincidental.

First Emily Bestler Books/Atria Books hardcover edition January 2026

EMILY BESTLER BOOKS/ATRIA BOOKS and colophon
are trademarks of Simon & Schuster, LLC

Simon & Schuster strongly believes in freedom of expression and stands against censorship in all its forms. For more information, visit BooksBelong.com.

For information about special discounts for bulk purchases, please contact Simon & Schuster Special Sales at 1-866-506-1949 or business@simonandschuster.com.

The Simon & Schuster Speakers Bureau can bring authors to your live event. For more information or to book an event, contact the Simon & Schuster Speakers Bureau at 1-866-248-3049 or visit our website at www.simonspeakers.com.

Interior design by Laura Levatino

Manufactured in the United States of America

10 9 8 7 6 5 4 3 2 1

Library of Congress Control Number: LCCN

ISBN 978-1-6680-8400-7
ISBN 978-1-6680-8402-1 (ebook)

Let's stay in touch! Scan here to get book recommendations, exclusive offers, and more delivered to your inbox.

SUCH SHELTERED LIVES

The Coroner

The body will be shipped back to its family. A shame, the coroner thinks; the body belonged to a person who had been young—relatively young—and beautiful.

So much life left to live, people might say. *Taken too soon.*

Most of the time, the coroner deals with elderly bodies: skin lined with wrinkles, marked by scars from surgeries and injuries and the bumps and bruises accumulated over a lifetime, the sort that never entirely fade.

Despite its relative youth, *this* body is mangled nearly as badly as those older ones, its skin scattered with remnants of the aches and pains it endured in life. The coroner surveys each blemish carefully, noting which are recent and which are from months, even years ago. Every line on the body is a clue. The family will want an explanation; when someone dies like this—unexpectedly, needlessly—there are so many questions.

Over the years, the coroner has told himself that his is an honorable job, that giving a family answers helps them accept the loss of their loved one. But now, for the first time in his long career, he wonders how much the answer itself matters. After all, he need only give the family *some* reason. Just last week, he prepared the body of a seventy-four-year-old woman for burial. She'd had metastatic breast cancer, though the true cause of her death may have been any number of contributing factors: According to her family, she'd been on high doses of painkillers for weeks and had all but stopped eating months ago, barely taking even sips of water. Still, he'd recorded her cause of death as *cancer*.

Would it have given the family more peace if he'd discovered that the true cause was dehydration? If he'd told them that the painkillers their beloved had taken for relief in fact hurried her demise? Or would it have been a burden to know that if only they'd forced more water down her throat, curbed her pain pills, their mother, or wife, or grandmother (depending on who'd been managing her care; the coroner doesn't know) might have lived a little bit longer?

Absently, he fingers his phone in his jacket pocket, wondering when it might ring again. It's cool inside the morgue, but his palms are sweating. It's hard work, conducting an autopsy: sawing open a body, lifting the organs one by one.

He finds it easier to think of his subjects as *bodies* than people. Some might consider him insensitive or cold, but he thinks it's simply fair this way. He treats each patient exactly the same, no matter their background. After all, they say death is the great equalizer, coming to the rich and poor alike.

He brushes the body's hair away from its face. He cleans beneath its fingernails, bitten to the quick. Perhaps this may begin happening more often, given the goings-on at the nearby recovery center. *This* being finding younger bodies on his table, troubled people meeting an untimely end. People don't go to a place like that because they're *healthy*. They don't go there because the rest of the world has been a safe place.

The center, the coronor knows, promises its guests the utmost discretion, but he and his neighbors will certainly be able to find out which Wall Street scion or Hollywood celebrity is taking up residence at any given time. His daughter works on the ferry, saving for her college fund, so he knows the island's arrivals and departures better than most.

He thinks it's fitting that the center is on Shelter Island, where his family has lived for multiple generations. He's always found the island's name comforting, conjuring images of a port against the storm, barricades against invaders, safety when the earth tilts off its axis, isolation from the noise and madness of the outside world. He understands why so many millionaires have chosen this small stretch of land for their lavish vacation homes. Many locals resent the summer people who take over the island each year, but as far as the coroner is concerned, the occasional crowds are a small price to pay for living in paradise.

He eyes the bluish cast around the body's fingertips. All the money in the world can't protect the wealthy from their own bodies, as vulnerable to the elements as anyone else's.

The coroner estimates the time of death to a narrow window—one hour, perhaps two. It will be a week before he receives the results of the tox screen, but he can suggest a cause of death without it. There are so many ways for even a young, healthy body to die: blunt force trauma, overdose, accident, hypothermia. There's even such a thing as death by misadventure. He looks at the body's blue knuckles and writes one word on his form: *exposure*.

Now, he must prepare the body for its journey home, shut tight in a casket for the flight. The family might hire another examiner—some expensive city type, no doubt—to verify his findings. Should someone else come to a different conclusion, the coroner might be questioned, but he won't be blamed. He's small-town, after all, accustomed to preparing bodies for burial, not investigation. No elite practitioner, charging, he imagines, more for one examination than the coroner makes in a year, would question his incompetence. It would merely confirm the wealthy's confidence in their wealth. Someone else might get into trouble, but not him.

The coroner is not a religious man, but he finds himself offering up a small prayer, wishing the body more comfort in death than it, apparently, found in life.

ENTERTAINMENT
EXTRA

ROCK AND ROLL'S BAD GIRL STRIKES BACK—LITERALLY!

Grammy's Best New Artist, Joni Jewell, recovering after attack, promises not to cancel tour: "The show must go on." Fans rally as Joni's tickets sell out in record time. Full story inside!

NepoBabiesRUs.com

Scott Harris's Daughter Wasting Away (Again!)

Looks like another stint "in treatment" for ABH. But is it really an eating disorder, or has she moved on to drugs—just like Mom?

 @ dismoi • August 19, 2024

Dunderhead Duke Parties All Night Long in the Hamptons.

Lord Eddie says a totaled Porsche and some damage to his leg is a small price to pay for the party of the summer. (DD's companion is under a doctor's care.)

1

Amelia Blue

L et me tell you what I know.

I know how many calories are in a serving of fat-free Greek yogurt (eighty) and how many are in the three frozen strawberries I chop and mix into it (six each; eighteen total). I know precisely how many miles there are between our house in Laurel Canyon and LAX (17.9), and approximately how many minutes it will take to get there (never under an hour, unless I'm taking a very early morning flight). I know the date of my father's death (December 8, 2001) and the time (4:17 in the morning), but I didn't know it before the general public. (I was only five at the time, and my mother waited days to tell me. By then I'd seen Dad's face plastered on the cover of magazines beneath headlines I couldn't read but could tell were nothing good.)

I know my grandmother's old landline by heart (914-555-0654) even though she hasn't lived in her East Coast apartment since January 30, 2002, when it became apparent that my mother was ill-equipped to raise me by herself. I know that my grandmother has never arrived at an airport less than two hours before her flight was scheduled to take off and that my mother has never arrived more than twenty minutes before her scheduled departure, not even if we lied to her about the time, hoping to get her there earlier. I know my mother's Social Security number and that my father's suicide note was dated two days before he went through with taking the drugs that ended his life. I know that particular fact not because anyone told me but because my mother posted the letter to her Myspace account two years after my father died for the whole world to see (Myspace being all the rage at the time), and eventually the whole world included me. There are, by my count, approximately seventy-seven conspiracy theories suggesting that my mother murdered my father, and that the date on the note somehow proves it. Personally I think my dad was so out of it by then that he didn't know what day of the week it was, let alone the actual date. I suppose it's strange that he dated his suicide note at all, but apparently Dad dated everything. Here's another number I know: In 2021, some billionaire bought a page of Dad's lyrics dated March 3, 1993, for five hundred thousand dollars from a fan who'd swiped Dad's notepad from his dressing room after a concert.

Right now, I know that my flight (American 29) is scheduled for take-off at 6:11 a.m. from LAX for a 3:02 p.m. arrival at JFK. Which means it is precisely 4:11 a.m. when my grandmother (Naomi) drops me off at the airport. Traffic is light, and the drive takes fifty-nine minutes; it's hard to say whether the other drivers on the road are early risers or still awake from the night before.

"You sure you don't want me to walk you to the gate?" Naomi asks. "I could park the car."

"You're not allowed past security."

"I could get permission."

They let her walk me to the gate when I was small, flying to meet my mother while she crisscrossed the country, ostensibly to work, though it looked to me like a prolonged party, stretching from sea to shining sea. Back then, I was an unaccompanied minor, often the first person to board. Naomi would hug me tight, and I'd walk up the Jetway alone.

When it was time to send me back home, my mother and I would arrive at the gate panting, winded, having begged someone or other to hold the plane for me, always certain they'd make an exception for her, for *Georgia Blue*, whose face they'd seen on magazine covers and posters and late-night talk shows. There was never time for hugs or kisses goodbye. Sometimes I wondered whether she made us late on purpose so she had an excuse not to hug me, like I was a child made of spikes, like she already knew I would become all bones and angles, not at all pleasant for a parent to hold.

All of this to say, another thing I know is how to navigate an airport. "I'll be fine," I tell my grandmother now.

I merely have to get from the curb to the gate in a timely manner. Then, sit in my assigned seat, where someone will tell me when it's time to fasten my seat belt, time to drink, when it's safe to stand, when it's safe to leave. If there's a delay, it's not my fault, and if we're early, it isn't because I did something right.

"And it has to be *this* place?" Naomi asks for the hundredth time. "There are dozens of other places that specialize—"

"I've been to those places," I interrupt, also for the hundredth time. "They haven't helped."

Naomi sniffs, and I hear the words she isn't saying, ghosts of arguments we've already had.

"You agreed this was the right choice."

"I agreed that you needed to go back into treatment. You insisted it be there."

In fact, I refused to consider anyplace else. I felt guilty for practically blackmailing my grandmother, but it was the only way I could get her to go to the bank and secure the funds from my trust to finance my stay.

"The best care money could buy. Even Georgia said so, remember?" I say. "They must have something all those other places don't."

Naomi nods, not because she agrees, but because this part of the conversation is over. We're at the airport; the tickets have been purchased, my spot secured: I'm going. She gets out of the car to hug me goodbye. "So skinny," she says, her fingers digging into my ribs like she's checking to make sure they're each still there. "You packed warm clothes?"

It's such a normal question that for a split second I believe that I'm magically leaving for college or grad school all over again. "Of course," I promise. I spread out my arms, indicating the oversize cable-knit cardigan I'm wearing even though the average high temperature in LA in January is sixty-six degrees. (Another thing I know.)

"Are you sure you don't want me to arrange a car to take you from the airport to Shelter Island?"

Shelter Island. The name should be comforting, but instead it makes me picture stormy waters and pursuing pirates. Things from which you seek shelter, not shelter itself.

"I don't mind the train," I assure her. I lift my bag over my shoulder and walk into the terminal.

~

Inside, I'm hit by an onslaught of smells: cheap food, cinnamon chewing gum, bare feet, anxious sweat. I hear children crying, businesspeople taking meetings on their cellphones, metal detectors beeping in protest, change being emptied from pockets. When I was little, I loved airports. Everyone at the airport, it seemed to me, was on their own private mission: checking their bags, getting through security, racing to make it to their gate on time. The people who work at airports wear uniforms with nametags fastened to their chest or on lanyards around their neck; they manage to look at once harried and bored. I used to play at distinguishing the business travelers from the vacationers, the people who are leaving home from the ones returning.

Today, when I reach the gate, I curl into a rubbery chair, circling my left wrist with the fingers of my right hand, pleased that I can do it pinkie finger to thumb, fitting like a loose bracelet. My phone buzzes with a text.

Abby, I'm getting worried. I clear the screen before I can read the rest of the message, before my heart can feel warm at the nickname Jonah gave me. (I really should block his number.)

I stand and pace. Moving burns calories, and there will be no choice but to keep (mostly) still on the plane. The next several hours of my life are literally mapped out, west to east: just under six hours to JFK, two hours on the train to Bridgehampton, followed by forty minutes in a car including ten on a ferry. It'll be long past dusk by the time I get where I'm going. This time of year, the days are short. Shelter Island is so far east that the sun there sets nearly fifteen minutes earlier than it does in Manhattan.

When they board us, I'm the last person to take her seat. My mother used to say, *Celebrities board last. We'd hold up the line with people stopping to gawk at us.* Not that I'm a celebrity. No one on the plane seems to recognize me, and why should they? It's mostly my name that's famous, not my face. And that's only to an ever-shrinking group of fans.

But if you're a certain age and like a certain kind of music, you've heard the stories. You know (because the press said so) that I was addicted to heroin when I was born in 1996. Maybe you read the tabloid articles "reporting" that I was kept in the hospital following my birth because I was going through withdrawal. They said that CPS came and refused to release me to my parents' care. They said my dad (Scott Harris, bass-playing Gen X god) paid off the agents who were supposed to keep me safe. They said it was disgusting that government employees would prioritize money and fame over a helpless child's welfare, and my birth story turned into a warning tale about government corruption. Meanwhile, I was (apparently) home with my parents, and my grandmother had taken charge (Naomi moved herself in until I was six months old), so I was fed and diapered and sleep-trained and whatever else you do with infants. If I'd gone through withdrawal, I certainly didn't know it.

When I was thirteen years old, I asked Naomi what really happened and she said the press exaggerated to sell papers, which isn't exactly a denial. I didn't bother asking my mother. (You know what they say: *How can you tell if an addict is lying? Their lips are moving.*)

The flight attendants walk the aisles to offer drinks, pretzels, stale cookies. The person sitting beside me pulls a paper bag from beneath the seat in front of him: McDonald's. I haven't eaten McDonald's for years, but the smell is so familiar it's like I'm five years old again. My seatmate rips his ketchup packets open with his teeth. I feel like sugar is entering my bloodstream through osmosis.

I root through my bag until I find a piece of gum. No minty freshness for me: I prefer watermelon, orange, strawberry, flavors made from artificial sweeteners packaged in colors that don't exist in nature. It's almost enough to overpower the scent of soggy french fries and overcooked meat. I chew so hard my jaw aches, trying to distract myself from the twist of hunger in my belly.

Six hours later, I watch pale winter sun glint off New York City's skyscrapers as the plane turns east toward JFK. I close my eyes, trying to imagine Manhattan in the early nineties, Georgia traipsing down one or another city block with her bad dye job, dark roots pulled into a greasy bun. Something else I know: The expression *jonesing* comes from Great Jones Street, because it's where dealers used to hang out. Now there are million-dollar condos on the same corners where my mother scored her first highs.

By the time I was old enough to notice, Georgia's celebrity was fading. Still, she always found a way to keep the world paying attention. So many times, I almost told her that *I* was paying attention, but I knew there was no point. One little girl's focus is nothing compared with the whole damn world.

For as long as I can remember, I knew that my mother was a drunk and a drug addict, too interested in her substances to spend time with her daughter, so interested that she found a way to score, time and again, even at rehab. That's what the tabloids said, the industry insiders, her manager, even her mother. It's what I would've said, too, had anyone asked me.

I squeeze my right wrist with the thumb and forefinger of my opposite hand until it feels like my bones are protesting against my grip, as if to say, *Don't you know you can't make your* bones *shrink like you can the rest of you?*

No, I want to tell my bones. *I don't know anything anymore.*

2

Lord Edward

I'm late to meet my sister for lunch. Each step I take through Midtown Manhattan is agony. The restaurant is only a block away, but I might as well be heading to China for all the progress I'm making.

I picture Anne waiting for me, her long brown hair coiled neatly into a bun at the nape of her neck. She's wearing a woolen blazer over pleated trousers, a belt cinched at the waist, a tailored white blouse, no wrinkles. She studies the menu, her face placid, her expression giving nothing away. Strangers wouldn't know how angry she is at her little brother's tardiness, wouldn't recognize how she works her jaw when she's annoyed, the way her pale white skin flushes pink. She's pretending she can't hear the people at the adjacent table staring, whispering, gasping.

Can it really be her?

What's she doing in the States?

Didn't you hear they sent the brother to school here?

Oh, that's right. I read he got kicked out of Eton.

That was years ago, I want to tell them. Since then, I've also been kicked out of Columbia.

Did they kick me out, or did I drop out? My leg hurts so much that I can't concentrate enough to recall. It doesn't matter. The result is the same. Lady Anne's good-for-nothing, undereducated baby brother, well into his twenties now, and utterly useless.

Anne studies the menu like it's a thousand-page novel, though she would never waste time reading fiction. *Frivolous,* I can hear her say, voice dripping with disapproval. Our mother's favorite book was *Wuthering Heights,* one of the few facts I know about her, and that only because it's a running joke between Anne and our father, who took it as proof of the former duchess's foolish romanticism. When I was a teenager, curious what all the fuss was about, I tried reading the novel myself. It didn't strike me as a romance so much as a cautionary tale.

Anne taps her fingers against the table, a subtle but sure sign that she's furious. Outside, I crumple to the ground, right in the middle of East Fifty-Seventh Street, but no one offers to help. Everyone is looking at me and I want to scream at them to fuck right off. They have their phones out, they're taking photos, recording videos. There's the sound of brakes screeching in the distance, and everyone starts to run, leaving me in a heap on the sidewalk, an out-of-control car coming straight toward me. I hear the crowd screaming for the car to stop, but it only moves faster, as though the driver mistook the accelerator for the brake pedal.

"Please fasten your seat belt, sir. The plane will be landing soon."

I open my eyes, shaking myself awake. I'm not in Midtown. I'm not in New York City. I'm not on the earth at all. I left London this morning, flew to JFK, then boarded a small private plane to East Hampton. Anne wouldn't let me go back to my apartment in Tribeca. She said everything I need will be waiting for me when I arrive. Anne believes she knows what I need, whether or not it's what I want.

I rub my left leg, digging the heel of my palm into my thigh until it aches. Aches *more*. It already hurt. It always hurts.

"I have to use the bathroom first," I say, and the attendant nods obligingly, walking away briskly in high heels, her gait easy and sure. She tucks an absent strand of blond hair behind her right ear.

I make my way to the back of the plane. Bringing a water bottle would've been too obvious, so I use water from the tap; it tastes sour. I wait a few moments and then flush, in case the attendant is listening.

It's not true that painkillers eliminate pain. They only make it seem far away, as if it's happening to someone else and you have no choice but to watch.

3

Florence

My ears hurt like they're gonna explode. I chew the gum Callie gave me before she left me at the airport—like a care package is enough to make up for sending me to the middle of nowhere—until my teeth ache, but it makes no difference. The plane dips, and I clutch the armrest, the guitar-string scars on my fingers turning even whiter than usual.

It's for your own good, Callie said. Like she's the authority on good versus bad. Really, she knew I couldn't argue, because she's the only person who hasn't abandoned me. Sometimes I want to remind her that *she* works for *me*, not the other way around. But then, everyone else who worked for me left no matter what I promised them, and not always peacefully. An old assistant threatened to leak stories to the press if I didn't agree to his exorbitant demands, which he called a "severance package." Callie said it was my fault for not making him sign an NDA before I hired him.

I make a mental list of my heroes: Janis Joplin, Stevie Nicks, Carrie Fisher, Jimi Hendrix, Jim Morrison, Kurt Cobain, Scott Harris. Stars and geniuses, every one of them. Every single one of them a troublemaker. And yes, every single one of them used drugs.

Only some of them died from it. For the rest, it was a rite of passage, just part of being a star.

That could be a song. "Rite of Passage." Angry guitar riff over a pretty melody. My voice, the one *Rolling Stone* once called "almost as shrill as Yoko Ono's," screaming the lyrics. They panned our first album, but I had the review framed.

Call me shrill?

On the second album, I went even higher-pitched.

Rite of passage.
What's your damage?
Everybody's going to rehab.
I'm gonna be a star.

Fuck that. I already *am* a star.

Carly Simon came up with her "clouds in my coffee" lyric on a plane, though I don't think she used drugs, at least not enough to make headlines. I release the armrest long enough to scribble the words into my notebook. I could sing it like it rhymes even though it doesn't.

Lazy, the Janis Joplin in my head accuses.

You need to do better, my mental Scott Harris agrees.

I've been hearing their voices for as long as I can remember. Every time someone died, they were added to the chorus. Not sure if I'm haunted, clairvoyant, or crazy.

I toss my notebook onto the empty seat beside me. Callie booked two seats. She knows I like to spread out. Plus the only way to avoid checking my guitar is to buy it a seat.

Two seats in first class. Not bad for a working-class Jewish girl who didn't set foot on a plane until she ran away from home at eighteen. I paid for the ticket with money from Mom's sock drawer. She never acknowledged the fact that I left a note promising to give it back, with interest. Back then, I flew coach.

The lyricism of Joni Mitchell paired with the barbaric yawp of the Sex Pistols.

That's from the *Stone*'s review of our second album.

Anyhow, the point is, plenty of stars get shipped off for talk therapy and group therapy and arts therapy and even electroshock therapy.

Callie said this wasn't that kind of place. But Callie doesn't know that these places are all the same.

These places have given me dozens of labels over the years: alcoholic, addict, borderline, narcissist, bipolar, postpartum.

I put enormous black sunglasses on before exiting the plane. Callie chose the red-eye, thinking a 6:00 a.m. arrival might protect me from the press, and she was right. The only person waiting for me at baggage claim is a man in a suit who recognizes me on sight.

There was a time when the paps would've woken up with dawn to catch a glimpse of me.

"Ms. Bloom?" I can't remember the last time anyone called me that— so polite, so professional. "I'll be escorting you to Rush's Recovery."

He says it like it's the name of a five-star hotel, not a mental-health facility. I keep my sunglasses on as he leads the way to the parking lot. He takes my phone from my hand before helping me into the car, then pockets it like he thinks I'm not going to notice that he didn't give it back.

What the fuck? Callie said I'd be able to keep my phone.

The car is a shiny black Range Rover with windows tinted so dark that I wonder how the driver can see through them. I didn't even know what a Range Rover was when I was a kid. Like, I'd literally never heard of that kind of car.

I don't ask the driver his name. I'm not being rude; it's just that I never know how to act in situations like this. Would it be weird to introduce myself? People who were born with money are probably also born knowing these kinds of things. But no one teaches you the etiquette when you make your own way in the world.

There's bottled water in the back seat, and that's in *glass* bottles, not plastic. Swiss chocolate in a pretty little box tied with a bow and the nameless driver explaining that of course it's nut-free, like that's supposed to make me feel safe and sound, well taken care of—pampered instead of put away.

I look out the dim back window as we drive east, watching the sunrise, pretty even over the streets of Queens in the dead of winter. It's so cold here that the bare branches on the trees lining the roadway are covered in ice.

When Callie told me this place was in the Hamptons, she'd widened her eyes like she thought she could trick me into believing this was all so glamorous. Even I know that no one who's anyone goes to the Hamptons in fucking *January*.

The first time I ran away—money from Mom's sock drawer, a guitar, and a seat in coach—I wanted to be found. *Discovered*, like I was a new

world and everyone else was an explorer who didn't know they were looking for me yet, like Columbus discovering America even though he was
looking for India.

It's been years since all those explorers mined my silver and gold, leaving me spent and hollow. Now, I'm running to Shelter Island to hide.

Do they think I'm seeking shelter or that they're sheltering the rest of
the world from me?

4

Florence

Pretty soon I get carsick from the winding roads, followed by a bumpy ferry ride, followed by even more winding roads. The streets here are narrow and crowded with trees, their bare branches touching overhead. I don't know how many turns we've made since we got off the ferry. I think about Hansel and Gretel, leaving a trail of crumbs in the forest so they could find their way home.

I lean my head against the cool glass window. Half the houses we pass are fancy mansions behind gates and long driveways, the other half clapboard ranches in various degrees of disrepair, so that one yard after another starts looking like a mismatched set of teeth: one large, one small, one jagged and cracked.

Gentrification, my kid would say, smart like that.

"You're not supposed to take my phone," I say to the driver finally. That's what Callie said. *It's not that kind of place.*

"Don't worry," the driver assures me. "You can discuss everything with your care manager."

Care manager? Not therapist, or doctor, or counselor? The word *manager* makes it sound like this is some kind of business deal.

I check the time on the Range Rover's console; it's just after 9:00 a.m. The driver makes a sharp right turn, and I gasp because I think we're about to run headlong into a wrought iron gate, but it swings open at the last second. Motion sensors, I guess, or maybe there's some hidden person controlling who gets in and out. The driveway is so long that it seems to go on forever, surrounded by bare hedges that look less like topiaries than twisted chains. I try to roll down my window, but apparently the driver controls it, not me.

The car bounces as the road shifts from asphalt to gravel. In the murky morning light, I make out a series of square-shaped buildings with sharp edges, the sort of modern architecture you'd expect in Malibu. The driver stops in front of one of the glass boxes. A bright white dusting of snow frames the building so perfectly it's like someone swept it into place with a broom. (Maybe someone did.) I have to wait for the driver to let me out—like the windows, the doors are set with a child lock, trapping me in the back seat. If the car caught fire, would the driver remember to release the locks before jumping out? There's a reason those locks were designed for parents—only a parent would stop to free their child before saving themselves.

A woman walks out the front door and down a set of broad, shallow steps to the driveway. She's wearing black wide-leg pants and a crisp white blouse; the only nod to the fact that it's wintertime is a camel-colored scarf wrapped around her neck. Her ice-blond hair is pulled back into a slick ponytail with a few pieces pulled out artfully around her pale white face, and she wants you to believe she's not wearing a stitch of makeup, but I can tell that she's got on foundation and blush. She isn't wearing any rings, no necklace. Tiny little diamond studs in her ears. I don't have to wonder whether they're real.

"Good morning, Florence." She says my name like we're old friends. "I'm Dr. Evelyn—"

"Hi, Evelyn," I say, cutting her off. I'm not about to call her Dr. So-and-So when she came out and called me Florence without asking. She pronounced it like *Eee*velyn, and I'm tempted to say *Eh*velyn just to annoy her.

She looks momentarily flustered but recovers smoothly, extending her hand for me to shake. "Welcome to Rush's Recovery." She says it like I'm an honored guest, which—at these prices—I ought to be. Callie promised I could afford it. This particular center is for particularly rich people, but really all of these places are for people with some degree of privilege—most aren't covered by insurance or, even if they are, not completely. Why do you think you hear so many stories about celebrities in rehab? We're among the lucky few who can afford to go back over and over again.

"I'll be your care manager while you're here with us. Let me show you around your cottage." She gestures to the building behind her without breaking eye contact. I'm not sure she's blinked once since I arrived. Even robots are programmed to blink so that they'll look human.

"Cottage?" I echo. There's nothing cottagey about it. For starters, it's huge, as big as the sort of house I would've called a mansion as a kid. (Before I found out what real mansions were.) Cottages are made of wood and stone with thatched roofs—at least the ones in the movies are. This whole building is a window, with exposed iron beams holding it together, framed by towering pine trees. The trees give the impression of being hidden while the gleaming glass walls make the place seem fragile and exposed.

Over the years, I've learned that rich people like to give their expensive belongings playful names, like calling the 2,000-square-foot guest house in their backyard their "shed," or calling their $150,000 vintage Bronco their "knock-around car," as though being poor is a charming affectation.

"That entire building is for me?" I ask.

"We respect your privacy here," Eeevelyn says, and I almost laugh. It's been years since anyone's respected my privacy, least of all at places like this, where I'm expected to share my deepest, darkest secrets and fears.

"But not to worry, Florence." She says my name again, as if to remind me of it. "I'll be available to you at any hour for the duration of your time here."

Time here is rehab-speak for *treatment*, but the only *treatment* I need is a quiet place where the paparazzi can't find me.

I wonder if Eeevelyn has heard Joni Jewell's latest hit, the one everyone knows is about me though she never says my name; it's oh so very *wink wink, hush hush*. The tune might be in Evelyn's head right now. It's nothing if not catchy; I have to give Joni credit for that. *Billboard* said it was full of *sonic surprises*.

Joni Jewell. God, I hate that girl's name. And it's her real name, too, I checked. I can still hear her nonthreatening little girl voice telling some interviewer that her parents named her after Joni Mitchell because they always knew she was going to be a songwriter. Her parents didn't give her a name they thought would look good on college applications and résumés, determined for her to end up as a banker or a lawyer, the sort of secure job that comes with a pension plan and a 401(k). The whole family moved to LA when she was fifteen, driving in their van cross-country like the fucking Partridge family.

No one ever called Joni Jewell *shrill*. Natural blond (unlike Evelyn; I can tell from years of dyeing my own hair, there's gray underneath her perfect highlights), skinny as a rail, perfect little double-A chest that doesn't need a bra, not one hair out of place, brown eyes so big and round she looks like a cartoon character.

She couldn't put a foot wrong if she tried.
So I walked all over her.

I reach for my notebook, but realize I left it in the car. My hands itch. I shiver, watching the steam of my hot breath hit the cold air. It was sixty degrees when I left LA last night, but I wore a fur coat on the plane. I bought it after our second album went gold. My kid hates this coat, animal cruelty and all that.

I run back to the car and grab my notebook from the back seat, scribbling the lyrics fast, like if I have to hold them in much longer, I'll be sick.

I walked all over her.

Even as I write it, I know I'll never turn it into a song, because it's a lie. If anyone's getting stomped on, it's me.

Callie said it all might have blown over if I hadn't threatened her. (Joni, not Callie. I never threaten Callie except threatening to fire her—an empty threat since we both know I can't. No one else will have me now.)

Drop off the grid until the Joni Jewell mess blows over, she said. *Wait a week or two, and some other starlet will offend someone, and no one will even remember what "Get Her Back" is about.*

"Let me show you inside." Evelyn leads the way up the stairs and into the cottage. The back wall is made of the same floor-to-ceiling windows, with ocean views as far as the eye can see. I know I'm supposed to *ooh* and *aahh*, but the sea looks gray and angry, waves tossing in the wind. What's the point of a house with glass walls, so easy to see into, so easy to break?

I swallow a sigh. Joni Jewell is currently on a twenty-city tour across America, and every night, her finale is "Get Her Back." There are videos of her performances all over the internet like the algorithms themselves are promoting her. Her record label is paying for security detail to keep her safe from me.

It's an easy story for the press to sell, tale as old as time and all that. The wrinkled crone and the good little girl. I'm the wicked witch to her Dorothy, the evil queen to her Snow White, the aging starlet to her ingenue.

Even when I was Joni's age, I was never what anyone called *sweet*.

5

Lord Edward

I close my eyes as we touch down, gritting my teeth when the small plane shudders on contact. There's a driver waiting for me on the tarmac of the tiny East Hampton airport beside a black Range Rover with dark windows.

"Sir," he begins. "I'm afraid there's been an accident."

The word *accident* conjures the sounds of screeching tires, twisting metal, and shattered glass, as though someone turned the volume up too loud. My head starts to pound.

"Lord Edward?" the driver prompts, looking at me expectantly.

"Oh no," I say finally. I try to look concerned. I must go too far, because the driver's face falls.

"Not that sort of accident," he explains quickly.

They should've sent him a list of words not to use around me: *accident, car, inheritance, leg.*

The driver's wearing a well-tailored dark suit and tie, his white collar starched and bright. He takes my bag from my hand—I do carry my own luggage, even if I don't always pack it myself—and leads the way to the Range Rover without missing a step. His gait is brisk and efficient.

I stuff my hands into the pockets of my overcoat. According to my phone, it's twenty-seven degrees, but it feels colder. The wind off the ocean, maybe, so much sharper than the wind rushing between skyscrapers in Manhattan, more than one hundred miles west of here.

Why can't you send me someplace in the city? I'd asked last month, my arms folded across my chest, standing lopsided beside Anne's desk in the drawing room. I wanted to sound authoritative and reasonable, but I felt like a little boy begging his parents to let him stay awake an hour after bedtime.

Anne scoffed when I referred to Manhattan as *the city* like a local, though I'd been living in Tribeca since being asked to leave Columbia's campus five years ago. I'm not sure, honestly, whether I still live there. The family might not let me go back.

Facilities in the city *could never guarantee your anonymity like this place.*

I couldn't argue, knowing the paps would hound me across New York City given the chance. But I wasn't about to let Anne know I agreed with her.

Don't they all guarantee anonymity? It's called Alcoholics Anonymous, *right?*

You can't go to AA meetings! Anne hissed. *How anonymous can it be when* anyone *is welcome to join?*

She sounded so much like Dad then that I laughed out loud, which only enraged her more.

Do you know how many celebrities and aristocrats have been helped by these people? No.

Exactly, she said. *Anyhow, I thought you'd feel more at home there.* She sounded so sweet that for a split second I thought she might actually mean it, but when I looked at her face, I could see she was trying not to smile. Sending me here—to this particular part of the world—is Anne's idea of a joke. *There isn't a more discreet center on the planet. Even when things go awry, no one finds out.*

Maybe nothing's ever gone wrong.

Anne scoffed, and I heard the words she didn't say: *With people like you getting sent there,* of course *things go wrong.*

Only Anne—and our father—would see a place's ability to conceal its fuckups as an asset.

"What kind of accident?" I ask the driver now, following him to the car.

"One of our guests got off at the wrong train station," he explains. He hasn't told me his name. People do that more often than you'd think, diminishing themselves because they think it's more comfortable to be waited on by a nameless person in a nondescript black suit than to acknowledge that the person opening your doors and carrying your luggage is a human being with a name and a home and a family.

Anne is careful to learn everyone's names, and the names of their spouses, their kids, their dogs. She says it's part of the job, and she is very good at her job.

The driver continues. "The guest exited the train at East Hampton rather than Bridgehampton, where a car was waiting for her. It's very cold outside, and unfortunately there's no indoor waiting area at the station—this area is more equipped for summer travelers than winter, as I'm sure you know."

He pauses so I can catch his meaning: The driver knows exactly how well I know the area. He knows when I was here last and what happened and why I've come back. At least, he knows the version Anne released to the public.

"So this guest, you see, we're so close now, though of course it's an unpleasant thing to have to ask—"

I realize I'm supposed to invite some stranger, some daft *idiot* who got off at the wrong station, to join me in my car.

I imagine the anonymity Anne held in such high regard vanishing into thin air.

"Of course." *The more the merrier,* Anne would say, and the driver wouldn't be able to sense the irritation behind her words. Anne is all smiles in public, no matter whether she's comforting a stranger in a hospital ward, attending a banquet after articles about our father's sexual peccadillos are splashed on the tabloids' front pages, or arranging yet another meeting about her troubled baby brother. I'm surely not the first member of my family to have an issue with alcohol, but I am the first for whom it's a problem rather than a charming personality quirk.

The driver beams. "I'm so glad you understand, sir." I can practically see him thinking that perhaps I'm more like my beloved sister than the rumors about me (selfish, spoiled, shallow) have led him to believe.

I get into the back seat, and the driver turns smoothly onto Highway 27.

The first time I came to the east end of Long Island was for the Hampton Classic the August I turned fourteen. In summer, the trees are bright with leaves, planted so thickly they join over the highway. At the time, I didn't notice the safety hazards: one-lane roads carved into the woods with no shoulder for idling cars. In the high season, the streets are packed with inexperienced city drivers speeding around town in expensive cars they rented for the summer. People who grew up in Manhattan are so used to taking cabs and subways that they barely know how to drive. And surely some of them, like me, grew up with security guards to drive them.

Now, it's January and the trees are bare. The streets are nearly empty without vacationers to crowd them. I look through the Rover's moon roof, gazing at the trees' bare branches stretching over the road like skeletons. It's hard to imagine they will ever be green with life again.

6

Amelia Blue

If I'd gotten off at the wrong station because I hadn't been paying attention, that would've been bad enough. But this is so much worse because I *was* paying attention. Someone else might have rented a car at the airport, driven themselves to Shelter Island, but not me—I don't drive. I was the only teenager in LA who didn't cherish her learner's permit, beg for her own car the instant she passed the driving test.

I stopped reading my book at Westhampton, knowing that after that came Hampton Bays, then Southampton, then Bridgehampton (where I was supposed to get off). I stood up, bag in hand, as the train slowed. But somehow I still missed the announcement that I was supposed to be in one of the first four cars to exit. (I was in the fifth car.) So now I'm shivering in the cold, waiting for someone to pick me up from the wrong station.

Toddlers can count to four, but not me. Add it to the list of things I can't do, the list of ways my body doesn't work like it's supposed to. I imagine dividing myself into pieces and packing them into boxes like I'm nothing but doll parts. I would send everything back to where it came from, the way you do with a dress that doesn't fit or jeans that won't button.

I stand firmly beneath the station's lone streetlamp. Everywhere else is pitch-dark: no other streetlamps, no oncoming headlights from down the street. I shudder as the light flickers, the fluorescent bulb buzzing as though it's filled not with chemicals but a swarm of bees.

The center promised that someone will be here as soon as possible.

I press my headphones to my ears, listening to the sort of music my mother would hate: Taylor Swift, the National, Bon Iver, music whose lyrics will make you cry if you listen too closely. Georgia used to say music stopped being worthwhile in the nineties, an era she never stopped trying to recapture: She kept wearing baby-doll dresses with Doc Martens and shooting up heroin well into the 2000s. As the former lead singer of the grunge band Shocking Pink (though mostly famous for being famous long before the Kardashians perfected that particular art), Georgia disdained squeaky-clean pop stars, stylists and makeup artists, sobriety coaches and promise rings and bare midriffs over low-rise designer jeans.

My phone buzzes with a fresh text, and I force my eyes open.

If I don't hear from you, I'm going to reach out to your grandmother. Just to make sure you're okay.

If Jonah contacted Naomi, I'd have to make up some version of events to explain why a stranger (to her, he would be a stranger) is asking after her granddaughter's well-being.

How would he even reach Naomi? I never gave him her number.

Then again, he always found a way to do everything he said he was going to do, like every word out of his mouth was a promise that couldn't be broken.

I blow on my hands until they're warm enough to write back: *I'm okay. I just need some space.*

I exhale when a black Range Rover pulls up in front of me, its windows tinted so that all I can see when I try to peer inside is my own reflection, my pale skin and frizzy hair, my chin jutting sharply. When the driver holds open the door for me, I practically dive into the light of the back seat.

It feels like I've been waiting a very long time—so much longer than a few minutes here at the station, a few hours on the plane, a few weeks while Naomi made the arrangements—to make it to Rush's Recovery.

I wonder whether Georgia felt that way when she arrived there.

7

Lord Edward

When we get to the train station in East Hampton, the sidewalk is empty except for a single person shivering in the cold. Even though it's winter, and we're in the bloody Northeastern United States, she's not wearing a coat, only a bulky gray sweater over a pair of black leggings. Sneakers instead of boots. I'd guess she was coming from someplace warm—Australia, maybe, Florida—but she's so pale it's hard to imagine her basking in the sunlight. It's dark enough that if it weren't for the streetlights, we might not have seen her at all.

The girl is tiny, and as far as I can tell, she's not wearing a stitch of makeup. The driver gets out and takes her bag—an oversize duffel slung over her shoulder—and puts it in the trunk. She doesn't so much walk as shuffle toward the car, her gait tight and compact. The driver opens the door, and she climbs into the SUV beside me. Close up, I can see faint lines peeking out from the corners of her eyes, one arch like a parenthesis on the left side of her mouth. Her skin is slightly loose over the bones of her face. I guess that she's older than I am, but still young, not yet thirty.

"Thanks," she says, her teeth chattering slightly, though she tries to control them. I'm not sure if she's talking to the driver or to me.

She takes earbuds from her ears and tucks them into her pocket, fastens her seat belt, then holds out a hand for me to shake. "Amelia Blue Harris," she offers, giving up any anonymity she might have retained in seven syllables. Her accent is American, with a slight West Coast drawl. I recognize her name; she's the late musician Scott Harris's daughter.

Amelia Blue Harris has hazel eyes and dark brown hair pulled into a messy bun on top of her head. When she smiles I see a crooked gap between her front teeth. I shake her hand but don't offer her my name. Normally, I don't have to. Her fingers are so cold that I find myself wanting to blow on them to warm her skin; the urge is so surprising that I drop her hand abruptly.

"Thanks again." She slouches in her seat, curled over herself like a teenager. "I'm sure you think I'm an idiot for getting off at the wrong station." Her teeth no longer chattering, she bites her lower lip. For a second, I think she's about to cry. Again, I'm struck by the instinct to reach out, rub her arm, to comfort her somehow.

"Not at all," I lie.

"They said it would take at least a half hour for another car to get here, and I was freezing. Did you come from someplace warm? Probably not, judging by your outfit. Or maybe you're just smarter than I am. Anyway, I'm probably not supposed to ask, right? I used to live on the East Coast, you'd think I'd know how to dress."

Dear god, she's bloody *chatty*. Mentally I calculate how long this drive together will be. I wedge the ankle of my left leg beneath the driver's seat just in front of me.

"Where are you from?" she continues. "I mean, your accent kind of gave you away, you must be British—"

She stops abruptly, and I know she's recognized me.

Anne pretends she cares about discretion, but what she really longs for is control. She'll leak the story—her wayward little brother in rehab—the next time she needs the press to turn a blind eye to one of Dad's unseemly acts.

Lord Eddie in a World of Hurt, the tabloids will shout. In the corner of the page will be some version of the headline they've been writing for years now—*Lady Mary Living the High Life*—alongside a picture of my mother at a cocktail party in Los Angeles or Majorca or Madrid. They never stopped calling her *Lady Mary,* even after Grandfather died and they ought to have called her the Duchess of Exeter. Of course, now she shouldn't be addressed with any honorific at all, having lost it in the divorce. I was only two when they split, far too young to understand what my mother was willing to give up to be free from the family.

Everything except the money, Anne would be quick to remind me. Mum received a handsome settlement in exchange for absenting herself from our lives.

"London," I answer Amelia Blue finally, though now that she's recognized me, she certainly already knows that. "I grew up in London." The third oldest private residence in London, in fact. When the family's not in town, they give tours to the public, pocketing the funds to put toward the property's upkeep, though of course the money's not nearly sufficient.

Amelia Blue's small hand disappears into her enormous handbag and digs around until it emerges clutching a pink pack of gum. She offers me a piece, but I shake my head. Anne and I weren't allowed to chew gum as children. For years I sought it out like other kids sneak cigarettes and alcohol. Gum was so gauche, so *American*. (Cigarettes and alcohol, Anne and I were given freely.)

I press the heel of my hand into my left thigh.

We drive past one mansion after another. In summer, these houses would be hidden behind elaborate landscaping, but this time of year, one can see through bare hedges up long, winding driveways.

"It's hard to imagine owning a home like this and only using it for a few weeks out of the year," Amelia says, the artificially sweet scent of her breath filling the back seat of the car.

I wonder if she realizes that in addition to the property in London, my family owns homes in Windsor, Edinburgh, and the Scottish Highlands, each larger than the mansions we're currently passing, and none lived in year-round. Technically, the family owns my apartment in Tribeca, too, though perhaps they've already sold it and the possibility of my return is a ruse Anne's using to keep me in line.

"No one who can afford it would be here this time of year," I point out. In the winter, they vacation in Switzerland or Aspen, the Caribbean or the South Pacific. Anne, her husband, and my nephews recently returned to London from Zermatt.

"Except for us," Amelia Blue points out.

I pretend to sleep for the rest of the drive—through the village of Sag Harbor, across the bridge to North Haven, onto the ferry that will take us to Shelter Island. Would Amelia Blue be surprised to learn that a bloke from London knows his way around, or has she heard about the time I spent here last summer?

The ferry sways in Long Island Sound, the current so choppy that it's hard to imagine that whoever named this particular body of water wasn't being ironic. Anne said that I wouldn't be able to run away from the recovery center like I did from Eton, from Choate, from Columbia. Where would I go, trapped on a small island surrounded by frigid water? She made my destination sound less like shelter than prison.

I find myself thinking, *Sirius Black escaped from Azkaban.*

Fiction, Anne would say disdainfully, *a children's story.*

The ferry rubs against plastic bumpers on either side as it pulls into port, groaning as though this is the last place on earth it wants to be.

Okay then, I imagine myself parrying, *the* real *criminal Frank Morris escaped from the* real *Alcatraz.*

Anne would point out that Frank Morris was a good deal more able-bodied than I am. Then she'd add, *Did you just call yourself a criminal?* pleased to have caught me in an accidental admission of guilt.

As though there's any denying what I've done.

8

Amelia Blue

Sitting next to Lord Edward is like being in the back seat with someone who isn't quite real, a person designed in a lab or dreamed up in a fairy tale. His light-brown hair falls across his forehead *just so*. His gray-blue eyes are narrowed slightly so I can tell that despite his good manners he isn't pleased to share his car with a stranger. After a few minutes in the car with me, he pretends (I think he's pretending) to sleep—exaggeratedly slumping his shoulders (otherwise, he has perfect posture) and trying to stretch his legs, his feet wedged awkwardly beneath the driver's seat. He looks more like a picture of a person than an actual human being. I wonder, if I touched him, whether his skin would be warm and pliant, or rubbery and smooth like an oversize Ken doll. If Georgia were here instead of me, she'd reach across the back seat to find out.

He didn't seem to recognize me, though strangers usually don't. A good thing, according to Georgia. Not because she cared about preserving my privacy (she used to say privacy was overrated) but because people might recognize her old nose on my face, and then what would she do? Didn't I know that I was supposed to have inherited Dad's cute little button nose? What did I think she'd married him for?

You married him for his nose?

I married him for your *nose,* Georgia corrected, as though a husband was no more than a series of features laid out for the picking. *Because I didn't want my daughter to have to do the things I did.*

My body's first failure, then: being born with the wrong nose.

I glance at Lord Edward, his eyes still closed. Like me, he was famous at birth, but the progress of his life was recorded not in grainy pictures on D-list celebrity blogs but in posed official portraits. I know about his parents' affairs and subsequent divorce when he was probably still in diapers. I know who designed his sister's wedding dress (Georgia hated it) and which boarding school he was kicked out of and what he wore to his father's second, and then third wedding. If he cared enough to search the internet, he could see what I wore to my father's funeral when I was five years old, to my mother's when I was seventeen.

The Range Rover wends down a narrow, gated driveway, finally stopping in front of a modern, glassy house. The driver opens the door on my side of the car.

"Ms. Harris," he prompts. I guess this is my stop.

"Well, bye," I say awkwardly, and Lord Edward opens his eyes so quickly that I'm certain he wasn't really asleep. "Thanks for the lift."

"I didn't do anything," he points out, gesturing to the driver.

Right. Add that to the list of things I've done incorrectly today. I bet even *Georgia* thanked the right person when she got here.

Actually, she probably didn't thank anyone. She wasn't the sort of parent who singsonged about manners and saying the magic word.

A woman wearing black pants and a crisp white blouse with black hair plaited into dozens of braids is waiting for me just outside the glassy house's enormous front door. She rushes to open it for me, introducing herself as Dr. Mackenzie, my care manager. The driver pulls away smoothly, barely disturbing the gravel beneath the car's wheels, as though the car is hardly touching the ground.

"We're so pleased to have you here at Rush's," Dr. Mackenzie says as she leads the way into my cottage.

I imagine my mother rolling her eyes at such a greeting when she arrived here ten years ago. She never thought there was anything the least bit *pleasing* about being sent to places like this.

Or maybe she was grateful to be here, relieved they had space to accommodate her. Maybe she arrived determined to *do the work*, exactly like you're supposed to.

I try to picture my mother participating earnestly in therapy, but the images in my head are fuzzy, her voice muted as though even my imagination can't make up what she might say.

I look around, hoping that being here will help to bring it—to bring her—into focus, but the pictures and sounds remain muddy.

Simply *being here* isn't enough.

9

Amelia Blue

Dr. Mackenzie shows me the kitchen and introduces me to Maurice, who will be my personal chef during my stay, and Izabela, the housekeeper. Maurice's hair is cropped close, military-style, and Izabela's dark hair is held tightly in place with one of those clips that looks like a claw. They're both wearing uniforms that look like a set of jet-black scrubs. Dr. Mackenzie promises they'll work out of sight but are available to me any time I need them. (When does anyone *need* a private chef or housekeeper?)

The kitchen is open to the living room (how exactly will Maurice do his work out of sight?), bisected by a long marble island that runs almost the full width of the house. Behind the island is a Viking range with six gas burners and a double oven and an enormous copper sink. The dishwasher and Sub-Zero refrigerator are gleaming stainless steel. The cabinets are painted dark, dark blue, almost black.

In the living room, there's a comfortable-looking white sectional facing a fireplace, inside of which is a roaring wood-burning fire. On top of the mantel is a row of candles, lit cheerfully and filling the room with the scent of lavender and mint. Hanging above the candles is one of those mirrors that's really a television in disguise.

"Do you give this tour to every patient?" I ask Dr. Mackenzie.

"We want each of our guests to be comfortable with their environment," she answers, subtly correcting my use of the word *patient*.

I wonder, but don't ask, about the patients who arrive strung out. There were days when Georgia was too high to know which way was up, let alone to appreciate a Nest thermostat.

Dr. Mackenzie gestures cheerfully to a large glass bowl of lemons on the kitchen island, the lone pop of color in the room. "Your grandmother told us you like lemon."

I always have. Maybe that should have been a warning sign. What kind of toddler is drawn to such a sour, bitter taste?

On cue, Maurice offers up a plate of lemon-scented shortbread. (Has he been holding the platter behind his back since I walked in?)

Over the years, doctors and therapists have tried to tempt me with "favorite" foods. When that (inevitably) didn't work, they switched tactics, forcing me to drink cans of Ensure to meet the weight they designate as *healthy*. They sent me home with meal plans that Grandma Naomi studied like maps, but I always lost my way, like Little Red Riding Hood straying from the path to meet the wolf.

I swallow a sigh. I bet other patients (*guests*) are offered exclusively healthy foods: organic, local, clean. I bet some people come here expressly to lose weight, abstaining from white flour, sugar, dairy. In another body, my eating habits would be praised, not pathologized.

The cookies are very, very pale yellow. Almost white. If I concentrate, I can picture the flour that must have gone into them. I can see flecks of lemon zest sprinkled throughout. I imagine Maurice running a lemon over a Microplane. Perhaps he was careless, looking away, and accidentally scratched his knuckle, so that a tiny droplet of his blood dripped into the dough before he baked it.

"I'm not great with gluten," I offer finally.

"Our apologies," Dr. Mackenzie says quickly. I don't know, and don't ask, whether Dr. Mackenzie is her last name or her first, like she's a talk-show therapist. "There wasn't anything in your medical records about a gluten intolerance."

Her polite apology isn't an apology at all but a challenge.

It doesn't matter how expensive this place is, how pristine the setting, how white the couch, how warm the fire. All these places have the same MO: Get patients to hit a goal weight, then send them home.

Slowly, I reach for a piece of shortbread, its angles sharp and precise. I break off a corner and place it on my tongue.

My mouth floods with sweetness. Then the sharpness of the lemon, the granulated sugar crunching like sprinkles between my teeth. It tastes like the cookies my grandmother used to make. No, they are those cookies *exactly*.

Naomi must have shared the recipe with Maurice. As I chew, the texture of the cookie turns sticky as glue. It's difficult to swallow.

Did some chef offer Georgia a personalized snack, too? Did Naomi send another one of her secret recipes? (Then again, Georgia never liked Naomi's cooking.)

"Mmm," I say finally, meeting the doctor's eyes. "Thank you, Maurice." The chef beams like he's already fixed me.

Georgia called anorexia a gateway diagnosis, like smoking pot before shooting up. (That had been her route of choice.) The first time I went to treatment, she said, *Maybe they'll find out what's really wrong with you.* After all, her daughter—Scott Harris's daughter—couldn't possibly be defeated by something as soft-core as a diet gone awry. Anorexia was too clean, too neat and organized for her taste.

I never had a chance to explain that there's nothing clean about teeth going rotten and breath that stinks because, without any food to digest, the acid from your stomach bubbles into the throat. Nothing clean about fingernails that are ragged and bowel movements that feel like you're coming apart at the seams, about hair growing thinner, more feathers than fur. This disease could kill me as messily and horrifically as the drugs and accidents that killed the celebrities she worshipped. Maybe if she knew that eating disorders are the second deadliest of mental illnesses, she would've been impressed. (Or maybe not, since opioid overdoses are number one.)

I picture her now, sitting cross-legged on the big round chair in the living room, facing away from the view of Laurel Canyon. Apparently, Dad was the one who cared about views. Georgia complained that he picked out the house, a bungalow in the hills, like he'd made music in the 1970s instead of the 1990s.

Georgia always called it *your father's house*. Once, when I told her I liked the house, she said, *You're your father's daughter.* I wasn't sure—I still don't know—whether she meant it as a compliment or an insult.

In my mind's eye, Georgia's wearing one of her cotton nightgowns, the sort that looks like it belongs on a five-year-old. The skirt is hiked up so you can see the scar on her knee from the time she fell down the stairs rolling on E, too high to feel pain. Her hair is bleached blond but her roots are showing, mouse brown and streaked with gray. She's waiting for her phone to ring, waiting for some expert to call and say her daughter was misdiagnosed all those years ago.

Here's what's really *wrong with Amelia Blue.*

Now, as Dr. Mackenzie continues to tour from one room to the next, the delicate cookie crumbles in my hands. Surely they don't expect me to eat *crumbs*. I leave the remains of the cookie on a bathroom counter.

"Would you like us to provide you with a coat?" the doctor asks.

"What?" I say dumbly.

Dr. Mackenzie smiles patiently, a teacher explaining arithmetic to a child. "I noticed you arrived wearing only a sweater. Perhaps you didn't think you'd need anything warmer, since our work together can be done indoors. But I'd be happy to walk the property with you. Some people prefer to practice therapy while walking through nature. Do you think you might like that?"

I imagine myself wearing a puffy black coat with the words *Rush's Recovery* (perhaps simply *RR*) embroidered across my chest like a scar.

The truth is, I would like a coat. It's freezing out, and I'm not planning on spending all my time here within the walls of the cottage. But I'm also not planning on being outside with a doctor by my side.

"No thanks," I answer. "I don't need a coat."

When I return to use the toilet a few minutes later, the cookie crumbs are gone, no doubt silently and secretly removed by Izabela, as if she were a mouse rather than a human being, like I'm Cinderella at the start of her story—birds and mice her only companions before the prince comes to rescue her.

But Cinderella was *so good*. She wanted to be rescued.

She *deserved* to be rescued.

10

Lord Edward

My care manager, Dr. Rush, does that thing most people do when they meet me: a slight tilt of the head, peering at his shoes as though there might be a scuff on them, not quite a bow, but not the complete absence of one, either. (I realize, belatedly, that Amelia Blue did no such thing.) When Dr. Rush bends his neck, I can see the beginning of a bald spot on the top of his head; his remaining dark hair is peppered ever so slightly with gray. Anne and my father seem to know what to do when faced with such a greeting—that is, they take it in as though it isn't the least bit absurd but perfectly appropriate. Now, I find myself mirroring the gesture slightly, trying to pass the movement off as a nod.

Dr. Rush at least calls me Edward, not *Lord* Edward. The chef and housekeeper do the same. Anne must've told them to use my first name. Or maybe it's a rehab thing—tearing one down before they build one back up again. That's what happens in the movies. Though none of the places in the movies look like this.

The doctor leads me around the cottage as if he's giving a museum tour. The fridge is stocked with my favorite flavored water, and there's organic crunchy peanut butter in the cabinets. Dr. Rush name-drops brands the way some people drop the names of celebrities they slept with: Sub-Zero, Miele, Viking, deVOL.

"A British brand," Dr. Rush adds enthusiastically about the last, as if it might make me feel more at home, though he must know that, excepting the past few months, I haven't lived full-time in England since I was fifteen. Still, I smile and thank him, like they picked out the kitchen cabinets with me in mind. The doctor beams.

In my apartment in Tribeca, I have similar appliances. My mattress is a Vispring; my sheets are organic cotton; the furniture is high-end but not custom, selected from catalogs. The first time she set foot inside, Harper pointed out that everything was brown or navy blue: brown leather couch, navy-blue bedspread, brown wooden furniture, navy-blue dining chairs. The color scheme was the result of a lack of imagination, not intention.

Spend too much time in this apartment alone and you might forget there's a world of color out there, Harper said. She left her pink underwear on the bedroom floor, shiny tubes of coral lipstick on my bedside table. She'd come home with travel magazines, ripping out pictures of the most colorful destinations, taping them to the refrigerator door. I promised to take her to each and every one.

We'll take each other, she said. *With our own money. Not your family's.*

I don't have my own money, I pointed out. Financial support from one's family isn't exactly unusual in New York City, though I don't imagine most people were receiving quite as much support as I was.

That makes you just like every other twentysomething I know, Harper replied. *We'll rough it.* She laughed at the idea of me staying in hostels, nothing but a backpack to my name. She was going to wend her way through the cities of Europe and the beaches of Fiji with her light, loping gait, as graceful as a cat.

Someday, when my father dies, my sister will be in charge of every cent I'm given to live on—an allowance, like a child—as well as which public events I can officially attend, in which of our properties I can reside and when, for which privilege I will pay rent from the allowance Anne determines. The concept of my own money, my own property, has never entered into the equation.

So get a job, Harper said, as if it were easy. *Go back to school.*

I suppose it was easy, in as much as most people did it. But to tell my family—impossible. They would laugh at the idea of my continuing my education when I barely made it through high school. My father's voice would drip with sarcasm as he asked what I wanted to be when I grow up, as though my hoping to be anything other than what they'd already decided was the punchline to a terrible joke. *We let him live in America too long,* Anne would say, *he's getting ideas.*

Of course, I will have a job eventually—sons and daughters like me are expected to—but it will be one the family selects, secured not by my résumé but by their connections. One doesn't talk about what one *wants* to do in my family; one does what one is told to do. It's been that way, literally, for centuries. Who am I to change matters?

Dr. Rush leads the way with a slow sort of amble as though he hasn't a care in the world. I try to match his stride, but it's impossible for me to step with that sort of ease. He's slightly taller than I am (six-one; you can look it up), his legs longer. He points to the Nest thermostat in the corridor, mine to control while I'm here.

"What if I like it really hot or really cold?"

"Then the house will be really hot or cold," Dr. Rush answers with a smile, as though his own comfort, and that of the rest of the staff, is so much less important than mine. I should be used to that sort of thing—certainly, Anne and Dad are—but it makes me queasy.

"So tell me, Edward," Dr. Rush says as the tour concludes in the bedroom. (Frette sheets, he points out. Hastens mattress.) He wears thick-rimmed tortoise-shell glasses with square frames, a white button-down tucked into gray slacks, a sweater vest on top. He looks more like a professor in a movie about some ivy-draped college than a therapist. "What can we do to make your stay more comfortable?"

I almost laugh out loud. I haven't been *comfortable* in months.

"Nothing. This is excellent." I smile politely. My back teeth ache.

"I'm so glad. Our goal is to make our guests happy."

Guests. I'm not a guest. I'm a prisoner sent away for my crimes, and Dr. Rush knows it.

Briefly, I wonder why the tiny girl I rode in with—*woman*, Anne would correct—is here. Heroin, maybe. Would explain why she's so skinny. Or perhaps depression zapped her appetite; with a name like *Blue*, she's practically predestined for a mood disorder.

"I'm afraid I must ask: Did you bring any drugs, medication, or alcohol with you?"

"To rehab?" I ask, playing dumb. This is all so civilized. No stomach pumped, no pockets frisked. I wonder if they strip search the guests who aren't members of the landed aristocracy. "Wouldn't that kind of defeat the point?"

At my joke, Dr. Rush smiles, though it doesn't reach his eyes.

"Your prescriptions were sent to the local pharmacy," he assures me. "So there will be no interruption in your pain management."

I clench my jaw. If there's a more absurd phrase in the English language than *pain management*, I've never heard it. As though pain is something to be controlled but not avoided, an unruly child that needs to be taken in hand. Permitted to be *here*, but not *there*. Playtime from *this* hour until *that* hour. Maybe if the people in charge of managing pain had actual experience with it, they'd see things differently.

"According to the notes your care team back home sent, you don't need your next pill until morning, yes?"

Fuck off, Doctor, I think. *You have no idea what I need.*

"Yes," I agree, ever polite.

"Then I'll give it to you with your breakfast." He slides his hands into his pockets, and I wonder if my pill bottles are rattling around with his keys.

In London, it's the middle of the night. I yawn widely.

"Excuse me," I murmur apologetically. "Jet lag."

"You've had a long day," Dr. Rush offers. "I'll let you sleep. I'll be downstairs if you need me."

"Downstairs?" I echo. The bedroom, living room, and kitchen are on the same floor; I limped up wide wooden steps to the front door.

"Of course," he explains. "Here at Rush's Recovery, you'll never be alone. During your stay, I'm available to you twenty-four seven."

He says it like it's a service to me, though of course it's a service to my sister and father. They don't want me left unsupervised.

"Good night, Edward." Dr. Rush slides the enormous barn door to the bedroom closed behind him. I'm surprised he doesn't lock it and pocket the key.

Four weeks. That's how long Anne said I had to stay. Actually she said, *At least four weeks. After that, we'll see,* which is code for *Behave yourself for four weeks and you can go home. Act up, and we'll add time to your sentence.*

I limp across the room and rest my forehead against the cold floor-to-ceiling window. It's too dark to see the ocean now, but I can hear the waves crashing against the sand below.

When I was ten years old, I broke my thumb playing rugby. At thirteen, a cricket bat to the face made my nose explode with blood. At fifteen, I broke my arm when I fell off the roof of our estate in Scotland. If someone had asked, before last year, I'd have said I had plenty of experience with pain.

I would have been wrong.

I keep one hand on the glass to steady me as I bend down, sticking my fingers into the space between my sock and my boot. I suppose it's not the most creative hiding place, but it's proven itself effective.

I pop a pill in my mouth, swallow it dry, and wait for the sweet click; not oblivion but distance, as though my body were happening to someone else.

Pain is my real punishment. This place will end, eventually.

The pain won't.

11

Florence

Joni Jewell's lyrics pound like a headache while Evelyn gives me the grand tour, as if this place is an art gallery.

Now all he wants is to get her back.
Just you wait, I'm gonna get her back.
But he's never gonna get me back, get me back, get me back.

Joni repeats the refrain *get her back* more than thirty times in a two-minute song. People on the internet praised Joni for her double entendre as though no one had ever done that before.

I could've done better. But the villain can't write her own revenge song.

"This is your housekeeper," Evelyn says, gesturing to a woman in a uniform: gray pants, gray top, her (graying) hair pulled into a sleek ponytail without a single flyaway out of place. "Sascha. And this is your chef, Andrew."

Andrew stands behind the kitchen counter. He's wearing the same uniform as Sascha, but with a black hoodie over the top, its sleeves pushed halfway up his muscled forearms. His dark-brown hair is cropped close to his scalp, and his cheeks are dotted with stubble, a five o'clock shadow a few hours early.

"Can I get you anything?" he offers, the slightest hint of a Southern accent sneaking its way between the syllables. Next to Evelyn's crisp diction, the roundness of Andrew's words is practically exotic. Without waiting for an answer, he reaches into a cabinet and offers up a white ceramic platter. I expect to see an arrangement of fresh fruit—strawberries sliced into bleeding hearts, kiwis cut into tiny stars—but instead the plate is covered in candy: Twizzlers, SweeTarts, Sour Patch Kids. I laugh out loud.

"Guess my tastes don't really challenge your culinary skills."

Evelyn answers before Andrew can. "Your manager told us that you prefer sour candy when you're—" She pauses.

"When I'm what?" I prompt, then shake my head. "I'm not going through withdrawal." Heroin addicts notoriously crave candy. "And I'm not here for rehab," I add. Callie was supposed to tell them that. She didn't even pretend she was sending me away to get clean. Included in the care package she gave me at the airport were a few joints, cleverly disguised in a cigarette carton, but I left them behind on the plane.

I don't like going into hiding, I'd whined when Callie announced she was sending me here. *It feels like admitting I did something wrong.*

Didn't you do something wrong? she'd quipped in return.

Didn't he? I asked, but what I really wanted to say was *Didn't she?* I was about to launch a solo tour when Joni Jewell cast me as the wicked queen to her perfect princess.

The song takes aim at both of you.

Yeah, but did Elizabeth Taylor disappear after Eddie Fisher left Debbie Reynolds for her? Did Camilla Parker Bowles disappear after Prince Charles cheated on Diana?

Callie bit her tongue before she could point out that I'm neither Hollywood nor actual royalty. Instead she said, *They both listened to their publicists.*

You're not my publicist.

No one else is.

The truth is, Callie is my everything: manager, agent, publicist, assistant. I can hardly remember which she was first anymore.

What about Nick? Joni Jewell's boyfriend, the ho-hum sex on the roof of the Roosevelt that caused this mess.

He's "retreated to the studio to work on his music." Callie used air quotes to show it was part of an official statement.

Why can't I do that?

Maybe you could've, if you hadn't attacked her.

I rolled my eyes. I couldn't believe how seriously everyone was taking a backstage scuffle.

It's not like I tried to kill her, I whined.

You threatened to.

Those were just words! Sticks and stones and all that.

I never told my kid, *Sticks and stones may break your bones, but words will never hurt you.* Personally, I'd rather someone beat the shit out of me than talk crap about me.

You broke her tooth! Callie insisted.

My guitar broke her tooth. It was an accident. Or it wasn't. I hadn't been aiming for her *teeth.*

Now, Evelyn says, "Our guests come here for all kinds of reasons. Rest, retreat, reset."

"Is that your motto?" I mutter.

If this place had a motto, it'd probably be in Latin so no one could understand it. According to Callie, it caters exclusively to UHNW individuals. I googled UHNW rather than ask Callie what she was talking about: ultra-high net worth.

"Really," I explain, "I've done the rehab thing a dozen times."

"Addiction is a self-diagnosed disease." Evelyn speaks in that awful tone people use when they think they know better than you do. Her unblinking ice-blue eyes are set far apart so she looks more like a doll than a person. If they made dolls of women in their fifties.

Usually, therapists at places like this are recovering addicts themselves, meant to inspire the rest of us—*look how great life would be if you got sober!*—as if anyone's dream job is listening to other addicts' sob stories all day. But it's impossible to imagine Evelyn sniffing coke or shooting heroin or even smoking a joint. The whites of her eyes are too white, her forehead too smooth, her teeth too straight.

How long does it take to hate someone? Is twenty minutes enough? Because I already hate Evelyn.

I grab a handful of Sour Patch Kids from Andrew's platter, catching a glimpse of a tattoo that peeks out from his sleeve and snakes around his wrist. I make out the words *never settle*, the title of a song off our first album. I grin, but Andrew lifts a finger to his lips, the universal sign for *shhhh.*

"Why don't I show you to your room?" Evelyn offers, apparently oblivious that her chef is a fan. "You can lie down, take a shower, get settled."

I can decide for myself when I'd like to lie down or shower, but I definitely want Evelyn to leave me alone, so I follow her obediently, stealing a glance at Andrew, who's rearranging the platter on the kitchen counter. I think he winks at me, but I can't be sure. I feel a rush of butterflies in my belly. He's taller and more muscular than the guys I usually hook up with, but handsome enough that I find myself smiling. I'm sure this is the kind of place that has rules about *fraternization*. I can practically hear Callie begging me not to give her another mess to clean up.

Everything in the bedroom is white: white bedspread, white sheets, white rug beside the bed. The walls in here are floor-to-ceiling windows, just like in the living room. It must cost a fortune to heat this so-called cottage.

I guess UHNW individuals don't think about that kind of thing.

Someone has brought my bags in from the car and placed my notebook at the foot of the bed. The pink ribbon on my black luggage is the only splash of color in the room.

"When do I get my phone back?" I ask.

Evelyn smiles serenely. I bet she's the kind of person who gets calm when others get angry. "Why do you need your phone?"

"I'm a mother." It's the truth but it feels like a lie. I'm the last person anyone back home would call if something went wrong. I'm usually the *reason* things go wrong. Without me, there's clean hair and homework and lights out at bedtime.

"I assure you that if we receive any messages from your family, we'll pass them along right away."

"I can't stay here without my phone," I insist. I try to sound authoritative, but it comes out as a whine. *Shrill.* "I'm a businesswoman. My manager might need to contact me."

"Of course, you can leave anytime."

I drop onto the bed. The soft mattress gives way beneath my weight like a waterbed. "Do you take everyone's phones?"

"Care here is individualized to meet our guests' needs," Evelyn says like it's a line she memorized from a brochure.

"What about me screams, *Take her phone?*"

"You said so yourself, you're not here for rehab." Evelyn smiles that same peaceful smile again, and I hate her even more.

"So?"

"Do you really believe you can rest, retreat, reset if you're bombarded by news from the outside world?"

Evelyn slides the door shut behind her, and I grab my notebook and start scribbling.

How long does it take to hate someone?
Call me an addict, and I'll take some more,
Smile while you try to control me now,
But you will never, ever hold me down.

Another lie. Of course they're holding me here. I can't leave, and Evelyn knows that.

I have nowhere else to go.

12

Amelia Blue

D r. Mackenzie walks me to the bedroom like I'm a little kid with a bedtime. "I'm downstairs if you need anything." She shows me a button
on the bedside table. "Press this and I'll be right up. Some of my guests do
their best thinking at odd hours," she adds with a wink, as though the reason other therapists failed to fix me is because they scheduled our appoint-
ments on, say, a Wednesday afternoon, instead of meeting my every whim.

Finally alone, I pick up my phone. According to my internet searches,
the *Rush* in Rush's Recovery is for a psychiatrist named Albert Rush. He and
his wife worked as therapists outside Atlanta, then sold their practice and the
home where they'd raised their son, putting everything they had into building the center here on Shelter Island. Albert Rush graduated from Duke,
then received his master's in psychology and clinical social work as well as an
MD at Emory. (His wife's credentials aren't quite as impressive. In her bio, it
says she grew up in the Northeast, moved to Atlanta to be near her husband,
and got her PhD by attending community college classes at night after their
son was born, her husband sparking her interest in psychology.) Albert Rush
claims to be a descendant of Benjamin Rush, one of the signers of the Dec-
laration of Independence and a pioneer of American addiction medicine,
like he was destined for this sort of work. Even the son went into the family
business eventually, earning his degree in clinical social work.

I google Benjamin Rush. He espoused the use of sober houses, embrac-
ing methods like forcible vomiting and compulsory attendance at religious
services.

I search for my mother's name next. A few weeks ago, Shocking Pink
announced that they were going on tour with a new lead singer, a recent
runner-up on *The Voice*. Even so, they're calling it a reunion tour. They'll
perform the songs Georgia lost all rights to because of a Byzantine record

deal she signed before she had an agent or attorney to vet that sort of thing. It didn't really matter in the end. Georgia only released two albums with the band before she realized she didn't actually have to make music to be famous.

If she could come back as a ghost, Georgia would be haunting her old bandmates right now, rattling chains in their attics, possessing the dolls in their children's bedrooms. How dare they do this, and so close to the ten-year anniversary of her death, claiming it was some kind of tribute? (The anniversary is another reason Naomi thought it was strange I wanted to come here now, but I told her it was a coincidence. That, at least, wasn't a lie.) I imagine Georgia back home, throwing her phone across the room hard enough to break into a million pieces, crawling the walls of our bungalow in the hills, the house Dad bought with the money he made from *his* first record deal, the house Georgia could never have bought on her own. (And even if she could, it wouldn't have occurred to her to do something as responsible as buy real estate or set up a trust for her daughter.) She'd be happy to see, at least, that across the internet, her fans—calling themselves the Justice for Georgia Warriors—are trying to organize a boycott of the tour.

I sigh as I scroll social media. Posts about Georgia populate my feed no matter how many times I tell the algorithm I'm not interested.

I turn to face the nightstand and stare at the little button Dr. Mackenzie showed me. If I pushed it, would she sprint to my room in her pajamas? I reach out, my fingers itching, like a child who's been warned away from the hot stove. Almost anything seems better than getting caught in a #georgiablue whirlpool.

There have been conspiracies and rumors about my mother since before I was born and long after she died—that her marriage to my dad was a sham, that she slept around so much I can't possibly be Scott Harris's daughter, that Dad wrote her music, that he only killed himself to get free of her. Only the most hardcore conspiracy theorists ever questioned the manner of Georgia's death, an accidental OD after (technically, during) yet another stint at rehab. They don't know what it's like to be on the receiving end of a phone call, a stranger on the other end explaining that your mother checked herself out, scored drugs nearby, and never woke up.

I'm not here for more whispers and conspiracy theories. I'm nothing like the superfans who look for Easter eggs in Dad's lyrics and in the clothes my mother wore.

But my phone continues to feed me #justiceforgeorgia, and it's harder to ignore them than it was a few months ago, as though each post is a car crash from which I can't make myself look away. So like Alice down the rabbit hole, I fall.

The Police Chief

His phone rings early in the morning, not even 6:00 a.m. The sound wakes his wife, sets the cat to meowing, demanding breakfast and to be let out back. Cats don't understand that when a police chief's phone rings at an ungodly hour, it's because something serious has happened, something that takes precedence over mealtimes and litter boxes and traipsing through the barren winter grass, searching for moles and voles and mice to torment.

In fact, that's why he'd wanted a cat in the first place. A creature who didn't know about his job; who didn't complain, as his kids did, about his long and irregular hours; who wouldn't wrinkle its nose, as his wife did, when he came home smelling like a crime scene.

Of course, it's not as though Shelter Island is a hotbed of crime. Last year, there were six overdoses, Narcan administered three times; the island isn't isolated from the opioid crisis. And certainly, in summertime, god-awful city drivers flood the streets with their Range Rovers and Jaguars, driving like they're three sheets to the wind even when they're stone-cold sober. July and August, the chief and his officers issue speeding tickets like candy; they give out more citations between Memorial Day and Labor Day than they do in all the other months of the year.

But now, early on a January morning, the streets are quiet. The chief is groggy enough that he has to ask the officer on the other end of the line to repeat himself.

"Sir, a woman—you know Clarice Bendersly, husband died six months ago?—she was out walking her dog this morning and found a body on the beach."

The chief wipes the sleep from his eyes, sits up straight. No one describes a living, breathing person as a *body*.

It's already been identified. Not officially; the officer explains that Clarice Bendersly recognized the body.

Someone from the recovery center.

When they broke ground on the recovery center, there was an uproar. People claimed the town council had been bought off, bribes paid to overcome zoning laws and building codes. The rich believe they can get away with anything if they throw enough money at it.

The people who work at the center, they may live on the island year-round, but they're not locals any more than the summer people are. The owners opened the center here not because of some history with this island—the chief heard they're from Georgia—but because they thought the island was an idyllic location, isolated and private, rustic but appealing.

And the patients—they're worse than the summer people, using up the island's sea air and sandy beaches like everything was put here for their benefit.

Just before the center opened, the owner met with local law enforcement, explaining that their patients would be on the property voluntarily, distinguishing them from the drunks and addicts the chief interacts with on the job, the sort who get sent to rehab as part of a plea deal to avoid jailtime.

The officer asks if the chief would like him to call the center.

No, the chief will do it himself.

He sets the coffee brewing before he makes the call. The center's owner doesn't sound groggy, as though the wealthy—and the chief certainly counts the folks running the shelter as *wealthy*, right along with the patients—are more well rested than the rest of us.

The chief can't help it. He's relieved that the body on the beach is one of *them*.

On the other end of the line, the owner expresses shock, dismay, murmurs, "What a tragedy."

In the absence of a family member, the center's owner will formally identify the body. Clarice Bendersly, batty old woman, is hardly reliable.

As he hangs up, the chief thinks, *A place like that recovery center will never work, not really. You want to get someone sober, you gotta break them down, remind them that they're nothing.*

People like that never believe they're nothing.

13

Amelia Blue

In the morning, Dr. Mackenzie knocks on the bedroom door. She doesn't wait for a response before letting herself in.

"Thought it best to let you sleep late. You're still on West Coast time, after all."

I blink a few times, giving my eyes a chance to focus. Dr. Mackenzie's outfit is almost identical to yesterday's (black pants, crisp blouse), this time with a soft-looking heather-gray wrap thrown over her shoulders. I'm not sure exactly when I fell asleep last night. My phone is on the bed beside me, the battery almost dead, Instagram reels still playing one after the other, old videos of my mother's antics. I swipe the screen blank as Dr. Mackenzie crosses the room. She places a familiar metal slab firmly on the floor in front of the bed.

I nod but ask to go to the bathroom first. Brush my teeth, scraping my tongue with the bristles until it bleeds. I spit the blood into the sink. In the mirror above, my reflection looks hazy and warped, my nose too long, my eyebrows too wide. My lips are dry and my hair is wild with sleep. It takes me a moment to realize that the mirror isn't made of glass but brushed steel.

Dr. Mackenzie tells me to take off my long-sleeved shirt and pajama pants so that I'm wearing only a tank top and underwear. She makes me roll the top up, tucked under my arms, so she can see my torso. She notes every beauty mark, freckle, and scar, describing it out loud as she makes a notation on her phone. I try not to shiver in the cool air, pretending that having my body inspected by a near stranger doesn't bother me.

Here's another thing I know: These places need a record of the state their patients arrive in, at least when they arrive for reasons like mine. (I don't, obviously, know if Georgia was subjected to this sort of thing.) I'm surprised the doctor doesn't ask me to open my mouth, make note of my bloody gums. (Would she consider it self-harm or poor dental hygiene?)

Finally, Dr. Mackenzie tells me to step onto the scale. I wait for it to beep and light up with a number between my feet. But nothing happens. For a second, I think maybe I'm too light to register.

I wait for Dr. Mackenzie to tell me the machine's not working, but she merely glances at her phone.

"The scale texts me the results," she explains.

"What if I want to know what it says?" I ask.

"We don't think that would be conducive to your journey with us," Dr. Mackenzie explains, slipping her phone into her pocket. Her face betrays nothing.

Places like this say they consider eating disorders and addictions diseases, but they *treat* them as behavioral problems, like addicts and anorexics are unruly children in need of stricter parents. They want you to feel powerless, because only when you're powerless do you stop resisting—whether it's eating what they tell you to eat, saying what they want you to say, doing what they want you to do. Maybe that's why Georgia couldn't stay sober. I can't imagine her admitting powerlessness.

"Why don't you get dressed and join me in the living room?" Dr. Mackenzie suggests with false lightness as she lifts the scale off the floor. She doesn't use the language treatment centers usually do: *weigh-in*, *goal weight*, *ideal weight*. (Incidentally, the same language people with eating disorders often use.)

I shower; the towels are plush but small. (Too large and they can be tied into a noose.) There's no full-length mirror, only the warped metal over the sink that renders my reflection slightly fuzzy. (Glass can be broken, used for self-harm.)

I rub my skin with the organic lotions on the counter. There's a blow-dryer, but it's battery operated. (Wires can be dangerous.) I dry my hair, soft and smooth down my back, even though I know it will end up frizzing later. It always does, but I established my morning routine when I was in middle school, and I haven't deviated since.

I must take too long getting ready, because Dr. Mackenzie calls out, "Everything all right in there?"

She opens the door without waiting for an answer. (Again: powerless.) *Why don't you get dressed and join me in the living room?* wasn't a suggestion but a command. Even though she's already seen me nearly naked, I rush to cover myself with one of the too-small towels. There's no bathrobe. (The belt could be used as a noose.)

"I'll be out in a minute," I answer, hands crossed over my body.

She and Maurice are waiting in the kitchen when I finally emerge.

"What would you like for breakfast?" Dr. Mackenzie keeps her voice cheerful, as though the question isn't fraught.

"Coffee would be great."

My new doctor doesn't suggest that coffee isn't a proper breakfast, simply nods at Maurice. He prepares a cup without asking how I take it. Black, two sugars. Sugar is worse for you than fat, but I went through a phase in high school where I ate exclusively fat-free foods, and sugar stuck.

"It's decaf," Maurice says apologetically as he hands it to me.

Caffeine is considered a mind-altering substance, so they don't allow it. Plus, I might chug it to burn extra calories.

Dr. Mackenzie gestures to the couch in the living room.

"You're not going to force breakfast on me?" I ask as I sit.

"Would you like me to?" Dr. Mackenzie asks. She faces me at an angle, sliding off her shoes and tucking her legs beneath her. I'm wearing sweatpants and a ragged oversize sweater. I feel underdressed and pull my sleeves over my wrists.

"Obviously not." I take a sip of the coffee. No shitty rehab sludge here. This is French press.

Dr. Mackenzie isn't holding a pad or a notebook, nowhere to scribble an observation in my file. She simply looks at me, as if I fascinate her. If this place requires a record of my weight, my scrapes and scars, then surely it requires a record of my doctor's thoughts, too. Maybe Maurice and Izabella are also expected to report their impressions of me and at the end of each day all three of them will disappear to scribble notes on what I said, noting every mannerism—that I sat cross-legged like a child, that I bit my nails or picked at my cuticles. I imagine all their notes neatly organized in a file with my name on it.

I meet my doctor's gaze. Her face would be symmetrical but for a smattering of mismatched freckles across her nose.

"So what's your approach here?" I ask finally. "Not CBT, clearly."

"Why not?"

"Because then you would've forced breakfast on me," I answer. In cognitive behavioral therapy, they focus on (you guessed it) the behaviors around your disorder, putting you on a schedule of what to eat and when, as though meals were a homework assignment.

I don't want Dr. Mackenzie to see how relieved I am that she's not forcing me to eat, so I keep talking, trying to sound clinical and detached, like this is all so boring to me.

"And not family therapy, either, because I'm here alone."

They tried that when I was younger. Grandma Naomi never missed an appointment. Mom's attendance was sporadic, and eventually the therapist agreed that we made more progress without her. (We didn't make much progress either way.)

"Internal family systems?" I ask. "That's all the rage these days. Or maybe you're out there with psilocybin? It's going to be more popular than Prozac before long."

"Have any of those approaches worked for you?"

"Obviously not," I say again, though I smile a little so she doesn't think I'm blaming the doctors, but myself. So she'll know I'm a *good* patient who wants to get better, not a difficult one who fights every step of the way. "I just like to know what I'm getting into."

"Why?"

"It helps me manage my expectations."

"And why do you want to manage your expectations?"

Apparently Dr. Mackenzie is taking a traditional talk-therapy approach. Answering all my questions with questions until I accidentally reveal my deepest, darkest secrets.

When I was underage, my therapists shared their observations with Naomi (and Georgia, if she remembered to ask), but after I turned eighteen, it was as though a wand had been waved and my family no longer had any right to hear about our sessions together.

Think of all the families who send loved ones to places like this, desperate for help, but not allowed to ask for details, blindly putting their trust into strangers who keep secrets for a living. The privileges of doctor-patient confidentiality spread far and wide. Even when a patient *wants* their data shared, it isn't easy: They have to fill out forms, sign legally binding documents.

I take a deep breath, picturing a room lined with tall cabinets filled with files for each patient Rush's Recovery has ever had: doctors' observations and diagnoses, the hints they're trained to pick up on as they gather information the rest of us don't know enough to recognize.

Files, including mine someday, stubbornly protected by doctor-patient privilege, even after each patient's death.

14

Florence

E velyn asks the questions therapists always ask, trying to get a picture of the life that led me to their couches. Halfway through her interrogation, sick of the way she stares at the tattoos snaking up and down my arms like she's searching for evidence of track marks between the ink and the skin, I say, "We could save a lot of time if you just look up my bio."

My mother hates my tattoos. They mean I can't be buried in a Jewish cemetery. I told her I don't want to be buried at all. *Cremate me*, I said, *turn me to fire and scatter my ashes to the wind*. Mom looked so horrified at the idea that I knew she'd ignore my wishes. Luckily, she'll die before me, statistically speaking. Probably, my kid will be in charge of what happens to me. Hopefully by then she'll be free of Mom's brainwashing.

"Why would you prefer I read about you on the internet than talk with you about your life right here, right now?" Evelyn asks.

I stretch my arms overhead. The couch in the living room is white and so deep that if I sit all the way back, my legs stick out in front of me, like I'm a little kid. Bet they did that on purpose, to make their patients feel helpless and small. Evelyn sits in a chair across from me, her feet firmly on the floor.

Little kid,
Little girl,
Made of id,
No one's pearl.

"This is boring," I sigh, dropping my arms and folding them across my chest. "I've told these stories a thousand times." I've lost track of how many therapists' couches I've lounged across, how many people have singsonged the question *And how did that make you feel?* I've heard the twelve steps so many times I can recite them, all the way from admitting powerlessness to having a spiritual awakening, though I've never personally made it past the ninth step, quick to quip that making amends would take up the rest of my life. Besides, the people who wronged me never bothered sending apologies my way.

Evelyn, I notice, hasn't mentioned the twelve steps. Guess she couldn't justify charging whatever it is she charges her patients if she trotted out the same program anyone can find for free in their local church basement.

Out the floor-to-ceiling windows, I can see waves crash on the beach, the water almost black in the dim January light. Who wants to be this close to the ocean in the dead of winter? Well, plenty of people, if you live in LA. I live thirty minutes from the beach, and I can't remember the last time I took my kid there. When she was little, I'd answer every request with a promise that we'd go tomorrow. The convenient thing about tomorrow is there's always another one. Eventually my kid caught on. Hasn't asked me for anything in a long, long time.

Ask me for anything.
I'll always say no.
Ask me for anything.
Unless you're asking me to go.

The Scott Harris in my head says, *Keep going,* but I ignore him. Can't listen to everything the dead-musician chorus says, even when they're being encouraging. People like Evelyn would think I'm even crazier than they already think I am.

Evelyn's icy blond hair is pulled into a bun so tight it raises her eyebrows, like a shitty facelift. It makes her look more like a simulation than an actual human being.

"Give me your phone," I say, reaching toward her. "I'll pull up my Wiki page, and we can sit here quietly while you read."

Evelyn doesn't flinch as I lean forward, but when I try to reach into her pockets, she holds up a hand. In an instant, the chef, Andrew, is standing between us. I hadn't even realized he was in the room.

"Florence," Evelyn says, hidden entirely behind Andrew's tall, broadly muscled body. "I'm going to have to ask you to sit down."

"What, you're not allowed to stand during therapy here?"

"You're not allowed to attack your therapist."

"I wasn't attacking you!"

The words I said to Joni—*I'll kill you for what you did to me*—will follow me around for the rest of my life like a stray dog. I bite my tongue to keep myself from saying something similar to Evelyn, the phrase in my thoughts like a birthday wish.

I picture Evelyn and Joni as roommates in hell, longing to exchange stories about me, but the devil stole their tongues, so Evelyn can't take her condescending tone and Joni can't sing.

"Are we going to have a problem?" Evelyn's disembodied voice asks from behind Andrew.

"What if we are?" I ask, feeling defiant. "Will you kick me out?"

"No, but we will sedate you."

Now, the housekeeper—I bet she'd be surprised that I remember her name, Sascha—steps forward, a medical bag in her hand.

"You're going to have the maid inject me with drugs?" I almost laugh at how horrified I sound, considering all that I've been injected with over the years.

"Sascha is a registered nurse."

She's surely had more training than half the guys—it was always guys—who'd shot me up over the years, if not quite as much experience.

"So you lied when you told me she was the housekeeper." Sweat springs on the back of my neck so that I'm tempted to twist my hair into a bun to cool off, but I don't want Evelyn to think she's upset me.

"She's also your housekeeper."

They must pay well here, to make a registered nurse clean up after me. Well, good for Sascha.

"And the chef doubles as your bodyguard?"

Andrew answers before Evelyn can. "Please, Florence. There's no need for things to get messy."

He's standing so close that I can feel his breath when he speaks, but he doesn't touch me. His face hovers over mine. In another context, I'd think he was about to kiss me.

I shake my head like this was all so ridiculous.

"Fine." I sit back on the deep couch. "But I'm not answering any more questions."

Andrew moves so I can see Evelyn's expressionless face once more.

"We can sit in silence if you'd like, though I don't think it would be the most productive use of our time together."

I roll my eyes, determined to keep quiet for as long as it takes. I wait for Evelyn to ask some other question, or to get hungry or thirsty or tired. But she just sits there, holding my gaze with her never-blinking stare like she's trying to hypnotize me.

After a few minutes—feels like hours—my leg begins to itch. And then I sneeze, and then I have to blow my nose. Then I have to pee. Then I start pacing, careful to keep my distance from Evelyn so she won't threaten to sedate me again. What kind of rehab tries to drug you? Then I turn on some music, because the silence is deafening.

"Would you like to stop for the day?" Evelyn asks. She has to shout to be heard.

"Yeah," I say. Her eyes are the kind of ice blue you can almost see your reflection in. "Let's stop."

15

Amelia Blue

"Let's start with this question." Dr. Mackenzie clasps her hands over her knee. "Why do you think you restrict?"

"If photographs of your most awkward moments were splashed across trashy magazines by the time you were in elementary school, you might be worried about how you looked, too."

Not only was I born with the wrong nose but (apparently) I grew the wrong hair, too. When I was twelve, Georgia took me to get highlights, complaining to the stylist that my dark hair clashed with my pale skin. I spent all of seventh grade waiting for the terrible stripes on my head to grow out. The next year, it was a chemical straightening treatment.

Eventually, I was no longer famous enough (rather, my parents were no longer famous enough) to qualify for even the Star Tracks section of *People* magazine, but there were still plenty of blogs and fan sites that tracked the lives of celebrity children almost exclusively, showing off, with wicked glee, the chubby little girl who didn't know better than to smile for the camera and, later, the pimply preteen whose bad posture added ten pounds to her frame. In the comments, people expressed their condolences, as though not inheriting my parents' good looks and speedy metabolisms were the real tragedies of my life. Unlike the rest of my generation, I never understood about *good angles* and *finding my light*.

"That must have been difficult," Dr. Mackenzie says, but I know she doesn't mean it. She's the kind of beautiful that doesn't have a bad angle, the sort of person who can consider makeup and diets superficial even as she turns heads every time she walks down the street.

Half the time when someone befriended me, it was only to get a photo they could sell later. When I got to grad school and people talked about the friends they'd had since kindergarten, I nodded along as though I'd built lasting relationships, too.

Dr. Mackenzie adds, "I imagine it's not uncommon among children of celebrities. Your parents spend their lives—their careers—seeking out the spotlight, but you're born into it, never given a choice in the matter."

There are, of course, endless videos and pictures of my parents on the internet. My father, the sort of skinny that would be gawky on anyone else, looking strung out and dangerous. His every move was serpentine, his fingers flying over the bass, his hair buzzed short and dyed orange for a music video.

Somehow, in every photograph Georgia looks the same, and not only because she never stopped dressing like it was 1992. As she aged her stomach grew less taut, the skin on her upper arms turned crepey, but her actual *weight* remained the same. And unlike me, she walked with her shoulders thrown back, like she was proud of every step she took.

I shift my gaze from Dr. Mackenzie to the wall of windows behind her, retracing the spins I took down the rabbit hole last night. Normally, I spend my time online creeping around the #proana and #promia corners of the internet. I've certainly never made contact with a Georgia fan. Over the years, they've attempted to contact me, sometimes quite literally: When I was little, there were fans who showed up at school drop-off and hugged me tight, like they couldn't believe they were in the presence of my DNA.

It's snowing lightly outside, not enough to stick but pretty as a postcard nonetheless, the front of which would have *Wish You Were Here* scrawled across it. There's a fire burning in the fireplace, but the wall of windows creates the illusion of being outdoors so that when I exhale I almost expect to see my breath.

"Is that why you feel safer restricting?" Dr. Mackenzie prompts. "For more flattering pictures on the internet?"

I try to imagine how Georgia would react to a reductive question like that (*Is that why you do drugs, so you can always be the life of the party?*).

I clutch my coffee mug like a stuffed animal. Dr. Mackenzie leans back in her seat, making herself larger like they say you should when confronted with a bear or mountain lion on the hiking trails back home. I always thought I would get eaten immediately.

"I restrict because of patriarchy, classism, fatphobia, sizeism, sexism, misogyny." I rattle off the words like I'm reading from a manual. "We live in a fucked-up world." I slouch and my stomach curls inward, a C shape. Hollow. Empty.

"Yes, we do," Dr. Mackenzie agrees.

I wonder if this place was designed to help its patients forget how fucked-up the world is. Sitting in this room is like sitting in a snow globe.

Then again, less than an hour ago, Dr. Mackenzie was studying my body for scars and bruises. Rush's Recovery may have thick towels, organic lotions, and fine coffee, but my stay here isn't a luxurious vacation no matter how hard they try to disguise it as one.

The center doesn't even have a website. If you search hard enough, you can find mentions of an unnamed center where the disgraced Hollywood producer went for sex addiction, the rehab where some billionaire hedge-fund manager went after he'd gambled away other people's money while high on coke, the recovery facility where a pop star went for "exhaustion," trying to salvage her reputation after a terrible scandal.

I shift the conversation. "Am I your only patient while I'm here?"

Dr. Mackenzie nods. "Each guest has their own care manager."

"How many 'guests' can Rush's Recovery accommodate at one time?"

"We have three cottages," she says, which isn't exactly an answer.

"How long have you worked here?"

"Just under three years."

"So you weren't here when my mother was."

"No."

"So for all you know, they used to run this place totally differently."

"While I don't know exactly how things worked before I came here, I can assure you that at every turn, our goal is to keep our guests safe and secure during their stay. We want Rush's Recovery to be a refuge."

The word brings to mind wildlife trapped inside fences where poachers can't reach them. Or my great-grandparents, refugees from a government that wanted them dead, forced to give up the lives they'd built in Germany. Refuges can keep you safe, but they come with a cost.

"You can't guarantee your patients' safety," I counter.

"Guests," Dr. Mackenzie corrects. Her expression softens, like she thinks I'm scared of what I might do to myself if left unsupervised. "I assure you that I will never be more than a few moments away. In fact, I checked on you overnight while you slept."

"You did?" The skin on the back of my hands feels hot.

"After you went to bed at eleven, I set my alarm to look in on you. Once at two a.m., and then again at five." She sounds as though she thinks I'll be relieved to hear it.

"So you're going to check on me every night at two and five?" I ask.

"Will it make you feel safer to know the schedule?" Dr. Mackenzie asks.

"Yes," I say quickly.

It's almost the truth.

∾

In the afternoon, a woman with an Australian accent who tells me her name is Leonie arrives. She leads me to a yoga studio on the cottage's lower level, passing (I assume) the bedrooms where Maurice, Izabela, and Dr. Mackenzie sleep, where Dr. Mackenzie sets her alarm to check on me like I'm her sick child.

The yoga studio has mirrors along one side, floor to ceiling, like the room where Georgia sent me to ballet class when I was little.

I always wanted to be a ballerina, she said. *But Grandma Naomi said that kind of thing was a waste of money. No one makes a living as a ballerina.* Georgia mimicked her mother's voice when she said that. I was supposed to laugh, but I didn't.

Six years old and you already take her side over mine.

There's a barre against one wall, and I resist the urge to stand next to it and plié, practicing first position, second position, all the way up to fifth. My ballet teacher said I had bad feet, and Naomi pulled me out of class in fifth grade.

Naomi also decided I should go to boarding school in Big Sur when I turned fifteen (harder for Georgia to show up smashed to parent-teacher conferences that were 350 miles away), followed by college in the Northeast, with the semester abroad (Paris) my junior year, followed by graduate school in New York City.

I think this may have been the first place I actually asked her to send me.

Despite the cold weather, Leonie is wearing only leggings and a sports bra. Her arms are long and lean, her legs tightly muscled, her obliques visible on either side of her torso. She leads me through restorative postures, putting her hands on my hips when I'm in down dog, and I can feel my spine lengthening as she pushes me, like she's trying to force me to get bigger.

This isn't the first treatment center that thought yoga would make me feel more connected to my body, more *inside* my body. They believe having someone else's hands on my skin will lead to some kind of breakthrough and I'll realize that *I take up space, I have borders and edges that can't be breached.*

They always talk about *my body* as though it's an entity all its own.

Love your body.

Feed your body.

Move your body.

Their words are like a refrain from a song I can't get out of my head. As though my body is a stray dog found by the side of the road that needs to be cleaned up before it can be adopted by a family who will love it forever. #Proana influencers like to talk about historical figures who were sainted for starvation. Of heroes who went on hunger strikes to protest an unjust occupation, a war, a right deprived. Suffragettes would pin ribbons to their chests, proudly announcing to the world for how many days they'd gone without. But no one holds people like me as heroic.

I wonder if my fit, cheerful yoga teacher knows that most theories about eating disorders (they're all about control, they're exclusive to rich white women . . . , etc) have been debunked, or at least augmented by other explanations. Some research suggests they may in fact be neurobiological, which means all those therapists who complained about ED patients, calling us "difficult," really ought to apologize, because we weren't being *difficult* when we resisted treatment at odds with out brains' wiring.

After yoga, I pick up my phone and see a text from my grandmother: *I love you.* I write back, *I love you, too.*

And another message from Jonah: *Take all the space you need. Just glad you're okay.*

Okay is a vague term, covering a multitude of scenarios Jonah (who grew up in a house both his parents called home, with Christmas dinner and family vacations to Disney World) can't possibly imagine. Not even after everything that happened.

Leonie and Dr. Mackenzie think I need to put on five, ten, fifteen pounds to be healthy. If I were *truly* healthy, I would be twenty-five pounds heavier right now, at least, but they don't know that.

No one does, except Jonah.

16

Amelia Blue

After Georgia died, Naomi boxed up everything that had belonged to her—clothes, books with bent spines in whose margins she'd scribbled, unsigned contracts, forgotten makeup. I was finishing my senior year at boarding school, and by the time I got home, all traces of my mother were stacked in plastic bins in the garage. Naomi told me she'd tried to organize everything, but it had proved impossible. Even when Georgia was alive, Naomi and I had never been able to make sense of how she arranged her belongings.

This past June, when I moved back to the house in Laurel Canyon after graduate school, I opened the boxes and bins for the first time. The contents still smelled like my mother, her unmistakable scent of hair dye and patchouli, sweat and ink wafting from the bins like smoke.

It was almost impossible to distinguish what should have been trash from what was worth keeping, but eventually I found the notebook that's in my hands now. I've read its pages so many times over the past six months that I can practically recite the contents, but I couldn't imagine leaving it behind when I came here.

The first page reads, *Twelve days sober. My sponsor says I should keep track.*

The next day: *Someone recognized me at the meeting last night. Up till now, everyone has at least pretended not to.* (*Pretended* is underlined twice.)

I had to read those sentences three times before I understood them, my mother's words like a song that I couldn't get out of my head even though I didn't understand the lyrics, as foreign as the Hebrew prayers Naomi taught me to say at Georgia's funeral without telling me what they meant.

Finally, I understood: I'd found my mother's sober diary, written, according to the dates scrawled at the top of each page, over the year before she died. Georgia had a sponsor. She was, apparently, going to AA meetings.

Eighteen days and the house is quiet with Amelia Blue away at school. Sometimes I forget Mom is here, she skulks around like a mouse. Not that any sounds Amelia Blue makes when she comes home are directed toward me. I can't remember the last time she spoke to me.

I didn't think she'd noticed when I stopped talking to her. She talked enough for the both of us.

Day 23: Sobriety is sneaky. It holds open the door for all the thoughts you tried to keep outside.

I stare at the page like I think more information will magically appear. But Georgia didn't bother explaining what thoughts she meant.

Thoughts about me? About my wrong nose, wrong hair, even the wrong disorder? All the reasons Georgia let Naomi raise me rather than doing it herself.

I read the diary for what must be the thousandth time. It's a plain spiral notebook, nothing like the journals I kept as a little kid—bound books that Naomi gave me with locks and keys, inspirational quotes on every other page, pictures of teddy bears and puppies dancing across the front covers. Scattered in between Georgia's day-by-day count are nonsense words and phrases, like sometimes she ran out of thoughts about sobriety and simply wrote whatever came to mind just to have something to do.

The final entry is dated January 2, 2015. Two weeks before she came here.

Day 203: New Year, still sober.

It's possible, of course, that the words in the journal aren't true. Georgia lied like she breathed. No reason to think she didn't lie to herself, too. We tell ourselves stories in order to live and all that.

I close the diary and scroll through my phone. But instead of a break from Georgia, my social media feed is full of posts about her, the algorithm encouraged by the rabbit hole I went down last night. There's a video of my mother performing at some dive bar in Downtown Manhattan, black tights ripped at the knees, pink lipstick smeared across her face. Another post shows a series of photos of my parents together with the caption "Is this the most nineties couple ever?" In the comments, people argue whether my parents are nearly as iconic as Kurt and Courtney or Richard and Cindy or Brad and Jen.

Another post, this one from @sonjalovesgeorgia, reads, *Big news, #JFG Warriors!!*

I glance at the caption, expecting to see news about boycotting Shocking Pink's reunion tour, but instead there's this: *Has anyone else seen the police report from the last time Georgia was arrested? Her tox screen was clean! The press lied, but what else is new? They've been telling tales about our girl since she burst on the scene. #boycottshockingpink #justiceforgeorgia*

I squint even though the words on the screen are perfectly clear. The last time Georgia was arrested wasn't particularly remarkable. Another drug-fueled brawl (according to the press), another night in lockup, followed by another trip to rehab (here), and another public statement about getting sober and managing the disease of addiction. Nothing (I thought at the time) that hadn't happened before. Even if the contents of the diary are true, she could've easily fallen off the wagon by then; the diary's final page is dated almost a week before the night she was arrested.

Of course, @sonjalovesgeorgia could be lying. Georgia's fans have posted plenty of nonsense over the years. Someone claimed that Georgia wasn't dead at all, she was in hiding in the French countryside, so that people posted grainy pictures they claimed were her like they'd sighted Bigfoot. Someone else insisted that my grandmother had murdered Georgia so she could control my trust and the millions that came with it. Another fan suggested I'd had her killed, and all my stints in treatment were for psychosis, not eating disorders.

I study @sonjalovesgeorgia's profile, holding my phone like an egg that might crack. Her hair is dark and parted down the middle, framing her face like curtains. White ink tattoos snake up and down her arms, and in most of her posts, she's wearing nineties-era vintage clothing: baby-doll dresses, floral headbands, ripped fishnets with motorcycle boots. Even though she technically looks nothing like my mother—black hair, aquiline nose, a dimple in her chin—somehow she resembles Georgia more than I do. Certainly, she's the sort of daughter Georgia would've had fun with, the sort of daughter who's spent her life publicly defending her hero, begging the rest of the world not to let Shocking Pink perform my mother's music without my mother there to take center stage.

All my life, I *knew* these people were crazed fans with absurd conspiracy theories, but then I also *knew* that Georgia was a basket case whose every move was determined by which substances she happened to be on that day. I look around the pristine bedroom, as though its right angles and white walls might reveal hints, telling me what's true and what's not.

I click on @sonjalovesgeorgia's most recent post, from two days ago, January 12, 2025.

I'm going dark for a while. I'll probably be offline 'til after the anniversary, but I promise to give you more before SP goes on tour this spring. Like and follow for more info soon! #boycottshockingpink #justiceforgeorgia #jfg

I sigh. Clearly, @sonjalovesgeorgia is an influencer trying to attract more followers. I scroll through her feed. Sprinkled between #georgiafan posts are paid advertisements for everything from toothpaste to pumice stones to lip gloss. Even if she did track down the police report (something that never occurred to me to do), she only did it to excite Georgia's fans so she can keep selling them moisturizer and sunscreen, no better than the classmates who pretended to be my friend so they could sell a photo to blogs and magazines.

I press my fists into my stomach. It's nearly midnight, more than two hours till Dr. Mackenzie's check-in and there's a bass thump filling the air. Somewhere, someone is playing music too loud. Overloud music was the soundtrack to my childhood, as familiar as a lullaby.

I drop my hand, cross the room, and open the bedroom door. I half expect to see Dr. Mackenzie sleeping on the floor outside my room, but the hallway is empty. I tiptoe toward the kitchen, my belly in knots.

17

Florence

Just you wait, I'm gonna get her back,
The whole world will know,
I'm gonna get her back,
There's nowhere she can go,
I'm gonna get her back,
Nowhere she can hide,
I'm gonna get her back,
Everyone will take my side.

I throw the covers off my body, suddenly hot. That fucking song is in my brain so deep it's showing up in my dreams. Or maybe I wasn't asleep. Maybe I *can't* sleep anymore. Maybe years and years of coke and speed and whatever-the-hell-else fried the part of my brain that knew how to sleep and dream, and now I have no choice but to lie awake for the rest of my days. It's not true that you'll die without sleep. The human body's more adaptable than we give it credit for.

When Callie suggested this place, she promised no one would know exactly where I was. She said it like that was supposed to make me feel safer. Now, in the middle of the night, without my phone, I feel stranded. If something happened to me here, no one would know.

I get out of bed, my bare feet cold against the hardwood floors. There's a tiny white rug beside the bed, no bigger than a bathmat. This place could use some carpeting. The floor-to-ceiling windows everywhere make everything so goddamn drafty.

Drafty,
Nasty,
My skin is pasty.

How am I supposed to write anything halfway decent when I can't get Joni Jewell's fucking lyrics out of my head?

The chorus of dead musicians in my brain asks, *What was your excuse before Joni released her song?*

Janis Joplin laughs. Anger tingles beneath my skin. Before I attacked Joni, multiple witnesses heard me scream,

I'll kill you for what you did to me.

I meant it, even though Callie was quick to point out that I didn't exactly have a good reputation before Joni released that song.

Anyway, just because I meant it doesn't mean I was going to *do* it.

Boy, did you lose your shit, the Kurt Cobain in my head says.

Joni Jewell's got nothing on you, the Scott Harris says, trying to calm me. Most fans don't know that Scott Harris had terrible stage fright. He had to get high before every performance. Not like me. For me, the performance *was* the high.

Callie told the press I didn't know what I was saying. So-called journalists called me *dangerous, unstable,* a *has-been,* like they were schoolyard bullies throwing out angry taunts. I wonder if they even remember the things they called me before: *visionary, important, ahead of her time.*

Mom's the only one who called me anything that stuck: Bad Mother.

Bad Mother, Big Brother's
Watching you
Bad Mother, mother fucker
Ain't you blue?

Mom called me shrill long before *Rolling Stone* ever heard my voice. Sometimes I think she wishes I were one of those stars whose drug use got the better of them, like Janis and Jim and Jimi. It'd be so much easier, with me out of the picture.

I walk to the Bose speaker in the living room and turn it on. Satellite radio. I scroll until I reach the nineties grunge station.

I turn the music up, but I can still hear Joni Jewell's incessant warble inside my head.

Louder still, so that it feels like the hardwood floor beneath my feet is thumping.

Louder still, until I can't hear anything but Kurt Cobain screaming in my ears.

His honest screams are so much prettier than Joni Jewell's weak falsetto, aping her namesake for all she's worth. When will the world notice that they've been hanging on to every word from a singer who can't even be bothered to find her own voice?

Be authentic, my husband always said. *People* want *to listen to something real.*

I used to be something real.

But they all stopped listening to me.

18

Lord Edward

I'm back in Manhattan and I can't move; it's as though I left the bottom half of my body somewhere else. Anne's waiting for me on the other side of the street, the paparazzi crowding her. The headlines will read, *Lady Anne's Good-for-Nothing Brother Leaves Her Waiting*.

That's too long for a tabloid headline. They'd be cleverer than that.

Lady Anne Waits, Lord Eddie Ditched Their Date.

They love a good rhyme.

I wake abruptly, pressing the heel of my hands into my eyes. My dreams are terrible—a side effect, supposedly, of the opiates—but being conscious isn't any better.

I roll over and discover what woke me: My phone is ringing. Set to vibrate and perched on one of the downy pillows, it makes the whole mattress shake. In London, it's morning. Whoever's calling must think I'm still in the UK, which means that Anne's campaign to get me here stealthily worked.

I look at the screen. It's not a number I recognize.

I was thirteen when Dad and Anne gave me my own phone. The calls started almost at once: unknown numbers at odd hours, a voice on the other line saying, "Hey, how are you?" as though we were old friends. Groggy and still half-asleep, nervous about offending anyone by admitting I didn't recognize their voice, I kept up my end of the conversation—where I was, what I'd done that day, when I'd last seen my mother, whom my father had been out with that night.

The very next day, the details of the call would be published on the cover of some tabloid. The voice on the other end had been a grown man pretending to be a classmate, or perhaps they had a son or daughter who'd done it for them. My father would scold me for falling for such an obvious ploy; Anne would roll her eyes in disgust. Even when she was my age, her expression communicated, she'd never been so dumb.

I stretch my arms overhead, fully awake now. For months, I've been living in the UK. The doctors thought it would be better for me if I recovered with my family close at hand.

Here, they have a physical therapist called Bryce on call. He took me through my exercises first thing this morning—yesterday morning, I suppose—before breakfast. Bryce promised acupuncture treatments, an hour in a hyperbaric oxygen chamber every day, a cold plunge in an ice bath if I'm willing.

"We'll get you on your feet again," Bryce had said, then blanched at his choice of words.

In August, the official press release stated that there'd been an accident in the States and my leg had been *damaged*. No further details were given regarding my condition. Was that Anne's idea, or mine? Will she leak the truth someday, when she needs a story to appease the press? When she wants to punish me?

I toss the covers off. This mattress is too soft. I'll tell Dr. Rush at breakfast so they can replace it with a firmer model. *Whatever we can do to make you more comfortable,* Dr. Rush will surely say.

The phone falls silent on the bed beside me, and now I notice a musical thump in the air, coming in through the windows so they're practically pulsing in time with the beat.

I pull myself out of bed and move awkwardly toward the wall of windows. I don't turn on the lights. I don't want to see my reflection.

Even though we're in the middle of nowhere—not a skyscraper or a signpost around to brighten the sky—it's not that dark out. The moon and starlight reflect off the water, creating the illusion of dawn though it's after midnight.

I can see two other structures from my bedroom, about ten yards away on either side, each a corner of an equilateral triangle. The one on the left is lit up. Through the glass, I make out a figure with a bleach-blond mop of hair, dancing.

I slide the terrace door open, hopping outside. The cold air feels thin, easier to breathe than the artificially warm air inside. The music is louder out here, though I can't quite make out what song is playing. I clutch the railing for balance, the metal so cold against my palms that it feels sharp.

On my right, the third cabin is dark but for a tiny dot of light on the terrace. It takes me a second to recognize it as the tip of a cigarette. Finally, I make out the silhouette of a small person smoking.

Amelia Blue.

The girl I met because the driver said *Sir, I'm afraid there's been an accident.*

Hasn't anyone else noticed the absurdity of using the same word to refer to a missed train or spilled drink that we use to describe a fatal car crash, a broken limb? My birth—or at least my conception—was surely an accident. My parents can't have possibly *intended* to have a second child so many years after Anne was born, particularly when they were on the verge of their inevitable divorce. They didn't need another child, their duty long since done. (Before Anne was born, Dad arranged it so that his estate would be passed down to his eldest child regardless of gender, breaking centuries of tradition, garnering praise from the public. The *progressive duke*, the press said.)

The music must've woken Amelia Blue. Or perhaps she never fell asleep. If she's here for coke or some such, there could be so many stimulants coursing through her system that she literally cannot close her eyes. I've heard that some people need to be sedated so the drugs they took recreationally have time to get out of their systems. In the car with her, I was too busy feigning sleep to notice whether her pupils were overlarge, the whites of her eyes bloodshot.

Before I can limp back to bed, there's a light flashing in my eyes. I raise a hand as if I'm blocking the sun. Amelia Blue is holding up her phone, the flashlight pointing in my direction. I'm grateful that the railing around the deck is solid rather than slatted. It blocks my bottom half.

She's waving at me.

Then she's moving—across her terrace, down the metal stairs that lead into the courtyard between our cottages.

Good lord, is she coming *here?*

Quick as I can, I make my way inside and ready myself, pulling on sweatpants and boots, shivering. I head back to the terrace and down the stairs, keeping my focus on the light from her phone, bouncing steadily with each step she takes. Her gait is short and quick, something of a shuffle as she doesn't pick her feet high off the ground.

On the streets of the cities where I've lived—London, Manhattan—there are a million different kinds of walkers: businesspeople rushing from one appointment to the next; tourists taking up entire sidewalks as they inch along, enjoying their vacations; groups of students bent over their phones while they gossip, each and every one so sure of their steps that they don't bother looking where they're going. Even the dogs have particular strides: sure-footed Labradors and golden retrievers, tiny chihuahuas rushing to keep up with their humans' long legs, puppies who haven't yet learned to walk in a straight line.

I wish I could recall exactly how I walked before. I hope, at least, that the dim light conceals my limp enough that Amelia Blue won't ask questions.

The metal handrail along the stairs has a thin coating of ice that cracks beneath my grip like glass. I wonder if Amelia Blue will be dressed more warmly tonight than she was when she arrived.

Someone could catch their death out here.

19

Amelia Blue

Here's something I learned only recently but that I know for sure: Brushing your teeth is an ineffective way to get the taste of vomit out of your mouth. The best way to get the taste out is to get another taste *in*, but eating something would defeat the purpose.

And so, when the purging started, so did the smoking. It's absurd, I know. You're supposed to start smoking in middle school, maybe high school or college, because you're a nervous teenager and it gives you something to do with your hands when you're alone at a party. Nearly thirty is the age to quit these kinds of self-destructive habits.

In between #proana posts and suggested reels of Georgia and my dad, I've also watched my former classmates commit to dry January, to daily exercise, to at last finishing the novel they started writing when they turned twenty-one. They're getting married and making babies and scraping together down payments. Meanwhile, I've reverted to adolescence. (Although there's growing evidence that women struggle with EDs into middle age and beyond, so maybe I'm right on schedule.)

I used to hear girls throwing up in the communal bathrooms of my boarding school, my college dorm. They would flush the toilet while I brushed my teeth at the sink below a spattered mirror, then come out and wash their hands. Once in a while, some girl would claim food poisoning and warn me against the egg salad in the cafeteria, but more often than not, they didn't bother lying. Every so often, one of them might catch my eye in the mirror and smile like we were in on something together.

I stand beneath the terrace's gas lamp, the flame casting shadows on my hands as it flickers above me. I note the other sources of light: the tip of my cigarette, moonlight reflecting off a thin layer of snow on the ground, squat lanterns planted beside the perfectly cleared paths that snake between my cabin and the next.

I take a long drag on my cigarette. Even *Georgia* didn't smoke.

Along the path, there are boxwoods covered in burlap to keep the deer away for the winter. Bushes of hydrangea are cut down to twigs, neatly manicured even when they're not in bloom. I get the idea that, were I here in summer, the plants would be trimmed into perfect circles, the sort of symmetry that doesn't exist in nature.

I see a shadow moving on the otherwise dark terrace of one of the other two cottages. For a second, adrenaline skitters across my belly. But then I hold up my phone, and the flashlight turns the shadow into a human being.

I slump, leaning back against the house. My grandmother texted me again this afternoon to ask how it was going, and I didn't know how to answer. Underneath her casual inquiry was a desperate plea: *Are you better yet?* As though an eating disorder is a bout of the flu.

The second time my grandmother sent me away for treatment, not long after Georgia died, she said, *Imagine if your mother had gotten help when she was your age.* As though the problem with Georgia was that she started going to rehab too late.

Georgia left home halfway through her senior year of high school. Naomi didn't know where her daughter had gone until she was flipping channels one afternoon and saw Georgia's face on MTV, broadcast from clear across the country. Even then, my grandmother wasn't sure she'd found her daughter: This woman's name was different, her formerly light-brown curly hair blond and straight, cut into a shag that framed her face in the least flattering way possible.

I only ran away once. I was five years old and it was an accident. (I didn't run so much as wander.) A police officer found me in a parking lot near Rodeo Drive, my hands caked with peanut butter, chocolate pudding matted in my hair. They fed me french fries while they waited for my mother to pick me up. *You must be starving,* they said. (To Mom's credit, she had the good sense to invite Naomi to live with us after that.)

Sometimes I think Georgia was disappointed that I never left home on my own with nothing but a dream in my back pocket, like she did.

It's not too late. There's still time for me to live up to the example she set. I could go into the woods right now like the heroine of a fairy tale, seeking refuge in the wilderness.

Eventually, Dr. Mackenzie would discover I'm missing. She might assume, at first, that I grew fed up with therapy and decided to go home. But then she'd notice my suitcase still stored in the closet, my wallet and ID still tucked into the tote bag beside the bed. She'd call my grandmother, maybe the police. The center would launch a proper search party, sparing no expense, hoping to avoid disaster, praying that my family would be spared another tragedy.

At last, they'd find my body sitting on the beach, as peaceful as if I were watching the tide come out and in and out again, an endless loop. Once again, the center would be blameless, as they couldn't have stopped me from leaving. In fact, holding a patient against their will would be illegal, as they were quick to mention ten years ago.

The figure on the other terrace holds up a hand.

I can't quite believe Lord Edward is waving at me, considering he pretended to sleep rather than speak to me in the Range Rover when we arrived. Despite the cold, he's wearing a T-shirt, and even from here I can see how fit he is: his arms taut with muscles, his collarbones straight beneath his neck as though he never slouched a day in his life. The terraces are edged with a fence made of solid cedar, cutting his body in half at the waist. It looks almost like he's floating, but his hands grip the metal railing along the top of the fence like it's the only thing holding him upright. I recall reading that he'd been in a car accident a few months ago.

I look beyond the path into the woods and shiver, the image of my lost, frozen body on the beach floating in my mind's eye. I wind my scarf around my neck, wiggling my toes in my shearling boots.

In stories, it isn't safe to meet a man you barely know in the woods in the middle of the night. But I don't want to go inside where the lingering scent of vomit wafts from the bathroom. When she was here, Georgia surely wasn't too timid to venture into the woods alone. For all I know, she stalked fearlessly through the darkness every night of her stay. If I do the same, I might be following her footsteps, seeing what she saw, experiencing what she experienced. Isn't that why I'm here, at least in part?

Sometimes I wonder what might have happened if my mother had been a little more frightened of the world, a little more careful. But then she never would've left home, never would've met my father, and I never would've existed to wonder anything at all.

I throw down my cigarette and walk toward the stairs.

20

Lord Edward

By the time we meet halfway between our cabins, Amelia Blue's smoking a fresh cigarette. She's wearing gloves, but they're fingerless, and the skin around her nails looks purplish, not entirely alive. I recall how cold her hand was when I shook it in the back seat of the Range Rover. I'd felt the urge to blow on her fingers to warm them, as though I were a big brother or a father, exhibiting the sort of caretaking instinct no one ever expected from me—the baby of the family, the problem child.

"Want one?" she offers, and I shake my head. "I know," she adds, as though I've said something she agrees with. "Disgusting habit."

"Maybe they can help you kick it while you're here."

She laughs—loudly at first, and then, as if remembering that we're surely not supposed to be out here together, more quietly.

"Where should we go, Amelia Blue?" I ask.

"Just Amelia's okay, Lord Edward."

"Just Edward's better than okay."

Amelia nods, and I know she only said my name to give me the opportunity to ask her to drop the *Lord*.

"It's supposed to be one name—*Amelia Blue*, like *Mary Anne*. I don't think my mother realized most people aren't up for that many syllables."

"You ever think about changing it?" My father's title, the Duke of Exeter, goes back hundreds of years. The notion of changing one's name is quite literally foreign to me, another of those American quirks I haven't internalized, despite living almost entirely in the States since I was sixteen.

Amelia cocks her head, considering. "No one's ever asked me that," she answers finally. "Actually, I wouldn't want to drop the Blue."

"Why not?"

"I know most people think my mother named me Amelia Blue because she has a thing for color—like, her old band's name was Shocking Pink, you know?"

I nod, but the truth is, I've never heard of her mother's band.

"But actually, her grandparents were the Blaus—German for blue—before they emigrated to America and anglicized it to fit in. My mother changed her name when she decided to become famous."

I raise an eyebrow. Having been born to fame—notoriety, at least—I sometimes forget that other people *choose* it.

"So to answer your question, I wouldn't change my name. I wouldn't throw away all that history."

"I'm actually the eighth Lord Edward of Exeter," I offer. "So we have that in common."

"What do you mean?"

"We both have names that aren't entirely our own."

Amelia nods thoughtfully, taking another drag off her cigarette as she steps down the path. "We can't go far," she says irritably. "I have to be back by two for my care manager's next check-in."

"What?"

"Didn't they tell you? They do bed checks all night long."

As soon as Amelia says it, I know it must be true, despite Dr. Rush never having mentioned it. Even if it wasn't their official policy, it's the sort of thing Anne would have asked for. The idea that Dr. Rush could see me, see my body while I'm asleep and oblivious, makes me grind my teeth. At this rate, I'll be lucky if I can still chew my food a year from now.

"They can't see everything," Amelia says, sensing my discomfort. "It's like the paparazzi, catching glimpses of our lives and thinking they can tell the world what we're really like."

My jaw loosens. "Luckily, years of boarding school made me an expert at sneaking around."

"Didn't you get kicked out of boarding school?" Amelia doesn't pretend not to know this particular bit of my history.

"Not for sneaking around."

"Why, then?" she asks matter-of-factly, as though it doesn't occur to her that my family went to great lengths to conceal the real reason.

Maybe it's the drugs blurring my edges, or maybe it's knowing that, having also been born to famous parents, people have probably been googling Amelia her whole life as well, looking up statistics about her height and education and the trouble she got into. Maybe it's because her name is every bit as complicated as my own, or because she didn't hesitate before asking the question, but I tell Amelia the secret Anne and my father worked so hard to hide: "I got drunk on campus."

Amelia shrugs, unimpressed. "Isn't that practically required at English boarding schools?"

"Yes, but most people don't destroy school property in the process."

In fact, plenty of students damage school property, but few have ever managed what I did.

Conflagrate was the word the headmaster used. *Obliterate.*

Then, *Someone could've been killed.*

Dad had rolled his eyes at that, not even pretending to respect the headmaster's authority. *Don't tell me my son's another angry young man,* he said, as though the truly disappointing thing was that I was a cliché on top of everything else.

In private, Anne compared me to the sort of sociopaths who torture toads and squirrels in childhood, moving their way up the food chain one animal at a time until they got to humans.

One day it'll be the police knocking on the door, she said, more to our father than me, *to tell us about the people you hurt.*

"What was the official story?" Amelia asks.

My family told the press I was failing my classes. They had no problem with the world thinking I was too thick to survive Eton.

"Let's make a deal," I say. "You don't look me up, and I won't look you up. We'll meet like regular people, without all the 'official stories' to confuse us."

"Regular people are all over the internet, too," Amelia points out, "but deal." She looks relieved, which almost makes me laugh out loud. Surely the stories I might find about her are more flattering than the ones about me. The tabloids labeled me the "Bad Boy Duke" when I was sixteen, despite the fact that my only chance at becoming a duke would be if my father, Anne, and her two sons all died.

Amelia takes another drag off her cigarette. We follow the path back to her cabin, and then she turns on her heel, wending her way toward the third cabin, the music growing louder with every step.

"What do you think they're in for?" she asks, nodding at the noisy cottage.

"Hearing loss?" I suggest.

Amelia shakes her head. "You shouldn't make fun of someone for having a disability."

Spoken like someone who doesn't have one, I think. Amelia drops her cigarette on the ground and stamps it out, then bends down and picks the butt off the ground, putting it in her pocket. I'm not sure if she's opposed to littering or if she's trying to conceal evidence that she was out here.

"Anyway," she continues, "this music isn't that loud."

"Isn't it?"

"Not compared to what my mother used to play."

"Usually parents are the ones trying to get their kids to keep it down."

"Not in my house," Amelia answers. "How about you?"

"How about me what?"

"What're you in for?"

"I don't think you're supposed to ask."

"I don't think I'm supposed to be out here in the middle of the night, either." She stretches her arms out wide. "How big do you think this place is?" she asks, moving on to another subject agreeably. "Like the actual *property*, how many acres?"

"Dunno," I answer.

"Dr. Mackenzie told me they only have three cottages. Don't you hate how they call them cottages, like we're at some rustic resort in the English countryside?"

"A resort in the English countryside wouldn't have Nest thermostats." The aristocracy loves an opportunity to prove they don't care for modern comforts like central air conditioning and well-insulated rooms. Our Scottish estate is drafty in winter and sweltering in summer.

"There's got to be more than three buildings to this place." Amelia gestures behind her cottage, where at least one shadowy structure takes up space in the milky darkness.

"Could be an administrative building of some kind," I agree.

"Right!" Amelia agrees enthusiastically, as if I've said something important. I get the sense that Amelia's the sort of person who looks at the resort map before she arrives at a hotel.

Maybe Amelia *wanted* to be sent here. Some people *ask* for help rather than have it forced upon them by others who don't have the slightest idea of what help really is.

"Alcoholism," I say. The answer comes easily. I like that Amelia didn't press me for not answering earlier.

"Huh?"

"What I'm in for." It doesn't feel like a confession. Perhaps it's easy to say because it's not entirely true. Anne thinks I take my medication "as directed."

Amelia stops walking to light another cigarette. I reach out to shield the flame from the wind. My fingers brush against hers, her skin so cold it's like being burned.

"Aren't alcoholics supposed to spend the first few days of rehab shivering and throwing up?" She sounds genuinely curious.

"I haven't had a drink in months."

Amelia's brow furrows with skepticism—what kind of alcoholic quits drinking months before entering rehab?—but I don't offer an explanation, though I know I'm supposed to say something more: I'm meant to lapse into a daydream as I recall the mineral taste of cold white wine on a hot summer day, the clink of ice in a glass, the ritual of raising a toast at some celebration—a wedding, graduation, even a funeral. I ought to explain that I've tried to fill the hole it left behind with exercise or historical biographies or knitting or macramé. Isn't that what addicts do, to keep their hands and minds occupied, literally too busy to take a drink?

"What about you?" I ask finally. "What are you in for?"

"It's complicated." Amelia waves her cigarette dismissively, dodging my question, though her non-answer feels less like a lie than my actual answer did. "Hey, is it true you dropped cake on the queen's shoes when you were ten?"

"Well, I heard you blew your nose on Eddie Vedder's sleeve when you were a baby."

"I was five." Amelia sounds as petulant as a child. "I got lost at the VMAs."

"He had to perform with your snot on his shirt."

"And the queen had to wipe off your frosting."

"You think she didn't have people to do that kind of thing for her?"

"So it *is* true?" I hesitate, and Amelia begs, "C'mon, I told you mine."

"Eddie Vedder isn't exactly Elizabeth II."

"I'll tell you a Paul McCartney story later. Eddie Vedder plus Sir Paul adds up to one queen."

"Debatable." I sigh heavily. "There was a luncheon at Buckingham Palace. They had cake. And we weren't allowed junk food at home."

I can still taste the cake—overbaked and dry, turning to glue in my mouth. *Not worth the calories,* Anne would say.

"So I parked myself next to the buffet and had at it."

Amelia laughs. Anne always emphasized the importance of telling a good story. No one will stop you from controlling the narrative when it's one they enjoy.

So I don't say how badly I wanted to hide beneath the table, or that I filled my mouth with pieces of cake, hoping to look busy so no one would talk to me.

"You try telling a ten-year-old to forgo sweets so he can meet some old lady," I say, and Amelia laughs again, covering her mouth.

I wasn't ten. I was fourteen, but the story's funnier if it happened to a little kid. At fourteen, it's sadder than it is amusing.

Anne was at Dad's side, tall and slim and poised. Eleven years older than I, she was already engaged to an appropriate man, nothing like the overgrown adolescent whose feet were too big for his body, whose chin was still surrounded by puppy fat. She'd met the queen before. So had I, but I'd been a toddler at the time; her majesty was technically a cousin of some sort. Anne would know the exact lineage, but I could never keep it straight.

When Dad gestured for me to stand beside him, there was still a slice of cake in my hand. I couldn't put it down. When Dad calls, he expects an answer right away.

I'd practiced my bow for weeks before the luncheon. As the queen's eyes traveled from Dad (bow) to Anne (curtsey) to me, I knew what to do. I don't know how it happened. One moment, the cake was in my hand, the next at my feet. Dad assumed I'd been drinking—the first time my drinking was referred to as a "problem"; getting kicked out of Eton a few months later was the second time. It would've been more humiliating to admit I'd been sober.

"So how about that Paul McCartney story?" I ask, but Amelia holds up her phone.

"Crap—one forty-eight!" She breaks into a run. "I'll tell you all about Sir Paul tomorrow!"

Without thinking, I jog after her. For a brief moment, it feels easy and familiar: racing back to my room to hide under the covers, avoiding trouble. But at once, a shooting pain travels up my left thigh. I stop in my tracks.

"Oh, I'm sorry," Amelia says, bouncing in place beside me as though trying to keep warm. I don't know how she manages without a coat. "You were in a car accident this summer, right?" She looks apologetic. "I swear I didn't look you up, but it's hard to avoid the headlines."

"Yeah." I nod, clenching my jaw so hard that it's difficult to speak. "Fucked up my leg."

"We're almost there," she says, putting her arm around my waist. I lean on her like a human crutch. I expect her to collapse beneath my weight, but she remains steady.

"You're stronger than you look," I say.

I feel her shrug. "Yeah, well, my mother used drugs for most of my life. I have a lot of experience holding someone upright."

The top of Amelia's head doesn't reach my armpit, but she's more sure-footed than I will ever be again. "You okay to get up the stairs?" she asks when we reach my cottage.

I nod again. "You go," I manage. I'm sweating bullets, but my skin feels like ice when the wind blows. "Hurry."

She pulls away. I wait, watching her move across the path between our rooms. She doesn't run so much as skip, landing on the balls of her feet, almost hopping between her steps. Her wavy hair bounces like pigtails on a playground. She disappears into the darkness of her room just as the music from the third cottage cuts out. It's suddenly so quiet that I can't remember what exactly I'm doing outside. Someone else might think they'd dreamed the whole thing, but the pain in my leg reminds me I'm awake.

Carefully, I limp up the stairs, going over the night's conversation in my head to distract myself.

I'll tell you all about Sir Paul tomorrow.

It's been months since I wanted to do anything other than take my next pill, but right now, I want to see Amelia Blue Harris again.

I feel a pang of guilt, as if I'm betraying Harper, then remember that I can't betray Harper anymore.

21

Florence

Tonight, after another day of useless therapy—*Let me help you get in touch with your anger,* Evelyn said, as though she, with her neatly combed hair, her salaried job, her gold wedding band, could possibly relate to what has me so angry—I can't sleep. I press the button next to my bed and ask for sleeping pills.

Evelyn's voice comes through the speaker: "I can't offer you mind-altering substances." She sounds groggy. I'm pleased I woke her up.

"You were so eager to sedate me a couple days ago."

I release the button before I can hear her response.

I get out of bed, the hardwood cool beneath my bare feet. I'm wearing a nightgown that stops just above my knees, no sleeves. I twist my hair into a bun on top of my head, but it falls loose immediately. When I still lived with my husband, he woke with me when I couldn't sleep, never angry that I'd disturbed his rest. At least, he never said so. Could be he was as angry as I am now, he was just better at hiding it.

I grab my guitar and sit cross-legged on the couch in the living room.

You want to know why I'm mad?
Ask my mother, she'll tell you I was born that way.
Ask my ex, he'll tell you I'm the reason he went away.
Ask my kid, she'll tell you I'm crazy,
Ask my talent, it'll tell you I'm lazy.
Just don't ask me,
Don't ask me,
Don't ask me,

Don't ask me—
Why?

At the sound of applause, I nearly jump out of my skin. What was I thinking? I know better.

Places like this, someone's always watching.

The Housekeeper

The morning they find the body, the housekeeper wakes before dawn, as she has every day since she began working here, cleaning the evidence of another late night before anyone else stirs.

There are all sorts of wealthy people, but the wealthiest, in her experience, prefer to forget that they're being waited on at all, so she tries to keep her work out of sight. Even her uniform is a sort of camouflage, dull and nondescript, designed to let her fade into the background, more forgettable than the furniture. The decor here is meant to be seen, noticed, commented upon. *She* isn't.

She begins in the kitchen, hiding any sign that it might have been used overnight, a clean slate for breakfast, a blank surface for another day. The half bath next, just off the living room, scrubbing the toilet so that it looks like it's never been used. These people, she thinks, like to forget not only that they're being waited on, but also that they have bodies that function just the same as poor bodies.

The bedroom and its en suite bathroom, she will clean last. She can't begin until they're no longer in use. This morning, she waits for the sound of someone stirring, anticipating the sweaty sheets she'll change, the damp towels she'll lift off the floor, the dirty underwear she'll wash and fold. Perhaps there will be vomit on the toilet's edges, remnants of an overindulgent night. As she waits, she considers the many reasons a human body might throw up: viruses and parasites, alcohol and drugs and eating disorders. There are so many ways for a body to reject nourishment, so many things that might poison it.

Finally, she tiptoes toward the primary bedroom, pokes her head inside. Instead of a sleeping body, she sees an empty bed.

If anyone had asked her—and of course, no one would—she could tell them what else she's seen over the past days and weeks. People with jobs like hers—doormen, housekeepers, gardeners—they know the wealthy's secrets: when they leave and come home, what they eat and drink, when they fall asleep and wake up and with whom.

The power dynamic, she thinks, is terribly lopsided, and not entirely in the wealthy's favor, though they're the ones who hire and fire and compensate. When blending into the background is part of your job description, people forget you're there, but your eyes and ears function all the same. Better, perhaps, senses heightened by your own silence.

The people she works for aren't stupid. They made her sign an NDA, of course, leaving her contractually bound to keep their secrets as though she were nothing more than a human safety deposit box. As though they can lock her up and pocket the key. But she understands that nothing known by a stranger can be entirely secret, no matter the paperwork that stranger may have signed. Even if she never tells what she's seen and heard, it will live inside her.

She enters the cottage's bedroom—that's what *they* call it, a cottage—and starts the work of cleaning it. She knows that eventually, someone will arrive and explain why the house is empty. They won't realize that she doesn't need an explanation. She may not be allowed to share their secrets, but that doesn't stop her making sense of them.

She already understands that the person who slept in this bedroom will not be coming back.

22

Florence

"Sorry." Andrew flips a switch, illuminating the kitchen island, and him standing behind it, appearing as unexpectedly as he did during my therapy session. "Didn't mean to scare you."

He's wearing the same gray uniform and black hoodie, though now his sleeves are down over his wrists. I wonder if he had to prove he could enter a room silently to get this job.

I swing the guitar onto the couch beside me. "I don't scare that easy."

"I thought you might want something to eat," he explains. "You barely had any dinner."

"What, they keeping track of that, too?"

Andrew shakes his head. "Just a chef trying to please his customer."

"I'm not a customer. And you're not really a chef."

"I've cooked every meal you've had since you arrived."

"Just admit that they hired you more for your muscle than your skills in the kitchen."

Andrew opens his mouth to protest, then smiles instead. "Fair enough." He holds his hands up like I've beaten him.

I move toward the kitchen and sit at one of the barstools across from him.

"Candy?" he offers.

I nod, feeling like a little kid. The light is dim enough that maybe Andrew can't see the wrinkles framing my mouth, the sun damage freckling my cheeks. I think about the celebrities who died young, beautiful, their faces still pristine: James Dean, River Phoenix. Kurt. Scott.

It's already too late for me to go like that.

The not-really-a-chef procures a bowl of Swedish Fish. I dig in.

"I like your ink." Andrew's gaze runs up and down my bare arms as he reaches into the bowl and pulls out a handful of red fish, popping them one by one into his mouth.

"I don't think your boss approves."

"My boss?"

"Eeeevelyn."

Andrew laughs at the way I say her name. "Yeah, she's not exactly punk rock."

"She make you cover that up?" I nod at his forearm. Andrew pulls up his sleeve, revealing the *Never Settle* tattoo. I reach out, running my fingers over my own words. The letters are slightly smudged, like ink is forever bleeding beneath his skin.

"Not really appropriate," he says.

"The tat, or what it says?"

Or the way I touched you?

"The tattoo." He leans forward, his arms flat against the cold kitchen counter. "Though I don't think Evelyn would get the reference."

Maybe if she'd looked me up online when I told her to, she would.

"You know, the label hated that song? They wanted it off the album." I twist my hair around my fingers.

"You're kidding."

"Yeah, they thought I sounded ungrateful."

"That was kind of the point."

"I know."

"Obviously *you* know," Andrew says, but he doesn't sound sheepish, the way some fans do when they tell you what your songs meant to them, as though the lyrics were about their lives rather than mine.

I never minded when fans took my words and made them theirs. It was everyone else I took issue with. Cover bands making money off singing my songs, the record label selling rights so some strangely gentle version could play in the background of a car commercial. I didn't realize just how much I was giving away when I signed my first contract.

In another context, Andrew would offer me a drink right about now. Maybe something stronger. But here, he says, "You must be freezing," and walks around the island to pull a creamy blanket off the back of the chair where Evelyn sits during therapy. He places the blanket around my shoulders, so soft I think it must be cashmere, then does that thing guys do to have an excuse to touch you, rubbing his hands up and down my upper arms.

"Better?" he asks.

"Better," I answer, though I wasn't actually cold. My husband used to say I ran hot.

Instead of returning to the other side of the kitchen island, he sits on the stool beside me. "You gonna keep working on that song?"

"What song?"

"The one you were writing." He nods toward the couch, toward my guitar.

"I already forgot it," I say, though it's not true.

He hums a few bars.

"I was just dicking around," I say dismissively.

"It sounded pretty good to me."

"You'd be in the minority." No one's wanted new music from me in a long time. Not that I've finished a song in years.

"No way." Andrew shakes his head. "Your fans would love to hear from you."

That's not what Callie says. Not what the record company says. Not what my former bandmates say.

"I'd love to hear from you," Andrew says softly.

His words hover in the air between us for a beat before he stands again, this time grabbing my guitar and strumming it absently. "Ask me why I'm mad," he says.

"What?" I say dumbly.

"That's how the song started, right? Ask me why I'm mad."

"Something like that."

Andrew picks at the guitar strings.

"You play?"

"Not like you play."

"Well, no one plays like I play."

Andrew grins. "That's true."

I feel like an old rocker reminiscing about the glory days, all sinew and faded tattoos while he insists that he used to sell out stadiums. Suddenly, I wish we were talking about something, anything else.

"Tell me something awful about Evelyn."

"Huh?" Andrew's handsome face falters.

"Come on, you must have some dirt on her, working here. Like, tell me her hair is a wig or she's got a hump beneath all that cashmere and crisp cotton. Tell me something so that next time I sit down across from her I can think about it."

Andrew brushes one pointer finger over the other, like *tsk, tsk, tsk.* "That's not very nice."

"I'm not very nice, haven't you heard?"

He rolls his brown eyes. "Joni Jewell is a hack. I mean, come on, what's less original than *I'm gonna go after the bitch who stole my man?*"

"When you say it like that, it sounds like a country song."

Andrew starts crooning, "Woman done stole my man." He exaggerates his slight Southern accent so much it makes me laugh.

"Come on," I beg, "tell me something about Evelyn that proves she isn't as perfect as she pretends to be."

"I really shouldn't."

"You probably shouldn't be talking to me in the middle of the night, either," I point out.

Andrew raises an eyebrow. "Fine," he says, as though I'm dragging the information out of him and he can't resist me any longer. I grin. "She's going through a divorce. Super messy. Her husband's trying to take everything."

"You're not supposed to make me feel sorry for her!" I moan. "Is her ex trying to take her money? Her kids?" I shrug off the blanket Andrew spread over my shoulders.

"Nah, her son's grown up so there's no custody battle or anything like that," Andrew assures me. "But they're in business together, so it's still complicated and awkward while they both try to treat patients without running into each other. Sometimes I think that's why they came up with this individual cottage thing." Andrew waves his hands to indicate the room around us. "Anyway, Evelyn wants to keep the profits to herself."

"Wow, so she's the bad guy?"

Andrew shrugs. "She's not the good guy."

I relax into a slouch. No one's trying to take a kid from their mom. It's just Evelyn henpecking her husband with rules and regulations, getting off on bossing him around like she does me.

"Have you always been a chef-slash-bodyguard?" I ask. Fans like when you're as interested in their lives as they are in yours.

Andrew shakes his head, but I can see that he's pleased to have a chance to talk about himself. "I used to be a waiter-slash-songwriter."

"What happened?"

"Turns out waiter-slash-songwriter isn't very lucrative when no one's interested in what you have to say."

"I used to be a waitress-slash-songwriter."

It's a lie, but it feels true. It's what I'd intended to be when I left home. I thought I'd get some shitty job to finance a shitty life until I hit it big. But instead I met some guy and slept in his bed and ate his food until I met some other guy, and then another.

Even after I hit it big, I met another guy, and then another. By the time I met my husband, I had a bad reputation, though he never believed what they said about me.

"What makes a waiter-slash-songwriter qualified to be a chef-slash-bodyguard?"

"That's a long story," Andrew says. "And not a particularly interesting one."

"You got somewhere to be?" I gesture at the empty room.

"Bed," Andrew says. It almost sounds like an invitation, but then he places the guitar in my lap, his hands hovering above my hips for a beat before he stuffs them into the pockets of his drab gray uniform. "Finish that song. Stay up all night if you have to."

I shake my head. "I never finish anything anymore." What am I doing, admitting that to a stranger?

"This time could be different," he says, lingering beside me. "Lemme know if you get hungry."

"I'm always hungry," I answer, and Andrew grins like it's a good thing. I can't remember the last time anyone looked at me like anything about me was any good.

Mom said that as a baby, I sucked her dry, till her nipples cracked and bled. They made me feed my daughter formula; for the first few days of her life, I was too sick to feed her myself. By the time I was well, she'd gotten used to the bottle, refused to latch onto me.

I walk to the stereo and find the grunge station again, landing on more Nirvana.

Maybe the real reason Kurt killed himself was because he knew, deep down, that he wouldn't be able to keep writing music as good as what he'd written before.

I take a deep breath. I can still smell Andrew's shampoo in the air.

23

Amelia Blue

My Paul McCartney story gives way to the story of how drunk Edward got at Will and Kate's wedding, when he was only twelve years old. I one-up the tale of the handsome celebrity who poured Edward a drink at Harry and Meghan's wedding with the morning in 2003 when I found two stunning A-listers tiptoeing out of my mother's bedroom before dawn.

"What were you doing up so early?" Edward asks. He blows a bubble with a piece of my gum.

I shrug. "I always got up early."

Back then, I woke with the sun to clean the detritus of Georgia's previous night. Naomi was an early riser, too (*Ach, who can sleep late?* she'd say, as though her daughter, sleeping past noon, didn't count), and we'd tidy (my grandmother's favorite word, *tidy*) the house together. I don't think Georgia actually knew that we picked up after her, not because she was too selfish to notice, but because she usually couldn't remember having made the mess to begin with. I once asked Naomi why we didn't have a housekeeper—the (rich) kids I went to school with all had at least one housekeeper—but my grandmother scoffed at the idea of a stranger arranging our clothes, folding our linens, touching our dishes. Georgia's messes, she firmly implied, should be kept in the family.

But Georgia didn't see anything messy about the way she left the house. More than once, when I moved one of the many pieces of paper covered in her barely legible scrawl scattered around the house like dust, she complained that I'd disturbed her *system*.

When I was fourteen, I bought a doorknob for my bedroom that I could lock from either side. I used a ruler to hang the posters on my wall perfectly straight. I arranged the books on my shelves alphabetically, by theme and author. Georgia said it was so clean it was like a hospital room. (That, I know she meant as an insult. I took it as a compliment.)

"What do other people talk about?" Edward asks me.

"When?" I say, though I know what he means.

"When you ask someone else—someone normal—"

I pull a therapy face, silently admonishing him for using the word *normal*, the way every therapist I've ever had has done to me.

Edward rolls his eyes good-naturedly, then continues, "When you ask normal people about their childhoods, what do they talk about?"

I shrug like I don't know the answer, even though I do. Jonah told me he spent his childhood sledding in the park behind his suburban house in the winter and learning to swim at a lake upstate after his mother had slathered his skin with sunscreen in the summer. If Jonah were here, he would call Edward's and my stories *surreal*, a word one of my writing professors told me never to use. (She also warned against using the word *suddenly*, or clichés including *furrowed brows* and *bitten lips*, even though people do both things.) Jonah traced my small scars with his lips as though he could *kiss it better*, the way attentive parents (the sort whose children aren't found by police officers, crying in parking lots) do for skinned knees and scrapes.

I told Edward my reasons for being here are complicated, but maybe it's quite simple. Maybe I'm here because I didn't have a childhood like Jonah's.

It's cold enough to see our breath. I picture my wool coat hanging in the closet in Laurel Canyon, forgotten after having been shipped from my tiny West Village apartment last spring. I skim icy fingers over my stomach. There's a tiny stretch of softness around my waistband, a reminder of my body's refusal to cooperate, its inability to do what it should, to work the way other people's (*normal* people's) bodies work.

"Let's do something different tonight," I say to Edward. I'm sick of walking in circles on the path between our cottages, circles that seem smaller and less productive with each revolution. If my mother used these paths, surely I've walked them enough by now to say I traced her footsteps.

"Bored with me already?" Edward limps slightly, almost as if he's wearing the wrong-size shoes.

"I'm bored with *this*." I gesture to the dirt-strewn yards between the three cottages, stretching out like an enormous, twisting Y.

Each day, I've done my yoga and stared at Dr. Mackenzie's symmetrical face while she asks her questions, and they've kept the fridge filled with so much Greek yogurt it looks like the dairy section in a grocery store, along with foods I loved as a kid (Naomi must have sent them a list): Rice Krispies and fresh milk, chicken cutlets, ready-cut slices of cheddar cheese, Golden Delicious apples. And always, a plate of lemon shortbread that scratches my throat when I throw it up.

I look into the woods, imagining the hundred-year-old oaks, maples, and willows that were surely chopped down to make way for panoramic ocean views from the cottage windows. The branches on the remaining trees curl over the angular buildings, closing in like they might crush the metal and glass boxes that took their siblings' place. Beyond the cottages, the woods are dense and dark, no solar-powered lamps stuck into the ground to lead the way. Still, the moonlight is bright enough that I can make out a large structure in a clearing among the trees, as far as I can tell, the only building on the property other than the cottages.

"Where do you think they keep files for all their old patients?" I try to keep my voice casual. Maybe they have stacks of things people left behind: sweaters and socks and books they meant to read but never got around to, an elaborate lost and found.

"*Guests,*" Edward corrects with a wink. "And dunno. Gotta be around here somewhere, right?"

"Okay, but how can they really guarantee confidentiality if they have file after file on every celebrity and tycoon type who stayed here?"

"You saw the security cameras by the gate. Hell, you saw the *gate* when we got here."

Edward was feigning sleep when we drove in, so he couldn't have seen that beyond the locked gate, cleverly hidden between the trees, were tall wire fences, sharp barbs along the top.

"Yeah, but they probably keep their files on computers. What if they got hacked?"

I'm not tech savvy enough to break into a password-protected computer.

"They can't," Edward explains, shaking his head. "Anne looked into it. This place is strictly analog. They wouldn't even set up the reservations over email. It all had to be over the phone. Landlines, even."

There's moisture in the air, and I can feel the ends of my hair curling. I kick one of my boots against the ground. I checked the forecast earlier: too cold for rain, not quite cold enough for snow. It's supposed to start sleeting at 4:00 a.m. I'm wearing two sweaters, a knit hat, and fingerless gloves, but when the wind blows, I shiver.

"Check it out," Edward says, picking something off the ground. Before I can stop him, he throws a piece of gravel at the windows of the third cottage.

"What are you doing?" I hiss.

"You said you were bored!"

"Yeah, but—"

"But what?" Edward grins. He tosses another rock. The stone hits the glass with a dull thud that's barely audible over the music coming from the cabin.

Edward says he's seen the third patient from his window; it's a woman, he thinks. Given her taste in music—my parents' sort of music—I guess she must be middle-aged. (Edward said he couldn't tell.)

"Gotta find a bigger rock," Edward says. "No way she'll be able to hear us otherwise."

"You'll break a window," I protest. I can picture her now, a nameless, faceless basket case. Getting high in the middle of the day, her children coming home to the smell of something burning, never certain if they were smelling the remains of burnt toast or a bong rip. Georgia was creative when she had to be, chasing the dragon with the same aluminum foil Naomi used to wrap my sandwiches.

I try to remember the last time I saw a sign of Georgia's drug use. Was it months, a year even, before she came here? It all feels terribly fuzzy, like my memories were printed on old-fashioned film that's been damaged.

I circle my left wrist with the opposite hand's fingers, trying to stay calm.

"You're supposed to be here anonymously," I remind Edward. "Anyone who plays music that loud isn't interested in discretion. They could leak your presence to the press like *that*." I snap my fingers like I have his best interests in mind.

"You didn't," Edward points out.

"Yeah, well, you got lucky with me. I already hate the press."

Edward hesitates before tossing another rock.

"Come on." I step off the path before he can change his mind, turning away from the ocean, tiptoeing past the lower-level rooms where our care managers, chefs, and housekeepers sleep and toward the building I saw in the woods. I know I'm being insensitive, asking him to walk farther on his injured leg, but I can't help it.

"How's the PT going?" I try to sound nonchalant. He's told me he has physical therapy every day.

"Fine," Edward answers, though he sounds unconvinced. "They made me do a cold plunge today."

"A cold plunge?" I echo.

"It's exactly what it sounds like. You get into a tub filled with ice water."

"You're describing a literal form of torture."

In fact, it sounds like a treatment from medieval times, like bloodletting or leeches. I've considered telling Dr. Mackenzie that my treatment here isn't all that different from the "rest cure" they used to prescribe to women in the 1800s. It had three core elements: isolation, rest, and feeding, with massage to combat muscle atrophy—not dissimilar from my yoga and bodywork classes. Patients were required to lie in bed for twenty-four hours a day, sometimes for months at a time, with a special nurse who would sleep in the room with them—just like Dr. Mackenzie living downstairs. Visits from family and friends were forbidden. The women were given "feedings," and if they refused any part of the treatment, they were prescribed more rest.

Nowadays, we (allegedly) recognize the damage such treatments did. I wonder what they will say about places like this in 150 years.

Edward shrugs, like being forced into an ice bath is perfectly normal. "It's supposed to have all kinds of benefits. Anti-inflammatory, accelerates healing, blah, blah."

"So if it works, your fucked-up leg will get better, right?" That's what he calls it, his *fucked-up leg*.

"Cured," Edward answers wryly. He makes the word sound like a punchline.

"At least your leg isn't alcoholism," I say. "Like, there might actually *be* a cure for it. That's the advantage of physical ailments over psychic ones, right?"

"Right," Edward agrees. "Is this what American summer camps are like?" he asks as we crush dead leaves beneath our feet with each step. "At Choate, I had a couple of classmates who went on and on about sleepaway camp."

"I wouldn't know." I rub my hands together. In between words, I count my steps, as though the numbers are breadcrumbs I'm leaving behind to find my way back. "The closest I came to sleepaway camp was spending July at a treatment center when I was fifteen."

Edward laughs like I've made a joke. I join in as though I don't re-member how they punished patients with isolation if we didn't drink our allotment of Ensure with each meal. When they sent me home in August, I hated the new shape of my inner thighs, my breasts that were a size larger than they'd been before. I fantasized about carving the new pounds off me like a butcher.

It's less windy the farther we get from the water. The mystery building in the moonlight turns out to be an oversize barn made of cedar shingles, with floor-to-ceiling windows like the cottages. I can make out the silhou-ettes of an exercise bike and an elliptical machine, looking ghostly in the darkness. I see a swimming pool on the other side of the building, covered up for the winter.

"At least they don't make you do your cold plunge out there." I shiver. I read once that when people remove the covers from their pools in the spring, they find creatures that slipped beneath the water in winter: mice and birds and rabbits; even, somehow, deer.

I reach for the handle on the sliding glass door, wincing as my hand makes contact with the metal latch. I'm not surprised that it isn't locked. I've spent enough time around wealthy people to know how careless they can be. Once inside their gated communities, in their apartments guarded by doormen, they don't bother with deadbolts, leave their jewelry strewn on countertops and hang priceless art in their bathrooms. This area—the Hamptons—is famous for waterfront mansions without alarm systems, unlocked Mercedes in grocery store parking lots, designer shoes left behind at the beach. Spend enough time in rarefied air and you start to think the air itself is protecting you.

"What are you doing?" Edward hisses.

I don't answer before stepping inside.

24

Amelia Blue

I tiptoe past the treadmills and elliptical machines. It feels, somehow, colder in this room than it does outside. There's a light switch by the door, but I rely on the thin stream of light coming from my phone. I wonder if any patients have snuck into this building before, to work out in secret. Some clinics forbid people like me from exercising. #Proana Twitter is full of workarounds.

Two sides of the room are made of glass: the sliding door we just walked through facing the woods, the back facing the pool. I find myself thinking about the story of the three little pigs, imagining a big bad wolf huffing and puffing to blow this house down. Would this building collapse like twigs and hay or hold fast like bricks? Were the architects who designed all these glass structures confident their walls would never shatter, come hurricane or blizzard or cyclone?

One of the solid walls is covered by full-length mirrors. I catch sight of my reflection in the darkness: the body that isn't the shape or size it should be, the wrong nose I was born with.

The opposite wall has two doors, one on each side. I take a deep breath and head toward the one to my left first.

"Amelia?" Edward asks hesitantly.

I take another step, then wrap my hands around the doorknob and twist it open. I hold my breath as I shine my phone's light into the room on the other side.

A bathroom. Not at all what I was looking for.

I pull a piece of gum from my pocket and fill my mouth with oversweet fake watermelon, then close the door behind me and try the one on the right.

It's locked.

I'm prepared for this. I reach into my pocket and take out my kit.

"What's that?" Edward whispers.

Georgia used to lock herself out of the house all the time. She couldn't be bothered with details like keys. It didn't matter (she said) because she knew full well how to pick a lock. She taught me so that I could manage when she was too out of it.

When I hear the latch click into place, I think two words I'm not sure I've ever thought before: *Thanks, Mom.* I turn the knob, feeling like a contestant on one of those old-fashioned game shows, hoping that whatever's on the other side of the door will fulfill their wildest dreams. A new car, a million dollars, a romantic getaway.

A room whose walls are lined with cold metal file cabinets.

I step inside.

"Amelia, seriously, what are you doing?" Edward asks.

It takes all my willpower to turn away from the cabinets to face him.

"Why are you here, really?" I ask. My hands are so cold I can barely feel my fingertips. I cross my arms, tucking my hands against my chest.

"What?"

"You said you haven't had a drink in months."

Edward blinks. It's dim in here, but in the light reflected from my phone, I can see his eyes are very bright.

"Like you said," Edward answers finally, a hitch in his voice like he's finding it difficult to breathe, "it's complicated."

"Consider this part of my complication," I explain, gesturing to the file cabinets. I open up the drawer marked *A–C*.

"Are you working for someone?"

"Working for who?" I don't look at him, keep my gaze focused on one name after another.

"Whom," Edward says reflexively, like the habit was drilled into him as a child, then adds, "My girlfriend hated when I did that. Corrected her grammar." He pauses. "My ex-girlfriend, I mean." He sounds, for a moment, confused, as though he's forgotten that I asked him a question.

"*Whom* do you think I might be working for?" I prompt him, ticking through the files with icy fingertips.

"A tabloid. The *Star*, the *Sun*, the *Enquirer*." Now there's suspicion in his voice. "Did they pay you to fake an eating disorder or something, like one of those actors who loses weight for a role, so you could dig up some celebrity's file?"

"Who said I had an eating disorder?" I ask defensively. "Did you google me?"

"We promised not to."

"Then did you get your care manager to tell you why I'm here?"

I run my fingers over the files, reading each name a second time, in case I missed the one I'm looking for.

"Of course not," Edward snaps. "It's just a guess. Anyway, my doctor wouldn't tell me even if I asked."

I slam the drawer shut.

"Since when do you have so much respect for the people who work here?"

"I don't! But you have no right to look through other people's files."

"I'm not looking for just anyone's file. I'm looking for my mother's."

I open the drawer marked *H–J*.

"Why?"

"Because this was the last place anyone ever saw her alive."

Edward's hand lands on my wrist, stopping my search. "Amelia, I had no idea."

"I thought you knew." This place may think it's protecting itself by forgoing a website and relying on word of mouth for referrals, but it's not exactly a well-kept secret. How can it be, when half the people who stay here are regularly stalked by the press? "Anyway, like I said, it's complicated."

"I get that, I really do." Edward's tone is gentle, like he doesn't want to startle me. "But imagine how you'd feel if your family read the notes your doctor wrote about you."

"My mother can't feel anything." I twist away from Edward's grip. "She's dead."

Edward can't understand what it's like to discover something entirely new about a person after they've died, simultaneously getting to know them and coming up against the impossibility of knowing them any better than you did before.

Unless, that is, they spent the end of their life being observed by experts.

Maybe someone misfiled her. I go back to the *D-G* drawer that I skipped, then move on to *K–M*, and then the next, and the next. I look for her stage name, the name she was born with, her married name. I pass names I recognize—celebrities and politicians and the like. Apparently, this place doesn't conceal their patients' identities with fake names, like when Georgia used to check in to hotels under the name Janis Cobain.

"Shit!" I shout, slamming the final drawer shut. "It's not here."

"Then let's get out of here." Edward doesn't wait for me before he turns toward the door, like he thinks just being in here, in proximity to other people's confidential information, is a violation. I lag behind, shining my flashlight into corners and on top of the cabinets like Georgia's file will magically appear. My light lands on a bulletin board beside the door. It's mostly covered with mundane information: *Lock Door Behind You*; *Turn Off Lights*; *Used Car for Sale!* But I notice a piece of newsprint with a headline that reads, *Rush's Recovery Opening Soon.*

I pull the article off the wall. It's from a local paper, the *Shelter Island Reporter*, dated December 2014, just over ten years ago. It mentions the Manhattan decorator who designed the interiors of the cottages, the landscape architects who planned the gardens. Whoever hung it here must not have noticed the subtle criticisms, like the suggestion that the Rushes paid off the local town council so they could convert property that had been a nature preserve into a rehab facility for the rich and famous. Below the headline is a grainy picture of three people standing in front of one of the glass cottages. The caption reads, *The doctors Rush with their son on the property*.

I suck on a papercut on my left pointer finger, my hands so cold that it doesn't even hurt.

"Come on, Amelia," Edward calls softly from the outer room.

I read the caption beneath the photo again. The article must have been written before the son got his PhD and joined the family business.

I'm determined not to leave this room empty-handed. So I tuck the article into my pocket alongside my lock-picking kit and follow Edward outside.

25

Amelia Blue

In the cold air, I recognize the beat of one of my dad's songs coming from the third cottage, a hit called "Mortality Salience." Georgia told me she came up with the title, but it's a theory from psychology, so I know that's just another one of her stories. For years, I tried to parse the lies she told from the truths she let slip, like my own private, endless game of two truths and a lie.

Eventually, I gave up.

I place a hand on my chest, feeling my thready heartbeat. Silently, I promise my heart that tomorrow, I'll add extra strawberries to my yogurt. The building behind me can't possibly be the only place where they keep patient information. Georgia's file has to be *somewhere*.

I spin in a circle like another building might materialize in front of me if only I take the right steps.

At once, the air is bright white.

"Shit!" Edward grabs my arm, tugging me backward, but then I see it, unmistakable in the brightness: the silhouette of a Cape Cod–style structure nestled in the woods ahead of us.

I try to take a step, but Edward's grip is tight, pulling me in the opposite direction, back toward the cottages.

I don't turn to follow, because there's a figure coming out of the structure in the woods. Whoever it is looks ghostlike, long hair streaming, white like a halo. I blink, and the figure becomes sharper, its arms outstretched, pale feet bare. Before it can take another step, someone else, someone tall, throws their arms around it from behind. For a second, I think I'm seeing a romantic embrace, but the smaller figure squirms beneath the tall person's grip, almost thrashing. I'm too far away to know for certain, but I think it's a woman being restrained by a man.

Edward tugs me down into a crouch until all I can see are the bushes and brambles surrounding us. I hear him gasp with pain as he kneels at my side.

"Floodlight," he says breathlessly, pointing to a light nailed to a tree above us. "Must be motion activated."

The light turns off abruptly, plunging us back into darkness.

"They must not have seen us," I say, pressing myself up to stand. They were too focused on each other to look into the woods.

"Who?" Edward sounds alarmed.

"The people outside that house!"

The weak light from my phone falls across the building in the distance. It's completely dark, not even a lamp over the front porch.

"There's no one there." Edward sounds relieved. "Your eyes must've been playing tricks on you. Believe me, trees cast weird shadows when a light pops up like that. I remember once, I snuck out in Scotland and thought I was surrounded by ghosts and goblins."

"I don't think we're surrounded by ghosts and goblins. I saw two people. A woman and a man."

I try to sound reasonable, but my voice is shaking. I did think, at first, that the woman looked like something from a ghost story, otherworldly without a coat, hat, gloves, or shoes.

And the man. He was enormous. He threw his arms around her like a creature from a horror movie.

"If there'd been someone there, they'd have come running for us the minute our steps activated the floodlight," Edward points out.

Maybe the light *was* playing tricks on me. Or maybe my brain is sending hallucinations to punish me for depriving it of the nutrients all the doctors and therapists tell me it needs so badly.

"We should go," Edward says urgently, taking a step toward the cottages.

Reluctantly, I follow.

26

Lord Edward

Being inside a gym didn't bring back memories of *pumping iron* and *getting ripped*—those absurd phrases I'd use to motivate myself—instead, all I saw was the machinery that my physical therapists had been coaxing me onto for months. I used to run on treadmills, my heels landing so hard the entire machine would shake; just months ago, a therapist set me on a treadmill so I could learn to walk again.

Amelia seemed ill at ease in the gym as well. She walked on her toes, as though trying not to make a sound. She seemed much more comfortable going through patient files, while I couldn't so much as step inside the room. The thought of my sister coming across my therapist's notes, even after I'm gone, makes me shudder. Yet I recognized something in the desperate look on Amelia's face. After all, I asked Anne if she could include updates on Harper's condition in the deal she cut with Harper's parents. (Anne laughed at my request, refused to even ask.)

Amelia wants to know why I'm here. I can't possibly tell her. She'd hate me. As it is, she barely seems to tolerate my touch when all I'm doing is holding her upright.

I could've come up with an explanation. I could have said, when she asked, that being here is the next step in my sobriety or some bullshit like that. From what I've heard, sober-speak involves so many steps and numbers (how many days since your last drink?; how many people did you hurt?) that she might have believed me. But I didn't want to lie. I haven't yet lied to Amelia, though I've let her believe my leg will "get better" with the right treatment; I haven't told her it's beyond repair. And I haven't told her that every night, no matter how engrossing our conversation, how exciting it is to sneak around like teenagers, some part of me is always distracted, longing to go back to my room, back to the relief that's hidden in my sock drawer.

I could've offered a small piece of the truth, explaining that in the deal Anne made, my sobriety seemed almost beside the point. It was the promise that I was going to be sent away that satisfied Harper's parents, I think, even more than the money or the therapy. The promise that I would be out of reach.

Now, I follow Amelia through the woods, trying to put my feet exactly where she puts hers. Her wavy hair curls—she calls it frizz, but it's not, it's lovely—in the moist air like magic. She's short and pale but freckled. Her hazel eyes turn an almost electric green in the dim light under which we've met these past few nights, and the gap between her front teeth makes it look like there's always something she's not saying, some secret she's keeping hidden inside her mouth that makes her so intriguing I often find myself staring.

Harper must be at least six inches taller than Amelia, blond and fair, long and lithe. Even Anne approved of that much; at least Harper *looked* the part. A born and bred New Yorker, Harper wore outfits she'd found in thrift shops, somehow making mismatched, occasionally ill-fitting clothing look intentional and chic. She'd pull her long hair back with scrunchies and banana clips, twist it into braids, knot it into buns.

My hands are so cold even in my gloves that I can't feel my fingertips. I don't know how Amelia manages without a proper coat. I want to offer her mine, but I don't think she'd take it.

"Shit," Amelia says suddenly, glancing at her phone. "It's one fifty-eight."

She breaks into a sprint. She's not an athlete like I once was, but she moves with ease, assured her limbs will do as she asks. In the dim light, I watch her take the stairs up to her terrace two at a time, rushing to open and close her sliding glass door. I imagine her diving into bed with her shoes still on, burrowing under the covers.

Much more slowly, I limp toward my cottage. My phone vibrates in my pocket. I look at the screen; another call from that unknown number, the stranger who believes I'm on London time. Perhaps they imagine me rolling over as the sun rises, too close to sleep to remember to be cautious before answering. As though a creature can ever forget they're being hunted, venturing into the open meadow without sniffing for wolves. I think of the deer on my father's land in Scotland; for most of the year, they live in peace. Do they ever forget that there are apex predators out there? Do they ever forget the brother or mother or child they lost in last year's hunt?

My father first took me stalking when I was ten years old. Of all the many things I've done wrong over the years, I don't think anything disappointed him more than my inability to pull the trigger when the time came. When I hesitated, he was forced to take a bad shot, and the deer—injured but not killed—fled. We chased it, following the trail of blood it left behind, listening to it panting in anguish, its pain entirely preventable, and entirely my fault.

Later, my father set into me: Didn't I know that culling the herd was for the good of the land? Didn't I know that meat, killed properly, would feed the locals? Now, flooded with adrenaline because of my blunder, the deer's meat was inedible.

What had I been thinking, he shouted. How could I be so careless?

Careless is a word that's followed me my whole life: on teachers' annual reports, in the media, from Anne and our father. But like *accident*, *careless* is a word with many meanings.

I had been careless that day with my father, failing to go in for the kill. And I was careless years later with Harper.

I could be careless tonight. All it would take is one little slip, one foot put wrong. My phone would fly from my hands, out of reach before I hit the ground. I picture myself like a turtle flipped on its back by some uncaring child, utterly helpless. The cold would seep into my body, inch by inch, penetrating my down jacket and fleece vest.

Instead, I watch my steps, slow and painstaking, as I make my way back to my cottage, where I'll be safe and warm. Amelia's already inside; she didn't want me slowing her down. For the rest of my life, my companions will grow sick of staying behind, going slow, hanging back, missing out.

Before she sent me here, Anne said it was for the best, adding, *You wouldn't have wanted Harper to be a* caretaker *for the rest of her life, would you?*

I'm halfway up the stairs when I hear the flick of a light switch. I look up, blinking in the sudden brightness.

Dr. Rush is waiting on the terrace above, silhouetted as if there's a halo above his head, judgmental as an angel come down to earth. His arms are crossed, one eyebrow raised. He looks pleased to discover that I'm every bit as bad as Anne surely told him I was.

27

Amelia Blue

I kick off my shoes, toss my sweater and scarf to the floor, and dive into bed, pulling the covers up to my cold cold ears. I shut my eyes and hold still like this is a game of hide-and-seek and Dr. Mackenzie's just shouted, *Ready or not here I come!*

I hear the door open, then Dr. Mackenzie's satisfied sigh when she sees me lying in bed.

Maybe I'm *too* still. Do most patients murmur and roll over when the doctor opens the door, their unconscious bodies sensing the presence of another person? But if I move, will Dr. Mackenzie come closer? Will she hear that my heart is still pounding from racing up the stairs, sense that my fingertips are still chilled from the January air?

Don't be ridiculous, I tell myself. Even if she stood directly over me, Dr. Mackenzie wouldn't be able to hear my heart or feel the cold radiating from my body. She's a human being, not a witch. So I keep still, muscles clenched, until I hear the door closing. Even then, I wait until the sound of her footsteps fades away. She shuffles like she's wearing slippers. Had I opened my eyes, I probably would have seen my therapist in her pajamas. The thought is oddly intimate.

I roll over and stare at the ceiling. There's enough moonlight streaming in the windows that I can make out the modern light fixture hanging down from the vaulted ceiling, a series of metal bars crisscrossing over one another, a tiny black ball on the end of each. It looks like something out of a spy movie, a cross between a weapon and a cage.

What if it is something from a spy movie? Not literally, but—what if there are cameras concealed in those metal bars, giving my doctor a 360-degree view of the room and everything going on inside it? I stand on the bed and stretch my arms overhead, but the light is out of reach.

I shake my head and drop my arms. If these rooms were equipped with hidden cameras, Dr. Mackenzie wouldn't check on me in the middle of the night. They don't need cameras to keep watch.

I sigh. Jonah isn't that far away. If I asked, he would get into his car and drive until he got here, despite what I did. It should be unforgivable, but he forgave me. He doesn't even blame me. He doesn't think it's my fault.

Jonah would show up at dawn and bang on the gate, scale the barbed wire fence, rescue me like a princess locked in a tower. If I asked, he'd spring Edward, too, and he wouldn't even be jealous that I'd been spending late nights with a man who's regularly featured as one of *People* magazine's sexiest men alive. Jonah would be happy I made a friend. He wouldn't think I was awful for leaving Edward behind to run up the stairs tonight, too concerned about saving my own skin to slow down in solidarity. Jonah would offer to help. He'd hold my hand through the dark of the woods, refusing to leave my side until I found what I'm looking for.

Even after everything that happened, Jonah doesn't understand that I'm the ogre under the bridge, the evil villain who killed the innocent princess.

I tiptoe into the bathroom and turn on the dim light over the mirror that's not a mirror, my reflection soft and slightly blurry as though someone has smudged my edges. I wonder if they switched out the light bulbs just for me, from eighty watt to forty watt so I wouldn't be able to study myself too closely.

I pull my shirt over my head, remove my bra, slide my leggings down to my ankles. I stand on my tiptoes. There are my tattoos—two of them, tiny, one in black ink and one in white. The white tattoo always looked like a scar, but even more so after what I did to it last spring.

My first morning here, when Dr. Mackenzie examined me, did she mistake it for a badly healed scratch like the ones on my inner thighs? There are others I don't think she could see, the repeated paper cuts hidden among the places where the skin wrinkles around my joints, my ankles and elbows, even between my toes. Only Jonah ever noticed those.

I turn on the hot water. I never go to bed without washing my face, brushing my teeth. Even when I was in college, sleeping in someone else's bed, I'd sneak into their bathroom and make do with whatever I could find—the makeup remover some ex-girlfriend left behind, toothpaste from a crusted tube. I would not be like my mother, her eyes raccooned by smudged eyeliner each morning, her teeth stained with the previous night's red wine, her hair matted into angry knots.

I pick at the paper cut on my forefinger, more out of habit than a desire to draw blood. Why wasn't Georgia's file in the cabinets I searched tonight? There must be some other place where they keep the files of their difficult patients, the ones whose treatment failed spectacularly.

Not just their files. Is there some other place where they keep the difficult patients themselves?

In my mind's eye, I see the Cape Cod–style building in the woods, two people struggling outside it. Edward says it was the light playing tricks on me, but he doesn't know as much as I do about places like this. He's never been sent to a treatment center where they force-feed you through a tube, tie you to a bed, isolate you in a padded room. Just because this place is shiny and luxurious doesn't mean it's really any different.

I asked Dr. Mackenzie how many patients this place could accommodate, but doctors lie to patients all the time, telling them that they've only gained two pounds when they really gained eight, as if a person can't feel the difference.

I trace my hipbones, twisting my torso so they jut out like handles, then slide my hands over my bottom and down my thighs. Places like this love to tell their patients that they're safe: *This is a safe space*, they say. *You can reveal everything.*

But if they knew why I'm really here, they might send me away before I find what I came for.

I close my eyes, seeing the dark house in the distance, the woman being restrained. Did I really imagine it? Could that building be perfectly innocuous? It could be empty, or used to store things as dull as outdoor furniture in the wintertime. Maybe I'm crazy to think it's anything more. (Of *course* I'm crazy. No one comes to a place like this because they're perfectly sane.)

Crazy or sane, there's a chance my mother's file is inside that building, which means I have to get inside, too.

Her file has to be *somewhere*.

28

Lord Edward

I clench my jaw as Dr. Rush continues his lecture: the danger of walking alone in the dark, in the cold. What if I'd slipped? What if I'd fallen? What was I thinking?

Fortunately, he assumes I was alone.

Dr. Rush pauses between sentences as if he expects me to argue, but I won't. It would only prolong this interaction, and all I want is for my doctor to go away so I can take a pill from my sock drawer. I decide that I won't swallow it whole; tonight, I'll chew it up, crunching it between my teeth like candy. I can already taste the bitter chalk of it in the back of my throat. I just need Dr. Rush to get the fuck on with it. Tell me he's phoning Anne, they're extending my stay, I can never leave. (What will I do when I run out of pills? That's tomorrow's problem; tonight I need only one.)

"I'm sorry," I offer when Dr. Rush's silence makes it clear he won't speak again until I respond. I didn't even apologize when I set fire to my school. "I needed some air."

The doctor's face softens. I've said something right even if I don't know exactly what.

"I understand," he says. "And if that's what you need, I want to help you have it. All you have to do is push that button"—he gestures to the bedside table—"and I'll be here. But you have to understand why we can't have you out there by yourself." He says it like we're on the mean streets of some nameless, dangerous city rather than one of the most exclusive hamlets in the world.

"Understood." I'm gritting my teeth so hard that I can barely get the word out.

"If anything happened to you—" Dr. Rush pauses, and the words he doesn't say hang between us.

If anything happened to you, I could get into so much trouble; if anything happened to you, the center could be liable; if anything happened to you, there might be a lawsuit; if anything happened to you, the press might find out you'd been here in the first place.

If anything happened to you, there would be such a mess to tidy up.

I apologize again.

"I appreciate that." There's a hint of finality in Dr. Rush's voice, and I think the lecture is over, that we'll resume therapy in the morning and put this awful business behind us. Instead, he says, "I'm afraid that starting tomorrow, I'll be securing the terrace door from the outside."

It takes me a beat to realize what he means by *securing*. "You're locking me in my room?"

"Of course not," Dr. Rush says. "The door from your room to the rest of the house will be unlocked, and you're welcome to move about the cottage freely. But every exterior door will be secured so that you can't go outside alone. If you find you need some air again, simply press the button, and I'll be happy to venture outdoors with you."

Most buildings aren't equipped with locks that trap their inhabitants within. This cottage was designed to be a cage.

"This is bullshit."

"I'm sorry you feel that way. I assure you it's for your own safety."

"Like hell. It's for *your* safety." I pause. "You don't have to worry about getting sued. My family won't want that kind of publicity." I try to sound authoritative, like Anne talking to Harper's family. She made her suggestions sound as though they were for the Steeles' best interests, not mine, not hers.

"I assure you, my concern isn't litigious. But since you mention it, I am contractually obligated to manage your care while you're here."

"I'm fully aware that you're being paid."

Dr. Rush ignores the venom in my words. When he speaks, he sounds as professorial as ever. I thought people who did this kind of work were supposed to be grizzled old addicts themselves, not so mild mannered that it's hard to imagine them sipping a glass of wine, let alone falling down drunk.

"Your family trusted me with your care. And perhaps more to the point, Ms. Steele's family trusted that you would submit to this process."

And there it is. The man with the elbow patches who proudly showed off the deVOL cabinetry and Sub-Zero refrigerator is making his position clear: One phone call from Dr. Rush and the deal Anne cut with Harper's parents will be off.

My eyes dart toward the sliding door, searching for something that could shatter it completely. Perhaps I could toss Dr. Rush himself through the glass. I picture shards getting caught in his hair, slicing his hands, shredding his tailored sports coat. Even now, in the middle of the night, he's wearing the same clothing he wears in the daytime: slacks, button-down, tweed jacket. It's a costume, I realize, and for the first time, I notice that the cuffs are frayed. A bead of sweat drips into my right eye, making it sting.

In my mind, I hear Anne's voice. *What did you expect? Did you really think you would get off scot-free after what you did?* If I'd been born into some other family, I'd probably be in prison right now.

When the doctor finally leaves, I hobble to my sock drawer, in so much pain that it's a marvel I'm still upright.

As I chew, the pill gets caught between my teeth and makes me gag when I swallow. Perhaps it's a placebo effect, but at once my heart rate slows and the pain dulls, though it certainly doesn't disappear.

I realize that I'm relieved Dr. Rush locked me *in* rather than *out*. Out there, there's nothing to offer relief.

It only makes me hate him more.

29

Florence

"Florence."

Evelyn says my name like a teacher losing patience with her least favorite student. I had plenty of those when I was a kid. They could always find something to complain about.

Florence doesn't pay attention.
Florence doesn't apply herself.
Florence disrupts her classmates.
Florence asks too many questions.
Florence stopped coming to class.

Didn't matter whether I was there or gone, quiet or loud. They hated me all the same.

"Florence," Evelyn repeats slowly, emphasizing each syllable like I may not know the meaning of the word. "I want to make our time together as productive for you as possible."

Evelyn may be the whitest person I've ever seen. I mean that literally: Her hair is white-blond, her skin white-pale, her eyebrows nearly invisible (though brushed into place). White tips on her fingernails, crisp white blouse, white-gold wedding band on her finger.

Thanks to Andrew, I know the ring is a lie, part of a charade to present herself as the sort of person who has her life together, the sort of person who has any right to tell other people how they should live.

I'm sick of your lies
As you sit there and therapize
Who are you to tell me how to live?

When your own husband cannot forgive—
You wouldn't last one day in my shoes
One hour with my blues
You'd fade so fast into gray
Never bursting into every shade
A rainbow that will never fade
Like me.

My first album was filled with lyrics about living life in Technicolor, Dorothy after she landed in Oz, leaving the black and white behind. Back then, I thought my life would never be dull again. I certainly never thought I'd bleed into the background.

This morning I notice that Evelyn's wide-set eyes are bloodshot, the whites run through with pink and red. Maybe her divorce kept her up crying all night.

"Define productive," I say finally.

Evelyn looks pleased that I'm responding, like this is *progress*.

We're sitting on the (white) couches by the fireplace. Evelyn's back is to the kitchen, where Andrew stands, preparing lunch. I can already see that it's some kind of salad, food you're *supposed* to eat, every vitamin from A to Z. The ingredients are probably all *local* and *organic*, those catchphrasey words I was supposed to care about as soon as I started making enough money to afford it. Though how produce could be local in this climate this time of year, I don't know. I'm tempted to ask, just to catch Evelyn in a lie, but I don't want her to think I'm the kind of person who cares, because I'm not. Andrew catches my eye and pulls a Snickers bar from his pocket, winking as if to say, *Don't worry, I've got you covered.*

I bite my lip to keep from smiling.

"*Productive* is something we can define together. What would you like to get out of your time here?"

I gaze at my guitar, propped in the corner where I left it last night. I didn't write after Andrew disappeared. It was like the song got snagged and stuck, unable to keep moving.

"Lady, we both know I'm just here to ride out the storm," I answer.

"What does 'riding out the storm' mean to you?" She makes my words sound like a punchline.

"It means I'm here till things settle down at home."

"What would home look like if things 'settled down'?"

Joni Jewell would be stricken from the radio, banished to the world of washed-up pop stars. My kid and my mom would stop conspiring against me, two peas in a pod leaving me out in the cold. My husband would show up on my doorstep after all these years, a smile so big plastered on his face like he couldn't remember whatever it was that made him leave.

"If what you want is to live a more settled life," Evelyn continues, "I can help with that."

"Can you?" I ask archly.

"Another word for *settled* is *stability*. And you're not exactly known for being stable, are you?"

"I thought you weren't interested in what anyone else said about me. Isn't that what you said the other day? You wanted to hear my version of events, threatened to drug me for suggesting you read my bio online."

I expect Evelyn to look humbled—I caught her lying—but she merely smiles. "It would be dishonest to pretend I don't know anything about your life, and I don't think dishonesty would help us build a strong connection."

I feel my gaze wither when Evelyn suggests that she wants to *connect* with me, like she isn't here because she's paid to be, like she actually cares about me, wants to know me. "I don't think there's much chance of us building any kind of connection."

"What makes you say that?"

"You're not the kind of person I have any interest in connecting with. Besides, there's all kinds of instability."

"What do you mean by that?"

"Like, financial instability. Whatever else has happened, I've been paying my own way since I was a teenager. Never missed a mortgage payment or a phone bill. Not once." I pay someone to keep track of all that for me—dates and deadlines aren't exactly my strong suit—but it still counts.

"And you know, my marriage ended, but we never got *divorced*." I emphasize it like it's a dirty word.

Outsiders never understood our relationship. Journalists said I made him miserable, snapping pictures of us that made it look like we were fighting on the street when we were really making fun of each other. Not to say we never fought. Of course we did. But the rest of the world had no idea what it looked like when we made up in private.

The press announced our engagement like it was a tragedy, shocked that I'd managed—as they put it—to *land* him, like I'd tricked him into loving me. They didn't know that he'd had to ask me to marry him once, twice, three times before I said yes. It wasn't that I didn't love him—I did, so much it scared me sometimes—but I wanted to make my own name before I became someone's wife. So I didn't say yes until our second album went gold. But when we announced our engagement, the press made it sound like I was just another groupie.

His female fans gathered outside our wedding venue crying. When I pulled up in my white dress, I saw someone holding a sign begging him not to go through with it.

After he left years later, I knew that all those people who said we were doomed were patting themselves on the back for having been right.

"We never battled over custody, never divided up our assets," I continue. "Not like *some people*, who spend years arguing over who gets what."

Evelyn shifts in her seat, so I know I hit a nerve.

"I'm proud of my marriage."

Evelyn scratches her scalp, causing a strand of hair from her perfect bun to come loose. As she presses it back into place, I can see that she's shaking slightly.

I add, "Whatever else I've done wrong, at least I know I didn't fail at *that*."

The lie tastes sour in my mouth, but I'm careful not to let it show. No one knows the truth of how things ended, I made sure of that.

In the silence that follows, I concentrate on the sound of Andrew chopping vegetables. It sounds like a drumbeat. I bet he's doing that on purpose.

"Lunch," Andrew announces finally, breaking the silence.

I stand immediately, patting my belly like I'm starving. "I guess we're done for the day."

This afternoon, a personal trainer will (try to) get me to exercise, and then a massage therapist will loosen up all the muscles I was supposed to be strengthening. I feel the soft flesh of my belly beneath my hands. My kid was an emergency C-section. I hadn't been scared, figured it was a routine procedure, happens every day. I was awake when things started to go wrong. I heard the panic in the doctors' voices when they saw bleeding where there shouldn't be. My kid and I stayed at the hospital for weeks. When they finally sent me home, I could barely walk.

In between bites of my salad, I hear a soft but firm *thump*. I turn and see that a tiny bird has flown into the wall of windows behind the couch.

Sascha, the housekeeper, is already outside, shivering in her gray scrubs. She pulls on rubber gloves and picks up the tiny ball of feather and bone. She doesn't check to make sure the bird is dead before dropping it into a plastic bag and tying it closed. I imagine that bird's heart still beating, imagine it flapping its wings, trying to escape.

It's the first time I've actually seen Sascha clean anything. This place is like a fancy hotel where the maids wait for you to leave the building before they clean up, so you walk into a spotless room without a reminder that someone had to get down on their hands and knees to undo the mess you made.

30

Florence

"What does she want from me?" I ask, crunching on SweeTarts, so hard I think my teeth may crack. It's after midnight and I'm starving. Andrew's healthy salad and one mini Snickers, followed by yet another bland and unsatisfying dinner, wasn't near enough to fill me up.

Does anything satisfy you? the chorus of musicians asks.

My husband used to cook for me. *Real* food: pasta, roast chicken, pancakes. He didn't mind when I ate off his plate. I think I haven't been full since he left.

"She's a therapist." Andrew shrugs. He picks out the flavors I don't like—the greens and the yellows—and eats them himself. "She wants you to tell her about your life."

No, I think, *she doesn't.* She wants me to reveal a hidden, dark secret that will explain everything: My uncle molested me in the closet when I was ten, or my father died in front of me when I was six. Without some childhood trauma, Evelyn's probing questions imply there's no excuse for my behavior, my failures, my mothering—no excuse for *me.*

"I already told her, there's nothing about me she can't find out online. Or if she wants a deeper dive, some *Us Weekly* reporter published an unauthorized biography in the early aughts. It's out of print, but I'm sure she could find it on Amazon or something."

I read it, actually. The guy interviewed girls who'd claimed they'd been in grade school with me, a boy who said I gave him a hand job in the ninth grade behind the gym, some old man who claimed I bought drugs from him when I was thirteen. I didn't recognize any of the stories, but Callie said there was no point denying it.

I crunch an orange candy, so sour my tongue tingles, just the way I like. "Usually other people's stories fill the silences."

We're sitting at the kitchen counter, our barstools angled so we're facing each other. Andrew's legs are so long and the stools are so close together that his right thigh is perched loosely between mine. He's acting like it's casual, but I know he sat that way on purpose.

"What do you mean?" Andrew asks, reminding me that he wasn't hired for his expertise so much as for his muscle. I have more experience at rehab than he does.

"You know, group therapy. Other places, you go around in a circle and people talk about their abusive parents, the teachers who went too far, the people who broke their hearts."

"What did you talk about when it was your turn?"

I couldn't tell them about my decent enough childhood (absent father, overbearing mother, nothing really all that wrong), the success I found young (though not as young as I wanted), the boy I fell in love with and married, the baby we made together. Unlike everyone else—the addicts with their tough childhoods, their genetic predisposition to addiction, the traumas they built up over the years—I have only myself to blame for what I lost.

"I mostly kept quiet."

"You?" Andrew scoffs, and I give him a playful shove.

"It's true!" I insist. "I never felt like I *belonged* there."

"No one feels like they belong in rehab. That's kind of the point, isn't it? Like, people denying they need to be there and all that? People thinking they're the exception to the twelve steps; it's okay for them to drink and get high and whatever else."

I shake my head, seeing the shaggy platinum tips of my hair in my peripheral vision. "I don't mean it like that."

"So what do you mean?"

I take a breath, tasting the artificial flavors my mother would disapprove of if she were here: *Tsk, tsk, tsk.* I can smell Andrew, the *maleness* of him. I haven't lived with a man since my husband. For so long, after he was gone, I didn't want to wash anything. I liked walking into the bathroom and still smelling him: his cologne, some forgotten T-shirt on the floor, his sweat on the pillowcase. For years afterward, I wore the same cologne, used the same soap and shampoo he had, but it all smelled different on me.

"I mean, I never felt, you know, *entitled* to be there. Like everyone else there was a member of a club I hadn't earned the right to join."

"You say that as if you *wanted* to join."

"I didn't like how it felt to be left out. I felt like a fake or something. An imposter." Just like I did at the fancy parties when our second album went gold, or when I went back to Yonkers to visit my mom, or walking down the aisle on my wedding day, or bringing my kid home from the hospital. I felt like this wasn't meant for me, like there was someone else out there, some expert, who knew how to navigate the world better than I did. "I guess I've been an imposter all my life."

Andrew cocks his head to the side like a puppy. "Sounds like a song." He reaches one of his long arms out to grab my guitar from the chair where Evelyn sits during therapy. He strums it and croons, "Imposter all my life."

"I was just talking," I say. "Not writing."

"You're writing music every time you open your mouth."

It's been a long time since anyone spoke to me that way—like I'm an artist. Even fans, when I meet them now, they're looking for a good time, not poetry.

I pull my notebook from the waistband of my leggings. I've gotten used to the feel of the spiral binding against my skin, like my waist is a hiding place for my darkest secret: I'm still trying, and failing, to write.

"I haven't finished anything in a long time," I confess. "See? All these beginnings, but no endings."

"These are some good beginnings," Andrew says, thumbing through the pages.

"I know," I say, and Andrew grins, a lock of his tawny hair falling over his forehead. I don't believe in false modesty or fishing for compliments.

"I know you know." Andrew slides my notebook onto the kitchen counter and fits my guitar into my lap, the backs of his hands lingering against my thighs. He puts my left hand on the neck, and moves my right hand over the strings. He's so much taller than I am, but his hands aren't actually that much larger. My fingers are long, my palms wide.

Like a man's, my husband used to say. *Like Jimi Hendrix, like Jimmy Page.* He made it sound good, like I was born to be a rock star.

"Sing it back to me." Andrew speaks softly, like we're lying in bed together. Goose bumps rise on my skin, and a pleasant shiver runs through me. "I've been an imposter all my life."

"Imposter all my life," I echo. I close my eyes. The fire in the fireplace is dying, burned down to embers, but still giving off heat. Or maybe the warmth I'm feeling isn't from the fire at all but from this man, so close to me that I can feel his breath when he exhales.

In crowded rooms of celebration,
In circles of strangers' consternation,
In the house where I grew up,
On the stage where I blew up,
Across the threshold where he carried me,
Alone with my baby.
You know I think that maybe
I won't even belong in the grave where they'll bury me.

I sing the words with a scratch in my throat, raw and aching. My husband used to say that music should hurt.

I swallow. "Another good beginning."

"A *great* beginning," Andrew counters. "Keep going."

He makes it sound simple. I let the guitar slide between my legs—between our legs—and down to the floor.

Andrew hands me my notebook and recites the words back to me so I can write them down.

"This time will be different," he promises. "This time, you're going to finish it."

"How do you know?" I ask, the words catching in my throat.

"This time you have me. Tonight you wrote one verse. Tomorrow night, we'll do one more."

"What'll you give me if I finish a whole song?" I ask, licking my lips.

Andrew winks. "I'll make it worth your while."

"You're going to have to do better than Swedish Fish and SweeTarts."

"Don't worry," Andrew promises. "I know what you want."

Of course he doesn't, but I smile, letting him think he does.

31

Lord Edward

At breakfast, Dr. Rush gives me my "use as directed" dose, pulling the pill bottle from the inside pocket of his tweedy jacket, held next to his heart for safekeeping.

I shiver through a cold plunge and sweat in the sauna. Before lunch I sneak back to my room—ostensibly to use the bathroom—and grab another pill from my stash, crunching it between my teeth while Dr. Rush waits for me in the next room for today's chat therapy. I put another pill in my pocket in case I need it later. Then another. And another.

"Why do you dress like that?" I ask as I sit across from the man who locked me inside. I stretch my leg out in front of me.

"Like what?" Dr. Rush asks.

"Like my father." Does he think it will make me feel more at home? I could tell him that dressing like my father is hardly going to set me at ease.

My father doesn't believe in ease. If I so much as slouched at the dinner table, I'd be sent to my room. The walls in my childhood home—the home in London where my father, Anne, and her family now live—are thick and ancient, but somehow my father always heard if I cried.

The Duke of Exeter wears a suit every day. In London, pinstriped, single-breasted jackets and pants in various shades of gray over crisp button-downs and ties, his collars held up by starch, so tight around his neck that when I was little I thought he might be choking. For the countryside, there are houndstooth and tweed, pants tucked into tall boots, unflattering hats to match. In the evening, we're meant to dress for dinner: tuxedos and cocktail dresses. I've never seen my father wear jeans, though I imagine if he ever did, his tailor would surely create a denim three-piece suit.

People like my family are anachronisms, but Anne acts as though we're saviors, holding up traditions and rituals—*a way of life*, she calls it—that would be lost if not for us.

I ask for a glass of water. When Dr. Rush's back is turned, I pull two pills from my pocket, slide them between my lips. Dr. Rush hands me the glass, and I swallow hard.

"So you're saying that your father's formal nature created distance between you?" he asks.

I shake my head. I didn't say that. I was thinking about my father's clothes, not pouring my heart out. Certainly not to Dr. Rush, jailer disguised as therapist.

Besides, I never said Dad was formal. Sure, he dresses the part, but I've seen him disheveled. The way the vein on his neck looks fit to burst when he shouts. The sweat shimmering on his neck when he grabs me, shakes me.

I feel as though I'm sinking into the couch beneath me, like the soft white cushions will swallow me whole.

"Did he do that often, grabbing you roughly?"

Did I say that aloud? No, I would never.

Was Dad rough? Certainly, he was never tender. He never hugged me or kissed the top of my head. He said I had no mother, so I had no reason to behave like a Mama's boy. He was quick to remind me that she left me without looking back. It was years before I understood that my mother hadn't been given much choice in the matter.

"And how did that make you feel? He belittled the impact your mother's absence may have had on you."

I shake my head. I mean to be shaking my head. Am I shaking my head? I stand, wobbly, but Dr. Rush doesn't question it. It'd be more suspicious if I were steady, all things considered. I go back to my room, into the bathroom, and run the water, splashing my face.

How did it make me feel? How do you fucking *think*, Doctor? My mother left and I wasn't allowed to act as though it meant *anything* to me.

I pull a pill from my pocket. I place it on the bathroom counter, white on white on white. I take the tumbler that's meant to be filled with water for brushing my teeth and crush the pill into powder. I've never done this before, but it seems simple enough. I bend over, pressing one nostril shut. I inhale so quickly that it makes me cough.

Holy shit. Why haven't I been doing this all along?

"You all right in there?" Dr. Rush calls from the other side of the door.

"Be right out," I shout back, hurrying to brush the remaining powder into my hand, into my mouth. I run the water, wipe my nose, blink my eyes open and shut.

I limp back into the living room and pat my belly. "Something must've disagreed with me." So polite, so genteel. I sit down, my posture stick straight. One may slouch *only* when one is leaning in to share a secret. Then, curl one's body into a C so the other person will know they're being confided in.

It makes them feel special, Anne told me once. When she cut the deal with Harper's parents, she rounded her back like a snake, her voice lowered to a whisper.

He'll go to rehab as soon as he's strong enough to travel. Tears in her eyes, silently reminding them that their daughter wasn't the only one who'd been hurt; her tortured, troubled little brother was suffering, too.

Eventually, the Steeles were convinced that Anne deeply cared about getting me *help.* It didn't hurt, of course, that Anne promised them more for keeping quiet than a judge would award them if they'd sued me publicly in civil court. Privately, Anne rolled her eyes at their naivete. She'd played into the Steeles' Americanness, their puritan certainty that I needed rehab rather than a stiff drink and a good kick in the head.

I don't think he'd survive a trial, Anne said mournfully. *He's already lost so much.*

My father likes to say that Anne will make an excellent duchess. Each time he says it, I know that he isn't talking about Anne at all, but about Mum, about me—how we'd failed by comparison.

What does it matter, Dad said, when Anne announced the terms of her deal with the Steeles. *It's not as though you could have* married *that girl.*

I couldn't have married her because I'm meant to marry an appropriate woman and play respectful in the public eye.

Appropriate is code for wealthy, like something out of another century.

My *appropriate* marriage will help finance our estates, since our income is no longer enough to maintain our properties. I picture the house in Scotland, the wallpaper peeling from the walls, the pots and pans the servants put out to protect the carpets when it rains.

"That sounds like an enormous responsibility to place on your shoulders," Dr. Rush says, all sympathy, like he's not working for Anne, like he isn't counting on my family to write an enormous check at the end of my stay.

What does Dr. Rush know? No, really: What does he know? I must have said something out loud, but I already can't remember what. My tongue feels like it weighs a million pounds.

Even if I brought in a million pounds, Anne and Dad would demand more.

"Good work today," Dr. Rush says.

The Dog Walker

For months, she's been waking early, rising before the sun, before the dog has a chance to nudge her feet with his nose and beg to be taken outside.

Absurd, she knows, to walk on the beach in the dead of winter, the breeze off the ocean so stiff and so cold. But it's been like this ever since her husband passed. Not a tragedy, they said; he'd been old, he'd been ill. Expected, they said, like that should cushion the blow.

They'd been married for more than fifty years. They had no children: It was the two of them and their collection of dogs. They'd moved to Shelter Island years ago, declaring that they didn't need a bustling city, they didn't need people and places and things—they needed only each other.

What did they think, she wonders now as the cold air snakes its way beneath her layers, goose bumps blossoming on her skin, that they would die at the exact same time, neither leaving the other alone? For good measure, did they think their last dog would die on schedule as well, and they'd leave nothing behind but a kitchen full of chipped pots and pans, a collection of books and letters and clothes, all of it trash for strangers to clear out?

Well, it hadn't happened that way, and now she's alone. She walks their dog for miles every day, the last dog that will ever belong to both of them, the last creature, she's decided, with whom she will share a home, a bed, a life. When they reach the beach, she unclips his harness, and he runs ahead. In the warmer months, he heads straight for the water, but he knows better when it's this cold.

She should be more careful with him, she thinks. If something happens to him, what would she do?

Suddenly panicked, she calls the dog's name. Normally, he comes right back to her side, but this morning—this cold, gray morning—he keeps moving, his nose in the air, like he's smelled something more interesting than she could ever possibly be. She runs after him, her aging bones moving slowly over the sand, calling his name over and over, her voice growing more high-pitched with each step.

By the time she reaches the dunes, she's crawling on her hands and knees up the incline. Twenty years ago, thirty years ago, she could scramble up the sand like a wild animal, but now she is out of breath.

The dog stands motionless now, but he still won't come when she calls. He lets out a whine, then paws at the ground.

It feels like it takes her ages to reach him. She notices footprints in the sand, a long winding path.

There is a person sitting cross-legged like a child where the prints stop. The dog nudges the face, and the person falls over.

At once, the dog walker recognizes that what she's seeing isn't a person at all. Not anymore.

The wind picks up, making her shiver, erasing the prints on the sand. The hair on the body's head moves in the breeze so that for a second it looks alive again, and without thinking, she moves closer, as if she could possibly help. But when the wind stops, the body stills again, and there is no denying its lifelessness. There are icicles on its eyelashes. Its lips are blue.

The body isn't wearing a coat. What was the person who used to be in there thinking, dressing like that this time of year?

Maybe they weren't thinking. That recovery center brings all sorts to the island, people out of their mind on god knows what. In the end, her husband was on so many painkillers he'd have gone outside in his underwear without realizing it.

Or maybe, the dog walker thinks, the person who used to be in this body *wanted* to die out here. The thought makes her angry, when she thinks of how badly her husband wanted to live, how badly she wanted him to live.

Then again, she understands longing for oblivion. She won't do anything to hurt herself while their dog is still alive—she has to take care of him—but she's considered what she might do after he's gone.

Her hands shake as she dials 911.

32

Amelia Blue

I'm counting. Counting the hours. Counting the minutes. Counting the seconds. Numbers are supposed to be objective, hard, absolute, but then how is it that seconds can feel like minutes, minutes can feel like hours, and hours can feel like days?

If even numbers are mutable, then perhaps nothing is solid.

Dr. Mackenzie watched me eat ("eat") dinner. She didn't suggest I try more than yogurt and strawberries, and she didn't insist we discuss the meal. But she didn't leave me alone, either. She watched like I was a riveting television show, barely blinking. Now, she's drinking tea on the couch while I sit with a book at the kitchen counter, waiting for it to be late enough to go to bed without arousing any suspicion. It feels like holding my breath underwater, like if I wait much longer, my body will simply give out.

At 10:04 (on the dot might arouse suspicion), I stand and say, "I'm heading to bed."

Dr. Mackenzie jumps to her feet, a soldier at attention. "I'll be downstairs if you need anything—just tap the button."

I wonder if she's bored with me. I haven't exactly been a forthcoming patient, going through the motions with her every day, recycling the stories I've told other doctors before. A few times, I even told stories that weren't mine, overheard after years of group therapy, just to fill the space between us, but I think she could tell I was lying.

I listen to her feet pad down the stairs, then head to my room. I run a bath and slip under the water. I haven't shaved my legs since I arrived. They must have confiscated my razor when I wasn't looking. I recall a scene in *Girl, Interrupted* (I read it in high school; didn't everyone?) when Susanna Kaysen shaves her legs in front of a nurse. I imagine Dr. Mackenzie watching me shave the way she watches me eat, her eyes on the razor blade to make sure I don't do anything I'm not supposed to do. Perhaps if I linger in the bath too long, she'll know somehow and rush upstairs to check on me.

I turn the water on again, so hot that it steams. I try to focus on the temperature instead of the clawing inside me, the ache in my gut that wants me to sprint to the kitchen. I wrap my legs around each other like I'm tying myself down.

When I finally get out of the tub, my skin is bright pink from the hot water. I don't bother drying myself, just pull on leggings and a T-shirt and rush out the door.

I open up the fridge and pull out cold chicken fingers. I don't stop to close the door before shoving meat into my mouth. The breading is so dry that I gag as I swallow, but I keep going.

I read once that for some people, anorexia is in part due to a hormonal imbalance: They simply don't experience hunger like everyone else.

I thought that was me. Georgia, I thought, was hungry enough for the both of us—for food, for fame, for drugs, for jewelry. The day the police found me and fed me McDonald's, I ate only because it seemed to please the officer. I can still feel the greasy wet fries between my teeth, lukewarm, smothered in ketchup so sweet it made my tongue itch.

All my life, I *knew* that uncontrollable hunger was Georgia's department, not mine. But over the past six months, everything I knew flipped on its axis, and a monster woke up in my belly, demanding food.

My hands shake as I open a cabinet and pull out a box of Rice Krispies, scooping handful after handful into my mouth, not bothering with milk. Some lemon cookie gets lodged in my throat. I stifle my cough—Dr. Mackenzie might hear.

My eyes dart around the room. Surely, if there were hidden cameras, the doctor would see what I'm doing and rush up the stairs to stop me. Then again, she might simply observe, like an anthropologist observing animal behaviors in the wild.

I hurry back to the bathroom, still steamy. How long since I got out of the bath? How much have I shoved into my body in such a small period of time? #Promia says it's impossible to truly purge every calorie you eat. Even if you throw up right away, your body, desperate for nutrition, will absorb *something*.

I catch my reflection in the dingy mirror. The skin on my face is blotchy, like I've broken out in hives. Even through my T-shirt, my stomach looks distended, almost as if I were pregnant.

I curl over the toilet, reaching my fingers past my lips, making a mess on the pristine white porcelain that Izabela cleaned earlier.

I sit back on my heels, my chest heaving like I've run a marathon, then stand and turn on the tap at the sink, splashing cold water on my face. Vomit doesn't taste like *vomit* when you throw up so soon after eating. It just tastes like what you ate all over again. (That doesn't make it any better, though it reminds me how wasteful it is to binge and purge, my disease itself a strange sort of privilege.)

I pull on my boots and my sweater and head to the terrace, tightening my scarf around my neck. Outside, I take a drag from my cigarette, my hands trembling. I lean back, situating myself entirely in the circle of light given off by the terrace's lamp.

I have to get moving if I'm going to make it to the building in the woods before Dr. Mackenzie's next bed check.

33

Florence

Even with a fire in the fireplace, even with my guitar in my lap and my fur coat across my shoulders, even with the heat turned up to seventy-seven on the glowing Nest thermostat—I'm still cold, and I'm never cold. It's these stupid glass walls. They're supposed to be high-end and luxurious, but I know the truth: It's just another way for them to control me, to keep me from being truly comfortable while I'm here. The rooms here may have doors, but there's no privacy, only exposure. I imagine paparazzi prowling the property with their high-powered cameras, enormous lenses and flashes capturing everything. They would climb the trees for a better shot, dangling from the branches like perverse Christmas ornaments.

"It's fucking freezing in here."

"I'll turn up the heat," Andrew offers, but in my mind I hear my husband's voice. *Bloody freezing,* he'd have said, if he were here. He wasn't British—the man was born in Nebraska—but he traveled a lot. All over the world, for work. He picked up words and phrases the way other people picked up magnets and snow globes. His souvenirs made their way into everyday conversation. I used to make fun of him for it, but he never minded. My jokes made him laugh.

I look out the window. It's past midnight, but it's not entirely dark outside. A flurry of tiny white snowflakes is falling, not enough to stick. All that white should call to mind cleanliness, purity, virginity. Snow White with her pale pale skin. I grab my notebook and scribble:

Even the princess, trapped in her tower,
Ever white, ever pure,
Is she aware of her power?

The sort of beauty that makes men battle dragons, take up arms,
Did she wonder, "Where do I belong?"
Was the tower her prison, or the wide world outside?
Was the prince her rescuer
Or another . . . another . . . another . . .

My thoughts are like a record skipping over the same line again and again. I throw my notebook across the room.

"It shouldn't be this hard to rhyme the word *outside*."

Andrew crosses the room and picks my notebook off the floor, sets it on the coffee table in front of me, then sits beside me on the white couch

"Of course it should," Andrew says.

"Huh?"

"Of course it should be hard." Andrew runs his palm over his cheeks and chin, brushing up against his stubble. "If it was easy, anyone could do it."

I nod like I agree with him, but I think he's got it backward. It *is* easy.

Or anyway, it used to be. It was easy for years. It was so easy that it felt like I was cheating, getting away with something.

My first couple albums, I wrote them drunk and high, late at night and early in the morning. Some songs took me twenty minutes and others twenty hours, but none of it was *hard*. I gave away lyrics and melodies to other musicians—I figured I could always come up with more. I used to think my career was an elaborate hoax, and all those people who admired me just hadn't tried doing it themselves and discovered how easy it was.

Until it became impossible.

"C'mon." Andrew pulls me up to stand, lacing his fingers through mine. Somehow, his hands are warm. He leans over and turns on the Bose speaker, still tuned to the nineties station. Miraculously, they're actually playing one of my songs.

Andrew starts crooning the words, closing his eyes. People used to do that at our shows: I'd look out into the crowd and see people screaming the words with their eyes squeezed shut, like they hadn't come to *see* me—they could *feel* me.

Andrew spins me around and pulls me close. I can smell his minty soap. I turn up the volume, until my voice through the speakers is so loud I'm surprised the glass walls don't shatter.

God, I sound so fearless. I *was* fearless, back in the days before a single social media post could take you down. Before my husband and I had barely gone on our first date, before Joni Jewell had ever picked up a guitar.

Evelyn said this place was a retreat. What if I want to retreat further, to my heyday, crowds screaming my name? Or more, to when my husband and I hadn't even met and my kid hadn't been born, and the only person I'd ever disappointed was my mother, and I was too disappointed in *her* to care?

What would I have done, at that age, in a place like this?

What would I have done, face-to-face with a man like Andrew?

I grab the waistband of Andrew's pants—jeans tonight, not the terrible gray uniform he wears during the day—and pull him to me. I lick his neck, tasting salt and sweat and aftershave. I put my face close to his, but I don't kiss him, not yet. Instead, I whisper my own lyrics against his lips.

Never settle,
Never beg,
Never let them tell you what you're worth,
You're a diamond,
You're a pearl,
You only have to be your own favorite, girl.

What happened to the woman who was so in love with herself she didn't care if anyone else loved her?

I know the answer. In my mind's eye, I can see my husband's face the way it was the last time I saw him, when I knew he would never, ever come back.

When I was pregnant, I talked to my belly, promising the baby inside that I'd found her a good father, one who wouldn't leave her like my dad left me.

I tried so hard to make him stay.

I failed so completely.

He left us both.

It's Andrew who closes the gap between us. When his tongue slides between my lips, I feel it in my knees.

Andrew backs me up to the couch. His hand slides under my night-gown, and his fingers trace the outline of my left nipple, sliding down my torso and around my back, down my pants. I unbutton his jeans, feeling desperate. My husband's face vanishes from my mind's eye. My song fades as the radio station cues up their next song. A DJ announces that they're playing music by *badass women* tonight.

Suddenly, I'm not cold. I'm so hot that I push Andrew off me and rush to the glass wall, pulling the sliding door open wide.

I breathe in the icy, thin air, and I sing:

Was the tower her prison, or the wide world outside?
Was the prince her rescuer
Or just another place to crawl inside?
Would she always be searching for somewhere that felt like home?
Some place she could be herself, unafraid to be alone?
No longer afflicted with Imposter Syndrome.

I look back at Andrew, wink, then rush out the door.

34

Amelia Blue

The gravel path crunches beneath my feet, louder than it seemed when Edward was with me, louder even than the music blaring from the third cottage.

I recognize the song that's playing. In fact, I've heard it more times than I can count. A relic from Georgia's glory days.

I know exactly how many weeks it spent on the *Billboard* top ten (eight), and I know that my mother thought eight weeks wasn't enough.

If she had been in the kitchen with me tonight, Georgia would've eaten right alongside me, but she wouldn't have called it bingeing and she wouldn't have felt the need to purge after. She would've been pleased to see me so hungry. To see me like her.

Something else I always knew for certain: I didn't want to be like her.

I walk away from the music, toward the driveway, and into the woods. Tonight, I don't flash a light at Edward's terrace, don't wait for him to join me. He didn't like me leafing through all those strangers' files last night. His reluctance would only slow me down, and tonight I have even farther to go. I keep my gaze focused on my feet, on the dim light coming from my cellphone, trying to ignore the incredible dark of the woods closing around me. Living in New York City, I was never scared walking down the street no matter the time of day or night. In Manhattan, the streets are never entirely cased in shadow, never truly empty.

But out here, the woods are deep enough to disappear inside. The quiet is disorienting.

And then I'm on the ground, the wind knocked out of me.

I can smell perfume, or maybe it's shampoo, or maybe it's just this person—a woman, I think—musky and hot, sweat mixed with vanilla. And something else, something earthy and moldy. As the person shifts on top of me, I realize that I'm smelling a fur coat, something dead. I tighten my grip on my phone, the flashlight now aimed at her face.

She presses her hand against my shoulder to push her body back to standing. She doesn't offer to help me up, and she doesn't apologize. Her hair is the sort of platinum blond you'd know is fake even if you couldn't see her dark roots, cut into a layered bob that frames her face.

"You the one throwing rocks at my window?" she asks, out of breath. Before I can answer, she adds, "Sick of waiting for me to come out and play, huh? Did it ever occur to you I'm *busy* up there?" She gestures to her cottage as if I'd dragged her out into the woods tonight.

Before I can point out that *she's* the one who crashed into *me*, she raises her eyebrows, lips circling into an *O*. "Holy shit. Amelia Blue Harris." She whispers my name like it's a secret I might not know.

I shouldn't be surprised she's recognized me, given the music blasting from her cottage. She looks me up and down like she's taking stock. I fold my arms across my chest.

"Talk about trippy," she says.

I can't remember which website was the first to report on my eating disorder, but the whole world knew the first time I was in residential treatment. (Or rather, the portion of the world who cared to know that sort of thing.) Rumors flew, suggesting anorexia was a cover story, really I was just as strung out and fucked-up as my parents, rumors Georgia did nothing to dispel.

"Don't worry," the woman says. "I won't tell anyone I saw you here. Long as you promise not to say you saw me? I want to manage how the story comes out." She speaks so fast that I wonder if maybe she's on something.

Despite her heavy coat, she looks naked somehow, exposed. Her body, when she fell against me, was hot, like she's some kind of otherworldly creature, impervious to the cold, able to survive when the rest of us would freeze to death.

I shake my head. Another thing I know: Every human body is as weak and vulnerable as the next, as likely to fail when it's deprived of what it needs (warmth, water, nutrition). A body can lose its extremities to frostbite, slurring words as the cold sets in, unable to think clearly or move well.

I know, too, that a starving body is more vulnerable to the elements, its immune system already compromised. Skin may be thinner, vulnerable to peeling, wrinkles, tears. The brain quite literally shrinks, the heartbeat loses its rhythm. Muscles will atrophy, and bones break more easily; even bone marrow may stop working. Fertility is affected.

All of that to say: I know better.

"No!" She almost shouts, as though I've said something she disagrees with. She stomps a foot hard against the ground. "It won't be another story. It'll be the *truth* this time, I promise."

She grabs my hands and looks into my eyes, holding my gaze like she wants me to take her promise to heart. Through my fingerless gloves, I can feel her nails, jagged and sharp, like she's been gnawing them.

"Just you wait, Amelia Blue." She says my name slowly, as though it's heavy on her tongue.

"I won't tell anyone I saw you here," I promise. I don't say that I haven't actually recognized her, that I have no idea what she's talking about. She seems so certain I know who she is, that this is all so terribly important.

Could she be the patient I (thought I) saw being restrained in the dark last night? The person looking for her—is that the person I (thought I) saw in the distance?

No; the person I saw was shorter, her hair longer, the Cape Cod–style house on the other side of the property.

And yet, this woman seems addled, maybe even desperate. Her eyes scan the woods around us like a feral cat's.

"I gotta go," she says breathlessly. "Got someone looking for me, if you know what I mean."

I wonder if her stay here, unlike mine, isn't *voluntary*. If she tried to check out, could they stop her? Before I can say another word, she winks, then rushes headlong into the darkness, leaving the scent of sweat and dead animal behind her.

I turn off my phone's flashlight. There are at least two people out there: The patient I didn't recognize, and whoever it is that's looking for her.

What would they do if they found me instead?

35

Lord Edward

Harper's laughing, her head thrown back, her mouth open wide. No; she's not laughing, she's screaming.

She's crying.

She's broken open, her insides streaming from her like tears

No; she's fine. She's whole.

We're at a party in Southampton. She's wearing a short pleated skirt, a ribbed white tank top. I'm running my fingers along the space just above her waistband, feeling her skin, cool and dry despite the summer humidity.

God, she was always so cool. Instead of sweating, she'd kind of *glow*. She was peach sherbet; she was a cold glass of milk; she was crunching ice cubes between my teeth.

I feel sweat along my hairline, gathering at the back of my neck, between my fingers and toes. I reek. I've been at the party too long. The drink in my hand is lukewarm, but I take a swig nonetheless.

"Don't you think you've had enough?" Harper doesn't pretend she's not concerned. She doesn't care if she embarrasses me. She doesn't keep up appearances.

I pull her close and kiss her. She tastes like strawberry ice cream.

No; my mouth is empty. She's not here. I'm not there.

I'm in bed, in this terrible place, and Dr. Rush thinks I did good work today.

She was going to break up with me. She told me that night.

No; we were going to get married. We were going to backpack across Europe and disappear into the Black Forest like creatures out of the Grimm brothers' fairy tales.

No; we were simply getting into the car.

I'd rented a sports car for the summer. Convertible, top down, leather seats. Harper was angry at me for using the family's money.

"I won't marry you unless you stop accepting their money."

"They're controlling you from miles away."

"It doesn't matter. They'd never let you marry me."

"You've had too much to drink."

"Let me drive."

I can't see the cottage, can't see the wall of glass leading to the terrace, the enormous barn door that opens into the hall. I can't feel the too-soft Hastens mattress beneath my back or the goose-down comforter over my body.

I'm playing with the radio, my eyes on the controls instead of the road.

The car was manual. I loved shifting gears as we pulled onto the high-way.

I can't feel the pedals beneath my feet. I hold my hands out, but it's like the steering wheel isn't there, there's only air.

I'm not in control.

I hear the sound of tires screeching, metal crumbling.

The whole world is shaking, humming.

No; my phone is ringing, vibrating against the mattress. My hands fumble as I try to silence it.

"Hello?"

Harper's screaming. The terror in her voice makes me shake.

Instead of cool winter air, I feel a hot summer night.

I feel the weight of Harper's body in my arms.

I feel the gravel of the road beneath my knees.

I think, *There's so much blood.*

It's dripping into my eyes, gluing them shut.

"Edward, are you okay?"

Harper's screams fade into whimpers.

Into silence.

36

Amelia Blue

"Edward, are you okay?"

He's squeezing his eyes shut tight, but there are tears edging out, tracing their way down his cheeks and over his angular jawline.

I sit on the edge of the bed, my left hip against his right. I slide off my hat, my gloves, unwind the scarf from around my neck, still cool from the air outside. My fingers, in the sudden warmth of his room, feel like they're on fire. "Please. Talk to me." His blankets are piled over him, twisted around his body like ropes.

After my run-in with the third patient, too scared to stay in the woods (she didn't exactly strike me as *stable*, though surely there are people who think the same about me), I'd followed the sound of music back toward the cottages, my steps falling in time with the beat in spite of myself.

When I knocked on his sliding glass door, Edward didn't seem to hear. The hollow thumping sound when I knocked harder make me realize the door was made of the kind of glass that doesn't shatter. At other recovery centers, they laminate the windows, but here I suspect they use military-grade materials, the sort of glass that can survive an explosion without turning to shards, breaking apart into solid pieces with edges too smooth to cause damage.

The door was locked, but it was easy enough to pick with my kit. Through the window, I could see that Edward's room was messy: His jacket and gloves were in a pile on the floor, his boots kicked off by the door, the bathroom light left on. Not nearly as messy as Georgia's room would've been, but far messier than my room across the courtyard, my studio in the West Village, my bedroom in Laurel Canyon.

As the lock gave way, it occurred to me, for the very first time, that

Georgia, who taught me to pick locks, easily could have undone the lock to my bedroom back home. She actually chose not to.

"I can't see." Edward's voice is soft, like a little boy's, his dark hair mussed, sweat glistening on his upper lip. "It's getting in my eyes."

I rush to the bathroom, grab a washcloth, and run cool water over it. I gently press the cloth over his eyelids. "I'm wiping it away," I say, though of course I have no idea what his nightmare is dripping into his eyes. "You're clean now."

Edward opens his mouth, but his words come out slurred, unintelligible.

Here's something else I know: what it looks like when someone's taken too many drugs. And exactly what to do to sober them up.

"C'mon." I tuck my hair behind my ears and slide my hands beneath his arms, pulling him up to sit. I feel the taut muscles of his back as I wrap my arms around him, so different from my mother's body, so much bigger than my own. "You have to help me get you to the bathroom."

I begin to push his blankets away, and at once he's wide awake, his hand gripping my wrist, stopping me.

"Edward, you have to get up." I used to have to beg Georgia the same way. "You need to purge."

I manage to twist my wrist from his grip and slide my arm back around him. I pull with all my strength. His muscles ripple with resistance beneath his soft white T-shirt, the sort that looks worn-out when you buy it new.

I wait for Edward to put his feet down on the hardwood floor. All this tugging and twisting can't be good for his injury, but he's flailing, reaching for the blankets, dragging them down after him.

Finally, I hear one of Edward's feet hit the floor, feel it when he starts holding his weight upright.

I step away, my hands flat on his back. His skin is hot through his shirt. I'm breathing so hard from the effort of moving him that it takes a moment to register what I see, reflected in the moonlight streaming in through the windows.

Edward's fucked-up leg isn't fucked-up at all. It isn't anything. It isn't *there*. His left leg is amputated at the knee.

37

Lord Edward

I don't think I've ever vomited so much. Or maybe I have and don't remember; I'm a blackout drunk after all.

I slide my body away from the toilet and lean against the wall opposite.

"Get the fuck out," I hiss, but my heart's not in it, and Amelia must know because she simply sits against the wall beside me.

If Anne were here, she'd accuse Amelia of invading my privacy, her voice terrifyingly calm as she threatened Amelia with some kind of legal action: That American girl had no right to enter my room, no right to remove my covers, no right to expose my broken body.

"Why did your family keep it a secret?" Amelia asks. She doesn't have to explain what she's talking about.

Anne said concealing the extent of my injuries was necessary to keep the press from discovering the severity of the crash. The official press release stated only that I'd sustained damage to my leg and that my companion—*companion*, not *partner*, not *girlfriend*, not even *friend*—was currently under a doctor's care. It was to preserve Harper's privacy, Anne insisted. To keep the press from sniffing for more details. The paparazzi had snapped pictures of Harper and me over the year prior, but the family never confirmed she was my girlfriend. *We don't do that,* Anne had said, though we both knew they'd have been quick to confirm had I been dating the sort of woman they wanted.

The word damage, my sister said, *covers a multitude of sins.*

"Maybe Anne thought it would make me less appealing on the marriage market." My family has kept so many secrets over the years, over the centuries: infidelities, addictions, deficiencies, madness.

"You make it sound like the eighteen hundreds."

I shrug.

"Did *you* want to keep it secret?" Amelia asks gently.

A lump rises in my throat. "I don't know." My voice sounds unfamiliar, as though a stranger has taken up residence in my vocal cords.

"You don't have to be ashamed." Amelia's voice is tender, but I shake my head.

The doctors and therapists tried to encourage me. They told me stories of former soldiers competing at an elite level in the Invictus Games despite amputations and injuries until I felt like a failure for not having a better outlook. Didn't they understand it wasn't the same thing? Those men and women had come by their losses honorably.

Nausea rises in my throat, and in a moment I'm hunched over the toilet again. Amelia doesn't recoil. She leans closer, rubbing my back.

When I'm done, Amelia puts her hands on my shoulders and pulls me close so that I'm leaning against her, her chin on my forehead. I almost ask if she has children; she seems to know exactly what to do, the way a mother would.

She shifts, straightening one leg out in front of her. She leans around me and takes off her warm boots and socks.

"Look," she says. "My toes."

Her foot is very white, her skin almost translucent except for a tiny heart-shaped birthmark just beneath her big toe. I look closer and see a series of nearly invisible scars between her toes.

"Papercuts." Amelia moves again, sliding out from under me. She lowers the waistband of her leggings, past her underwear, until I can see the top of her thighs. There are more cuts there, longer ones, though just as thin. The lines are neat, perfectly parallel like the pages of a book.

"I started doing it in high school," she explains, "while I was studying for the SATs. It was the only thing that made the tests bearable." She chuckles softly, then lifts her shirt and shows me another scar, this one beneath her left breast. It's a series of slashes over what appears to be a ruined tattoo. I can't make out what it used to be.

"I did this one just a few months ago," she says.

"Why are you showing me this?" I ask.

"Because you're not the only one with a ripped-up body," she answers.

She pulls her shirt down and sits back beside me. She's so small that I have to lean down so she can rest her chin on my shoulder. I can smell the lavender from her shampoo.

"Can I ask you something?" Amelia asks.

I nod.

"Were you trying to kill yourself?"

I look at my hands, so much larger than hers, than Harper's, than Anne's.

"No," I answer softly. "I was only trying to quiet the voices in my head."

Amelia circles the wrist of one hand with the thumb and forefinger of the other. "Sometimes I think my mother was actually trying to make the voices *louder*."

"What do you mean?"

"I told you, she took everything she could get her hands on. I thought the real world—you know, without chemical enhancement or whatever—wasn't enough to hold her interest. Like she needed, more, more, more to make it all worthwhile. Nothing like me. If anything, I wish the world would be less, less, less."

"Is that why you want to find your mother's file?" The thought still makes me squeamish. What if Anne or my father came here one day, rifled through Dr. Rush's notes? "To understand why you're so different?"

Amelia inhales sharply. For a moment I think she's crying, but her voice is steady when she answers. "Not only that," she says. With each syllable, she drums the side of her hand against her thigh. "I'm trying to make sense of how she lived the way she did, and I live the way I do."

My sister certainly wouldn't look to me—or to Dr. Rush's opinion of me—to make sense of *herself*. She thinks her place in the world is perfectly logical; she is exactly whom she was born to be. *I'm* the one who's out of step. Anne doesn't want a doctor to explain *why*; she wants me fixed until I fall in line like generations of second sons before me.

Amelia presses her hands against me, pushing herself up to look me in the eye. "What would've happened if I hadn't been here tonight?"

"I don't know," I answer heavily.

"What if I'm not here next time?"

"I'll be careful," I promise.

I can tell from the look on Amelia's face that she doesn't believe me.

I gesture toward the bed outside, the button on the nightstand. "Why didn't you call for help if you were so *worried* about me?" I say *worried* like it's an accusation.

"I would've, if I couldn't get you to your feet." Amelia's eyes widen as she realizes her poor choice of words, but for once, I laugh instead of cringing. In a second, Amelia's laughing, too, so hard that she doubles over.

"Do you think your care manager has any idea?" she asks as the laughter ebbs and quiet falls over us.

"About what?"

"That you've been sneaking pills."

I think of the doctor carefully meting out my dose each morning, and shake my head.

"They don't know how much it hurts," I say.

"No," Amelia agrees. "They never do."

38

Florence

"It's from Evelyn's stash." Andrew holds up the wine bottle like he's a kid at show-and-tell.

Of course this is what he thought I wanted. Over the years, it's gone this way more times than I can count: I meet a fan; I tell them something they don't know about my music; they tell me something I don't know about my music (how much it meant to them, how they interpreted it, etc., etc.); then they offer me a drink or a pill or a bump because they want to go home and tell their friends they partied with me. It got so partying was part of my job, another way to keep the fans engaged.

"Her stash?" I echo.

Andrew nods. "She's got countless cases hidden around the property. She won't notice a missing bottle or two."

I grin as Andrew opens the bottle and hands it to me to take a swig.

"Cheers," he says. I bring the bottle to my lips, inhaling the aroma of the wine. At so many dinners, the person sitting across the table from me would swirl their glass, breathe deeply, take a tiny sip. I never understood how they could drink so slowly. What was the point?

"Didn't peg you for a wine guy," I say, passing the bottle back to him.

"I'm not," Andrew admits as he settles beside me on the deep couch where we screwed last night. During therapy this afternoon, I was amazed Evelyn couldn't smell it. Then again, maybe she wouldn't recognize the scent. "It's Evelyn's go-to, though."

It's hard for me to imagine Evelyn drinking something so dark, so rich. Isn't she scared of staining one of her crisp white blouses?

"I bet you've got a local hangout where they know your favorite beer," I say. "Like, you can walk in and say, *My usual,* instead of placing an actual order. Where the bartender knows your name."

"You're making my life sound awful wholesome."

"The bar for what I consider wholesome is pretty low."

"Well, you're not that far off. I do have a favorite spot in town. Shelter Shack." He grins like an old man remembering his glory days as a high school quarterback. "Used to sing at their open-mic night, thought someone might discover me."

I picture Andrew sitting on a sticky stool in a dimly lit bar, and giggle. "Who exactly did you think would discover you out here?"

I can feel Andrew's muscles tighten beside me, and I know I've offended him.

"I just meant—"

Andrew sits up, his body no longer touching mine. "You meant that someone like me doesn't have any kind of chance of getting discovered."

"No! Just that maybe this island isn't the right place for that kind of thing."

Someone, hundreds of years ago, *discovered* Shelter Island. Or anyway, they thought they did, but it had long since been discovered by Indigenous people. Before that, by the animals and plants who'd thrived here. Before that, by the sea and air itself. Places don't actually get *discovered* any more than people do. People and places get *found*.

Andrew takes another swig from the bottle. "You know, the Shelter Shack gets bigwigs. Plenty of important people have second homes out here. They come even in the offseason 'cause they have to for their taxes."

I nod, even though I don't know the first thing about what taxes have to do with visiting your summer home in the dead of winter. Gently, I place my hands on Andrew's back. I press my thumbs into the curve of his shoulder blade, loosening his tight muscles.

He relaxes his body against mine, and I decide to return to safer territory. "Will Evelyn notice you snuck a bottle?"

Andrew shakes his head. When he speaks, his tone is lighthearted again. "Not likely. Besides, she can't accuse me of taking anything without admitting there's something to take." He turns and winks, clearly pleased with himself for being so clever.

He passes the bottle back to me, and I study the label. The words are all (I think) French. "Looks like she gets drunk on good stuff." At least, I think it's good stuff. I could never tell the difference. I always took whatever I was handed, whether it was a crystal glass at a party in the Hollywood Hills or a forty in a parking lot on Hollywood Boulevard.

"A discerning basket case," Andrew agrees, taking another drink, then leaning back against the couch. "I swear, her divorce has tipped her into full-blown alcoholism."

I imagine Evelyn's husband, trying to take her business from her while she gets drunk in secret and bosses people like me around.

Sounds like karma to me.

Maybe she's barreling toward her *rock bottom*—that's what they call the worst day of your life in AA—right now. I try to picture what Evelyn would consider a bad day—her hair out of place, dark roots showing, wine-stained teeth, her husband shaking his head with disgust—and compare it to my worst day.

If Evelyn had a *rock bottom* like mine, she'd need more than wine to numb the pain.

"How do you know so much about your boss, anyway?"

"I've been gathering gossip to make you happy." Andrew smiles like he's risking his job just to please me. I lean in and kiss him. I can taste the wine on his lips.

"You ready for another verse, baby?" he whispers, his lips hovering over mine.

I reach for my guitar:

How dare you tell me how to live
when your life is a disaster?
All these people want me to be like them—
Don't they know I'm getting there faster?
Candy is dandy, but liquor is quicker,
don't pretend not to know.
Turns out I'm not the only imposter here;
I just hope you'll reap what you sow.

Andrew starts kissing my neck. "Sing it again," he whispers. "Sing it from the beginning." He reaches his fingers into the waistband of my baggy jeans.

My husband and I used to stay up all night writing music.

Instead of hearing my own voice, I hear the song he and I wrote together before our kid was born, a song about how badly we wanted to become parents, all the promises we made to do a good job. I never guessed that a cowriting credit would start an avalanche of rumors: that he'd written my music all along, never mind that my first album came out before I'd even met him. It explained so much, they said—the critics, the label execs, the fans who turned on me after he left—no way a *girl* would write the way I claimed to.

They said he was the *real* artist. Sometimes I wonder if I would've married him at all if I'd known that I was going to be more famous for being his wife than I'd ever be for my voice.

Sometimes, I hated him. His star burned so much brighter than mine.

Maybe he knew I hated him.

Maybe that's why he left, no matter how I begged him to stay.

39

Lord Edward

Before therapy this afternoon, Dr. Rush said, *You're now welcome to explore the property.* He smiled as if he were offering me a gift. Like I was a little kid being rewarded for good behavior. No, even less than that, a puppy allowed out of his crate once he's been potty-trained. Did Dr. Rush think I couldn't see the shadow of a smirk on his face? He knew there was no chance of my going very far, even if they unlocked every door and flung open each window.

Locking me in was never about keeping me safe, but reminding me who's in control. Now, pleased with the "work" I did in therapy yesterday, freedom—if you can call it that—is my reward.

~

Just before midnight, I tap on Amelia's glass door. Her room is softly illuminated by a light on her bedside table. There's music in the air.

Last night, Amelia helped me to bed. She pulled the covers around me tight. I thought how much more pleasant it would be, from now on, to meet inside, in the warmth of one of our cottages instead of wandering around between them. It's terribly American, I know, my pull toward comfort; I'm meant to stalk about in the muck, my wellies full of country mud, never complaining when there's neither heat nor central air conditioning. Our estate in Scotland barely has electricity, and it certainly doesn't have Wi-Fi. But comfort takes on a different meaning when your body no longer functions as it should.

I open the sliding door and gingerly step inside. The heat makes my hands tingle.

Amelia's room is the mirror image of mine: king-size bed flanked by modern furniture, hardwood floors, a thick throw rug beside the bed. The enormous sliding door that leads to the hall is shut. There's a light coming from the en suite bathroom, the door ajar, the sound of retching drifting from within.

I rush across the room and peer inside.

She's crouched beside the toilet, her body coiled over the bowl. Her wavy hair is pulled into a messy bun on the crown of her head. The veins on her neck are bulging. She's wearing sweatpants and a ribbed tank top, but she seems more exposed than she did showing me her scars last night.

It takes me a second to register that her fingers are in her mouth, her knuckles pressed against her top teeth so hard that I think she'll break the skin. Her eyes are open wide; it looks like they could burst right out of their sockets. The room smells strange: an odd combination of comfort food and illness.

"Oh god, Amelia," I murmur, folding myself as best I can into something resembling a crouch beside her. When I reach for her, to rub her back the way she rubbed mine, she scurries away as though my touch burned her.

"What are you doing here?" she hisses.

I close the toilet seat.

"What are you doing here?" I echo, softly, sadly.

It's not like I didn't know she was sick. She taught me to make myself vomit last night. But seeing it—seeing *her*—is wrenching in a way I didn't expect.

"Please don't do this to yourself."

"You're one to talk," she snarls.

"What I'm doing is different," I say. "The doctors don't know fuck all about the pain I'm in."

"And you don't know fuck all about the pain I'm in." Her words land like a punch.

"I know your body deserves the nourishment it needs to survive." I hate how trite I sound, surely no different from all the doctors and therapists who failed her before.

"No," Amelia counters firmly, "it doesn't."

40

Amelia Blue

Last night was so familiar: getting someone else out of bed, forcing fingers down another person's throat. I can't remember a time when I didn't know what to do.

Forcing Georgia to purge didn't only teach me how to make someone else throw up. It taught me how to make myself vomit as well. #Promia social media is well and good, but I didn't need tips from strangers to master that particular trick.

I flush the toilet, then pull myself up to sit on top of it.

"I thought—" Edward begins, then pauses. He looks so sad and surprised that I want to slap him. Or hug him. I don't know which, any more than I know whether I want to keep throwing up or force thousands more calories down my throat. If I start making a list of the things I don't know instead of the things I do, I'll never stop.

Finally, Edward says, "I didn't know you were doing that to yourself."

"I didn't always." I used to be so much better at starving.

"What happened?"

First, Jonah happened. The goofy boy from my writing workshop, the one I hadn't intended to sleep with, the one who called me Abby like we'd known each other so long we had secret names for each other. Licks from his ice cream cones, bites of his pizza. My body was changing, but for the first time in my life, I wasn't keeping track.

Then, late April, I was fast asleep when a wave of nausea woke me, so powerful that I barely made it to the bathroom in time. Jonah heard and came to sit beside me on the bathroom floor.

Food poisoning, we figured. I was eating then, but mostly off Jonah's plate, still unsure how to fill my own. We both pretended not to notice when he served himself portions large enough for two.

I crawled back to bed. The next day, I felt better.

Two days later, I was sick again.

I thought maybe, after all those years of denial, my body didn't know how to digest a normal number of calories. Maybe my stomach had shrunk so much that there simply wasn't enough space, like someone who'd had gastric bypass surgery.

I bought the test on a whim. For years, anorexia had made my period erratic.

And then, there it was, the little pink line.

I was older than Georgia had been when she had me. I'll inherit my trust when I turn thirty, and the house in Laurel Canyon is in my name, bought and paid for. My child would grow up thinking that Naomi was her grandmother. Georgia would be a strange, absent woman we hardly spoke about. Jonah would move to LA with me. We'd give our baby everything my parents hadn't.

I pretended not to notice when I began eating less all over again. Then I told myself I was simply being healthy: I needed to take it slow, give my body time to adjust. I read that plenty of women had such severe morning sickness that they actually lost weight in their first trimester and still had perfectly healthy pregnancies and nobody accused them of having eating disorders. I wasn't doing anything wrong. I was being gentle on myself, being *careful* by letting myself be just a little bit (I told myself it was only a little bit) anorexic.

I started bleeding one day in May, so much I couldn't believe it. Then, a mad dash to the emergency room. Waiting to hear a heartbeat as the technician moved the sonogram wand. The doctor's mouth, set in a straight line. Jonah's voice, telling me it would be okay.

"Amelia?" Edward asks gently.

"I lost it." The words feel sharp in my mouth, like knives. I hate that phrase, *I lost the baby*, as though it were something I misplaced.

No, my baby *fled*. It knew I wasn't a safe place, my body with the wrong nose, the wrong hair, the stomach that's nearly flat instead of round with life, the brain that can't count train cars.

Jonah brought me soup. He lay beside me and held me. He kissed the top of my head. He told me he loved me no matter what.

It's remarkable to think how many human beings are the result of an accident, thoughtlessness, carelessness. I certainly hadn't been *planned*; my mother's pregnancy, like my own, was a surprise. I know this not because she told me, but because she was pregnant when they got married and no one actually *plans* to have a shotgun wedding. (Also, when did Georgia plan anything?) Jonah would have married me, if I'd wanted, but I didn't want to use our child to tether him to me like I suspected Georgia did with Dad. Maybe it was the only reason she had me at all. I thought I was better than that. Better than her.

But she got to keep her baby, and I lost mine.

It's not your fault, the doctor said. *These things happen.*

Jonah believed it, but I know better.

So I left. I packed up my things and flew home without saying goodbye. I moved back to the house in Laurel Canyon and searched the boxes and bins where Naomi stored Georgia's belongings years ago, making a mess even Georgia would have approved of.

I was determined to find something that would explain *why* I survived in her body longer than my baby survived in mine. I thought there might be some clue, some hint, in her unpaid parking tickets and baby-doll dresses and unreplied-to fan mail. Instead, I found the sober diary.

November 3, 2014. The last time I was sober this long was when I was pregnant. Not so much as a sip of wine.

"The press said I was born addicted to heroin," I tell Edward.

He shrugs. "When I was born, they said my parents were happily married." Edward knows better than to believe the things the press says.

But *I* believed it. My whole life, my birth story was part of how I understood myself, understood Georgia.

"It turns out, my mom almost died giving birth to me," I tell Edward now.

After I read the November 3rd entry, I confronted Naomi. She looked surprised that I wanted to know the details of my birth. She'd told me, she said, that the press exaggerated to sell papers, didn't I remember? But this time, I pressed for details. Georgia, she said, developed a condition called preeclampsia. They wheeled her in for an emergency C-section so quickly that the epidural hadn't even taken effect by the time they started to slice her open. When I asked why she hadn't told me all this sooner, Naomi answered that she could hardly tell this story to a child; she hadn't wanted to frighten me.

The hunger hit me in the middle of the night after Naomi told me the truth, waking me from sleep just as nausea had in the spring. I found myself in fast-food restaurants and ice cream parlors, as surprised to be there as if I'd sleepwalked.

The press hadn't *exaggerated* to sell magazines. They had lied, inventing a story to fit their narrative. Georgia hadn't stayed in the hospital after I was born because she was detoxing; CPS never came to keep my parents from bringing me home.

"It's confusing," Edward says. "When the press prints a lie with as much authority as they would the truth."

With the hunger came the purging. It led me to the bathrooms of gas stations and department stores, the sorts of places where Georgia had shot up back in the day, so unsanitary it was a wonder she hadn't contracted tetanus on top of everything else. Now I was the one making a mess in public toilets, sticking dirty fingers down my throat, hands that still tasted of the grease and ketchup I'd been eating minutes earlier.

I lost so much weight, so rapidly, that Naomi agreed when I asked to come here. I didn't tell her that I wasn't hoping to be saved by yet another round of therapy and yoga and acupuncture and meal plans.

I came here to learn what I don't know. Because I may know how many miles from our house to LAX and how many books I read last year and how many calories are in a strawberry, but I don't know how Georgia turned out to be a better mother than I. She was able to give up her disease (addiction) for her child—a child she barely paid attention to, didn't even seem to like—while I couldn't give up my disease (anorexia) for mine, a child I desperately wanted, a baby I already loved.

That's the real reason I came here. The help I need is the explanation buried in my mother's file. Surely, this place's experts (the best care money can buy) will have the answers that elude me, will be able to tell me which parts of her sober diary are true, and which are lies. Because if it's all true, then how could she keep her sobriety—something she surely knew I'd hoped for my whole life—secret?

Did she know, all along, that she was going to fall off the wagon yet again?

A breeze wafts through the sliding glass door. I hear the pipes groan as the heat turns on, like there's something inside the walls trying to get out. Edward moves to close the door, but I stop him. I prefer the sound of music coming from the third cabin to quiet.

"I met her last night," I tell him. "She crashed into me on the path between our cottages."

"Is she famous?" He doesn't add, *like us.*

"I didn't recognize her, but she seemed to think I should."

"Could you tell what she was in here for?"

I shrug, recalling her fur coat, her bare legs. "She looked like the sort of person you'd expect to see at a place like this. A basket case."

"It's not nice to call people names. Didn't you say that?"

I shove him affectionately, like he's my annoying little brother. "I said it wasn't nice to joke about a disability."

"I have a disability." Edward grins. I think it's the closest he's come to making a joke about his leg.

"So you should know better."

"What's the tattoo on your shoulder?" Edward asks, changing the subject. He must've seen it when I showed him my scars.

"SH," I explain, saying it like *shhhh.* "My dad's initials. Scott Harris."

"And the other one?"

He means the tiny white tattoo beneath my left breast, the one I destroyed in May.

"It was my mom's initials." Georgia was never as famous as my dad. More than once, someone identified me as the daughter of Scott Harris and *what's her name.*

"Why did you ruin it?" Edward asks.

I close my eyes and hold my breath, recalling how it felt when I pressed a blade to my skin, the initial pain followed by sweet relief as my mother's initials disappeared. People say bodies are temporary, but they're not, not for the people trapped inside them; for us, a body—its aches and pains, its scars and tattoos—is permanent. It's only temporary for the people around it, the ones who outlive it.

Finally, I answer, "It felt better to ruin it."

"Why?"

I don't answer.

The truth is, I don't know.

41

Florence

Holy fuck this is boring.

How many times can I tell the same stories? Yes, my father left when I was young, but whose doesn't? And sure, my mom tried to control everything in his absence until I was desperate to get the hell out of Yonkers, to talk to strangers without her dragging me away like she thought I was about to be abducted. And then there were the teachers who said I didn't live up to my potential, the reviewers who said I had no potential, the DJs and VJs and record execs who thought it was okay to grab my ass or my tits, the way I let them because I wanted what they had to offer and couldn't see another way to get it.

And the drugs that made it all so much easier.

I mean, I know *Evelyn* isn't bored. I know how to tell a story, put on a show. But it's like performing the same songs over and over and over again. It gets to a point where it doesn't matter how much fun it was to perform the first few times. You start to live for the unexpected moments—when some audience member crashes the stage or a band member forgets a chord and you have to improvise, change the set list, make up a new song and dance on the spot.

Take it from someone who's taken every drug there is: *Nothing* in the world beats that high.

I can't wait to get out of here and do it all over again. But I have to time my comeback exactly right if I'm going to emerge like a phoenix from the ashes, performing my brand-new song solo.

I just have to finish it first. In the meantime, I need to find smaller highs to get me through the day.

Which is why, halfway through therapy, I ask to use the bathroom, like I'm a first grader who needs permission from her teacher. And why I wink at Andrew, absently wiping the kitchen counter, on my way. And why I give him a blow job when I'm supposed to be peeing, even though I fucking hate giving blow jobs (maybe *that's* why my husband left?). Unexpected fellatio is the closest I can come to changing the set list.

"Everything all right?" Evelyn asks when I return. Andrew came fast, but I guess it still took longer than a normal bathroom break.

The sour taste of Andrew's sweat lingers in my mouth. He hasn't reappeared in the living room yet. He's smart enough to stagger our departures and returns.

Now that I know about Evelyn's drinking, I can see the telltale signs on her face: dark shadows beneath her eyes, puffiness around her nose. She has no idea I was studying the label of one of her fancy wine bottles on this very couch less than twelve hours ago. Her ignorance gives me another tiny high.

Evelyn's hair is brushed into its usual tight, eyebrow-raising bun. I imagine each strand coming undone when she screams at her husband, or cries in her lawyer's office, or sips from her secret stash. She's wearing her usual uniform: crisp white blouse, smooth black pants. I imagine a pile of blouses twisted into a wrinkled heap at the foot of her bed, stained with burgundy and streaked mascara.

Evelyn lights an enormous candle on the coffee table between us. It gives off a scent of roses and vanilla, so sweet and so fake that I want to gag. Despite the fact that I've been sleeping and screwing in this cottage for days, this place doesn't smell like anyone actually *lives* here. They keep it too clean for it to fill up with the odors of food and laundry and sweat. Personally, I like a messy house. I hate the smell of floors that have just been scrubbed, dishes just rinsed. Homes shouldn't be so neat; there *should* be scattered papers and mislaid clothes and chipped glasses in the sink. Anything else is so fake, like lipstick that doesn't smudge, hair that doesn't move in the breeze, hems that fall *just so* instead of dragging across the floor.

"So you own this place, right?"

Evelyn looks surprised by the question. It's the first time I've seen her startled.

She quickly regains her composure. "Yes," she says evenly.

"Okay, but unless you're some kind of billionaire, I'm guessing you couldn't afford to buy all this land on your own. So like, you must own it with other people, right? Investors?"

"I don't think you need the details of how I run my business."

Her business. "You started it with your husband, right?"

"Correct. We're both psychotherapists. He's an MD," she adds, "a psychiatrist. And I have a PhD in social work." Her voice drops on the last few syllables.

"It's complicated, isn't it, working with your spouse?"

I smile like I'm offering empathy instead of contempt. Evelyn thinks she knows better than me, but she doesn't know I'm sleeping with a member of her staff. If she'd asked me, I'd have told her never go into business with the person you're screwing, especially a man with more impressive credentials.

My life is such a shitshow that no one ever wants my opinion—which is completely ass-backward. I want to tell them all to *listen to me! Learn from my mistakes!* My kid most of all. She thinks I don't know that she struggles. She thinks I don't have any of the answers.

I guess I have only myself to blame for that.

∼

After midnight, the final verse of "Imposter Syndrome" tumbles out of me.

I used to think he'd be the one to bring me,
Build a house where I would be at home
I used to melt every time he'd sing to me
But he only left me alone
Take me, raise this, baby
You're not a real mother
I found someone to take my place
Let her take everything over
Till I forgot the love I wanted to create
I only have myself to blame, myself to blame, myself to blame.

I sing the whole song: three verses, a chorus in between, a bridge, then the shift in the final chorus that changes the meaning of the song. It's the most vulnerable, personal thing I've written in years.

"Holy shit!" Andrew shouts, raising the bottle of wine over his head. The only light in the room comes from the flames in the fireplace. I breathe in the smoke, as unhealthy as cigarettes, though no one ever acts like sitting next to a wood-burning fire is some kind of personal failing.

"I think we've got a hit on our hands," Andrew says excitedly.

I bristle at the word *we*.

I'll thank him in the liner notes. He'll be thrilled to see his name in print. (That reminds me: I should ask for his last name.) Maybe some exec will notice it and it'll help his career. Once I'm back on top, I can introduce him to people. But not now. Now he's kissing me, singing the final words of my new song into my mouth.

Imposter all my life
Never belonged anywhere
Imposter all my life
Wandered round everywhere
Imposter all my life
Someday, I'm gonna get there
Baby, I can take you there.

Does Andrew think I've been singing to *him* all these nights, that *he's* the person I want to bring with me? Does he think I'm calling him *baby*?

For years, all these unfinished lyrics, these fits and starts in my notebook—all my attempts to explain what it feels like to be me, why I am the way I am—I've been writing it all for an audience of one.

Doesn't Andrew know I'm singing to my kid?

The Bartender

The bartender guesses it was only a matter of time before someone from that place made a scene. It's not actually much worse than the crap the summer people get up to. Every year, from Memorial Day to Labor Day, the bar transforms from local haunt to millionaires' hot spot, though his tips don't increase nearly as much as they should. In fact, most locals are far more generous tippers than most of the summer people. After all, they know him. They know his son. They know what kind of car he drives and when the trim on his house needs to be touched up.

He'd suspected that the center's clients might make their way to his bar from time to time, looking for a fix of whatever it is that got them sent there in the first place, or whatever they could find that was closest to it. He imagined one or another of them might find their way to one of his barstools, looking for a sympathetic ear to listen to their troubles.

The thought is nearly enough to make him laugh out loud. People like that, living such sheltered lives, didn't have *real problems*, but *rich-people problems*. He'd like to be a fly on the wall during their therapy, whining about what drove them to drink and drug. He'd like to bring their stories back to his own AA meetings—seven years sober—to share. It'd be good for a few laughs. What does rock bottom look like when you're one of *them*? Barfing Cristal all over the dash of your Lamborghini?

Of course, his patrons took out their phones, snapped pictures, recorded video. He supposes he could have told them to stop, insisted that even people like that are entitled to their privacy, but why should he? It was a free country, this was a public place, and the people from the center were making a scene.

The police will ask him for details later, and he'll tell the truth. He hadn't interacted with the folks from the center, hadn't served them drinks or food, hadn't been close enough to see if they were on something, and certainly had no way of knowing if they'd come to the bar looking to score.

Later, he'll wonder whether he should've called the cops after they stormed out. Inside the warm, crowded bar, he forgot just how cold it was out there. Maybe he should have been alarmed, more concerned for a stranger's well-being.

Maybe if he had, things would have ended differently.

42

Lord Edward

Tonight, we're on the floor in Amelia's cottage. I lean back against the bed and look at her: her hazel-green eyes, the gap between her teeth, her wavy brown hair. So different from Harper and yet, the only other person on the planet who's ever really spoken *to* me, instead of speaking around me, about me, or for me.

The effects of the *approved dose* Dr. Rush gave me tonight are barely noticeable, and I don't have any of my own pills left. I grit my teeth, bracing myself for the pain to come, so bad that when I open my eyes, I see double. I've heard of phantom limb syndrome, but this is something else. I know my leg is gone; I am, in fact, acutely aware. It's the ache that won't dim.

I can't dull the pain, or silence the sound of Anne's laughter, Harper's scream, tires screeching.

I move closer to Amelia, feeling as I do that I'm dragging my prosthesis behind me, more a dead limb than the one they amputated.

"You said I didn't have to be ashamed of my body. But look what you're doing to yours." I smile as if it's a joke, how she's undermined her authority on the subject. But the truth is, I already didn't believe her.

"Your body didn't kill the person you loved most in the world."

I inhale sharply. "It almost did."

"What do you mean?"

"The accident last year. It wasn't an accident. I mean, it was—of course it wasn't intentional—but it was my fault."

I recall the ease with which I navigated the world for so long: two legs, sturdy and strong beneath me, foolishly convinced that so much wealth and privilege would protect me from a bad outcome.

Is that why I didn't hesitate to get behind the wheel?

Amelia's face flushes, and I know she understands. "How did your family cover up your drinking?"

"How do they hide anything? Money." Anne probably even paid off the doctors, already bound by confidentiality, just to be safe.

I was still in hospital when Anne and the family attorneys showed up to pepper me with questions.

I slammed on the brakes.

I must have; I can still hear the way they squealed uselessly.

I don't know whether she was wearing her seat belt.

I have no idea if I was wearing mine, so how could I be expected to recall if she was wearing hers?

Of course I thought I was okay to drive.

It's gotten so I can't remember which parts of the story are lies and which are the truth.

I don't remember when asked how we got from the car to the side of the road where our bodies lay when the ambulance arrived. *I don't remember* when asked why I didn't call a taxi as we left the party. *I don't remember* when asked what it was that made me swerve: a deer in the road, another car, a figment of my imagination.

Anne lost her patience and the questions stopped. Drunks like me, she said, aren't exactly known for having reliable memories.

They said—of course I don't recall—we must have been thrown from the convertible on impact. Someone told the paps where to find the car before it was towed the next morning—a police officer charged with cleaning up the scene, maybe, eager to earn some extra cash—and photographs of the destroyed Porsche were splashed across the internet within a day. The images show smoke still rising from the wreck.

"Your girlfriend was in the car with you?" Amelia asks.

"Harper." I can't remember the last time I said her name out loud. I had a million nicknames for her: Harps, Harry, Hazzy, Haps. Now, the endearments feel foreign, as though I'd been speaking another language during the months we spent together. I feel careless, like I should have been paying closer attention, counting the syllables, aware that there would come a time when I'd never get to say them again.

"She agreed to keep quiet for money?"

Anne put out a press release. I'd swerved to avoid a deer. There was no mention of my blood-alcohol level.

"She would never." If it were up to her, Harper wouldn't have accepted a penny of my family's money. But she was in a coma when Anne cut the deal with Harper's parents, offering so much more than money in exchange for their silence.

"I had to agree to stay away from their daughter."

Anne even made me change my phone number so Harper wouldn't be able to reach me when she woke.

If she wakes up, Anne said when she handed me my new phone.

"Is she okay?" Amelia asks.

"I don't know." The words get caught in my throat.

I don't know if she's still in a coma.

I don't know if she woke up with brain damage, memory loss, blindness.

I don't know if she remembers me.

I doubt she wants to.

43

Amelia Blue

Edward looks different somehow, and it takes me a moment to realize he's slouching, his shoulders hunched, as though perfect posture hadn't been drilled into him since birth. I recall the story he told me our first night together about dropping cake at the queen's feet. For a second, I can see the boy he used to be, his chin tucked into his chest, his eyes downcast and solemn. I think he's about to tell me more about his girlfriend, some detail about her smile or the way she laughed, but he surprises me by saying, "You don't look like you've put on any weight since we met."

"Where did that come from?" I ask.

Dr. Mackenzie still won't let me see the number on the scale, not that it matters. At home, when I can see the scale for myself, I sometimes think it's a trick. Maybe I'm imagining the number, along with the size of my jeans, my bras, my T-shirts. Sometimes I think, despite the years I've spent studying my body, I have no idea what I really look like.

"I was just thinking—after last night—maybe you need to be someplace that specializes in eating disorders."

"I told you, I need to be *here*."

"But you already know what happened to your mother here. She came for rehab, she couldn't stay sober. It happens all the time. It's happening to us right now. You're still bingeing and purging. I almost OD'd."

"Don't you think that's strange?" I fold my legs beneath me, sitting up straight as if to make up for Edward's slouching. "I've been in treatment before. They don't usually give you the freedom to hurt yourself."

"For what we're paying, it's not like they can lock us up."

"They *did* lock you up, remember?"

"Only because that's what Anne would've wanted and she's the one footing the bill."

"Okay, but that's sketchy, too. It's not in your best interests to do what your sister wants just because she's the one paying for your treatment. It's unethical."

"This place must be doing something right to have the reputation it does."

"Maybe all they're doing right is tricking rich people." In my head, I hear Georgia's voice trilling, *The best care money can buy*, as though the expense itself was proof of efficacy. "Plus there were the people I saw in the woods—the man restraining the woman."

"That was the light playing tricks on you."

"You don't know that for sure."

Maybe someone held Georgia, just like that woman in the woods, until Georgia would've done anything to feel free again, even if it meant sacrificing her sobriety. Maybe that's why she left the property, searching for drugs.

"I know *I* didn't see anything."

"You weren't looking!" I manage to stop myself from shouting, but I'm exasperated. Why won't Edward at least *consider* that this place is sketchy? Then it hits me. "You don't want to investigate because you're scared of being caught and having them take whatever's left of your pills."

"That's not—" Edward begins, but I keep speaking, my certainty rising with each syllable.

"You would choose your addiction over anything and anyone else. How else can you explain why you got behind the wheel with your girlfriend in the car?"

At once, I can't bear to look at Edward's handsome face. Another addict who let down the people he was supposed to care about.

After all, last summer, the night of the accident, Edward was with his girlfriend in a beautiful place. It was, ostensibly, a good night. Nothing was wrong, and yet everything was wrong, and so he drank.

I swallow a sigh. It doesn't matter if this place is sketchy. Georgia didn't need a catalyst to give up her sobriety, any more than she did all the times she'd used before. She fell off the wagon time and time again because the sun rose in the east, snow fell when it was cold, she woke up on a day with a *y* in it. Georgia was no different from Edward, despite the fact that they surely have nothing else in common: Nothing was wrong, and yet every-thing was wrong—just as it had been every day of her life before she came here.

"Just leave." *Please,* I think, but don't say.

Edward's head drops, his gaze on the floor. He pushes himself to stand and heads toward the sliding door and onto the terrace without another word.

44

Florence

Andrew's dozing on the couch, the first time he's ever fallen asleep in front of me, the first time we've been silent together. Before, there was always chatter or music—what I'm writing or what's blasting on the speakers.

It's so quiet that the song I haven't thought about for days snakes its way back into my head.

Just you wait, I'm gonna get her back
But he's never gonna get me back.

Joni fucking Jewell. Right this very minute, she's probably on a private plane, jetting from one tour stop to the next, her band getting high a few rows behind her while she pretends not to notice because she's *such a good girl.* Maybe she's faking sleep like I did when I was the one on planes and tour buses, when I was too exhausted to talk to anyone, sick and tired of the drugs that would wake me up for showtime.

The truth is that I didn't love getting high. I did it because it was expected, and sure, the right drugs would put pep in my step when I was too tired or let me sleep when I was too wired. I did it because the drugs would numb me out when the real world was too much to take. But eventually, I did drugs mostly because it was part of the persona I created, the character I was playing, the one with the (fake) blond hair and the (rehearsed) dirty mouth and the (self-selected) better name. The woman who never turned down a party and never apologized for causing a scene.

But all along there was a tiny little person inside me, someone I kept hidden like a secret. A person who dreamed of a quiet life with her husband, her child, a life in which she'd make music just because she loved it, not to sell out stadiums or even pay the bills.

That person would never have thrown her guitar at Joni Jewell, would never have screwed Joni's boyfriend, would never have been on the roof of the Roosevelt Hotel instead of tucked into her own bed, listening to her child's breathing through the thin walls of their old house.

The tiny person only comes out at times like this, when it's so quiet that I can hear her soft voice, telling me to go home, quit the business, sell the house, take my kid to the middle of nowhere and raise her where no one knows my name.

My husband and I used to talk about living that way someday. Maybe he got sick and tired of waiting. Maybe if I'd found that life for us sooner—if I were willing to give up the *bright lights, big city*—he wouldn't have left.

I sit up, shaking my head.

Probably all celebrities have voices like that once in a while, imagining a *normal* life away from the flashbulbs and the marquee billing.

Anyhow, just because that voice is *there* doesn't mean it's what I really *want*.

If it were, then why has my other voice—my big voice—always been so much louder?

Except right now, my big voice is silent, and the tiny voice won't shut up, and I can't tell which is the real me.

I slide off the couch and crawl on my hands and knees, almost crying out when I bang an elbow on the edge of the coffee table.

I reach for Andrew's jeans, crumpled on the floor. I smell weed and sweat and cheap cologne, plus the fancy organic soap that's on the kitchen counter. I stick my hand into his pocket and pull out his phone. I don't know why I'm being sneaky: Over the past few nights, Andrew and I have had sex on every surface in this room. We've broken plenty of rules already.

Callie has a Google alert for every version of my name—married, stage, maiden. She keeps track of my husband's mentions, my kid. For years, she's been the one to tell me anything I need to know.

Now, I google myself. I click on the first link, a *People* magazine article.

"I apologize," the former pop star tells People *exclusively. "Joni Jewell is a rising talent in the industry, and she deserves my respect. I've checked myself into a facility to*

finally maintain my sobriety and learn to manage my anger, and I wish Joni all the best for her tour this year. 'Get Her Back' is a brilliant song—congratulations, Joni!"

The tiny voice vanishes. The big voice is screaming.

Former pop star?

Congratulations, *Joni?*

A brilliant *song?*

Manage my anger?

Finally *maintain my sobriety?*

I scroll down to the comments section. Surely my fans have flooded the page with conspiracy theories: They know me well enough to know I'd never say anything like that.

But instead I see words like *has-been, jealous, old, washed-up, serves her right.*

"Fuck!" I shout, startling Andrew awake.

"What's going on?" he asks groggily.

"Did you know about this?" I hold out his phone. He blinks, taking in the article. "It says the statement was released days ago."

Andrew shrugs. "I figured you agreed to it."

He's acting like it's no big deal. Isn't he supposed to be a *fan?* Doesn't he know I would never apologize?

I'd like to see Joni Jewell live my life for two goddamn minutes without getting angry. That goody-two-shoes pop star accused me of stealing her boyfriend and wrote a song about it, a song that only became a hit because the public knew it was about *me.*

A person can't *steal* another person's boyfriend.

Something that's stolen has no agency—a necklace, a ring, a wallet.

"I would never have agreed to that," I spit.

"It's not like *People* just invented your statement," Andrew points out.

"Callie," I say shortly. She must have submitted the statement to the magazine in my name.

This can't continue. I've got to salvage what's left of my career before my so-called manager completely wrecks my reputation as the sort of person who never says *sorry.* My anger is a reasonable reaction to this fucked-up world. Callie's the one acting like a madwoman who needs to be locked away in a tower.

Fuck! I never should've let her talk me into coming here, never should've let them take my phone. I'd use Andrew's phone to log on to social media right now and refute the statement, but of course I don't know any of my passwords. Callie set all that up for me.

How could I have let her take over so much?

I guess that's my MO, isn't it? I let my mother take over raising my kid, after all.

I feel it bubbling in my belly, the same sort of rage that made me attack Joni. I get to my feet and stumble to the kitchen, so hungry that I think I'll never be full.

I'm halfway through a carton of ice cream when I come up with a plan.

I don't need Callie anymore, not now that I have a new song to set the world on fire.

My stomach settles, and I put the spoon down.

I know exactly what to do.

45

Amelia Blue

"There's something we need to discuss."

I wish I had the data on precisely how many times that particular sentence has been uttered, so I could calculate what percentage of the time it was followed by something good versus something neutral versus something bad versus something catastrophic. Then I would know, statistically speaking, what to expect from Dr. Mackenzie right now.

From the solemn look on her face, I don't imagine it's anything particularly good. Then again, I don't think I've seen her smile since I've been here. Sure, I've seen plenty of that therapist half smile that's supposed to make you feel like you're confiding in a friend, but not one *real* smile, the kind that reaches the eyes or precedes a laugh. Someone should tell therapists that their half smiles and nonresponses make them seem less than real, as though you're pouring your heart out to a simulation rather than an actual person. (Not that I've poured my heart out to Dr. Mackenzie.)

"What?" I sound like a sulky teen. It's midafternoon, and milky winter sunlight streams in through the glass walls. I feel strangely hungover, as though my body is having trouble metabolizing the fight Edward and I had last night. A nurse was here earlier, to check my vitals, run an EKG. Maybe Dr. Mackenzie wants to discuss the results of my tests. I shiver from my spot on the couch, wondering what secrets my bloodwork revealed. I never asked exactly what they're testing.

There's a fire in the fireplace, filling the cottage with a warm, smoky scent that somehow reminds me of summertime, someone grilling hot dogs and hamburgers in their backyard, family dinners, children running through sprinklers. I move one of the couch cushions to my lap, covering my (empty) stomach, imagining it round and full.

"I think we should talk about your bingeing and purging."

I glance at the kitchen: Are there hidden cameras after all? At once, I'm on my feet, looking up at the canned lights above the marble island.

"Amelia?" Dr. Mackenzie prompts, following me to the kitchen.

I climb onto the counter, reaching up to the ceiling. Somewhere on this property, is someone watching a recording of me stuffing calorie after calorie into my mouth? My hands tremble as they trace the ceiling.

"How long have you been watching me?"

"What?" She holds up her arms as though she thinks she can catch me if I lose my balance.

"You said you'd check on me twice a night, at two a.m. and five a.m. My very first day here, you lied to me."

"I didn't. Amelia, no one is watching you."

"Then how do you know about the bingeing and purging?"

"Maurice noticed less food in the kitchen each morning. Izabela cleaned up after you in the bathroom."

Maurice is standing at attention beside the stove, a soldier waiting for orders. One word from the doctor and he might grab me, restrain me, perhaps sedate me. Could it have been Maurice I saw in the woods the other night?

I fall into a crouch, swing myself onto the floor. I suppose there's no need for cameras when you have spies.

"Please, Amelia." Dr. Mackenzie sounds so reasonable. That's another thing they must teach therapists in school: how to sound perfectly calm even when there's legitimate cause for alarm so patients feel crazy when they're simply having a normal human response. "Sit down. I want to talk to you."

In the past twenty-four hours, the bingeing has gone from my secret to something known by Edward, Dr. Mackenzie, Maurice, and Izabela. (Though Maurice and Izabela have probably known for days.) I wrap the fingers of one hand around the opposite wrist and squeeze so tight it hurts.

Georgia was right: There's a cleanliness to starvation, an order. Hunger is disorganized. Vomit is messy. I'm *proud* of my ability to starve. I started when I was so young, skipping breakfast before third grade to see what would happen. Then skipping lunch every day of fifth grade to prove that I didn't need the kind of mother who remembered to cut the crusts off her daughter's sandwiches.

I sit on the couch and Dr. Mackenzie settles into the chair across from me. "I don't want to talk about the bulimia," I say finally. I fell hook, line, and sinker for the stereotype of the bulimic as a failed anorexic, as though bulimia isn't also a disease of extraordinary denial, as though it doesn't take enormous discipline to do something as unnatural as sticking your fingers down your throat to rob your body of food.

"I don't think you have bulimia," Dr. Mackenzie answers, surprising me.

I fold my arms across my chest. "I'm bingeing and purging."

"Yes, and those are the behaviors of bulimia, but I think it's your anorexia manifesting in a new way."

It's the first time Dr. Mackenzie has said something that hasn't been said, in some form, by one of the many doctors who came before her.

"It's not only that you don't know how to eat—you don't know how to be *hungry*. Your brain has tricked you into believing that hunger is all or nothing."

Hunger *is* all or nothing. My bingeing is proof.

Dr. Mackenzie continues. "No one ever modeled hunger for you."

Is she kidding? Georgia modeled nothing but hunger.

As though she can hear my thoughts, Dr. Mackenzie continues. "Your mother was an addict—you were raised in the chaos of her seemingly infinite hunger. Your grandmother was the polar opposite: keep everything tidy, orderly, don't lose control. Between the two of them, you never saw moderation."

Dr. Mackenzie adds, "Children of narcissists often struggle to find a middle ground between self-absorption and self-erasure. They don't believe that they can do something as simple as celebrating their birthday without sucking all the air out of the room."

I feel an unexpected lump in my throat. I've always hated my birthday.

"Amelia, are you willing to talk about any of this?" she asks. "If you can't be open with me, then we're not going to make much progress here."

For years, doctors have remarked on my *progress*. The ones who tried behavioral therapy, family therapy, IFS. They all said I would get better.

Slowly, like my head weighs a thousand pounds, I nod at my doctor.

Dr. Mackenzie's gaze flickers to Maurice, and he walks toward us, a bowl in his hand. As he approaches, I see that the bowl is filled with dry Cheerios. (More likely, some healthier, whole-grain, organic alternative.)

Therapists always start like this when initiating cognitive behavioral therapy. Cheerios, M&M's, jelly beans. Something easy to count.

"I don't want to force you to eat like the therapists you've had in the past," Dr. Mackenzie says as Maurice puts the bowl down on the coffee table in front of me. "I want to teach you to eat when you're hungry and stop when you're full."

I look at the bowl. The cereal is the color of cardboard.

My hand feels like it's in slow motion as I reach for the bowl, like I'm moving through thick syrup. I try to take a deep breath, but my throat won't cooperate. Maybe they're pumping something in through the heating vents that's changing the quality of the air.

I intend to select three pieces of cereal. I mean to bring each one to my mouth, to chew, to swallow. I definitely don't plan to pick up a handful and toss them at Maurice, the spy who gave me away. I don't mean to crush another handful beneath my feet into the carpet, creating another mess to punish Izabela for telling Dr. Mackenzie what she saw. I don't intend to pick up the bowl and hurl it across the table, nearly hitting Dr. Mackenzie in the face. I don't want to smile when I see the bowl smashed into pieces on the ground, the tiny little *O*'s of cereal mixed among pieces of shattered pottery. That's the sort of thing Georgia would do.

I wait for Dr. Mackenzie to shout at me, to tell me I could have seriously injured her. But she doesn't move from her chair, doesn't crouch to clean up the mess that I made.

Instead, she says, "I wish we had more time together so I could try to give you what you need, but this place doesn't work that way."

This isn't how it works at other treatment centers. There, you refuse to eat and they lock you in your room until you cooperate. They threaten you with a feeding tube, explaining the process of sewing it to your nose with such detail that you know they're getting sadistic pleasure from it and some part of them wants you to be difficult so they can force-feed you.

"You're sending me home?" I sound breathless, as though I've been running. "Because I wouldn't eat a few lousy Cheerios?"

I say it like the cereal is beside the point. If it were so unimportant, then why couldn't I eat it?

"I'm afraid there's no choice in the matter," Dr. Mackenzie answers. "I was hoping we'd make some progress today and I'd be able to convince the owner to make an exception—"

She makes it sound like today was my last chance, a test I didn't know I was taking.

"I'm not ready to leave," I protest, desperate. I need more time. I have to make it to the house in the woods. I have to find Georgia's file. "I'm sorry. I'll try again."

Dr. Mackenzie shakes her head slowly.

"Amelia, you need to leave the property as soon as possible."

46

Amelia Blue

"What do you mean *as soon as possible*?"

"Unfortunately, you can't stay here any longer."

"I'm sorry about the cereal," I say, scrambling. "I don't know what I was thinking. I wasn't thinking. It was like an out-of-body experience."

Dr. Mackenzie's shoulders relax, and she almost smiles. "You know, I think that's the first honest thing you've said to me."

"That's progress," I say hopefully. "A good sign, right?"

Dr. Mackenzie takes a seat on the couch beside me. "Yes, but that's not the problem."

I press my fists into my belly. "What do you mean?"

"We were unable to complete the payment for your stay."

Relief floods my body, and I release my fists, resting my palms onto my thighs. This is something I can fix. I can literally *buy* myself more time here. "I'll call my grandmother," I say. I'll tell Naomi the therapy is helping. She'll be happy to dig into my trust if she believes I'm getting better.

I reach for my phone, but before I can dial, Dr. Mackenzie says, "I spoke with your grandmother last night." Her face looks so solemn that I almost laugh. "I convinced the owner to let you stay for one more night to give you the day to arrange your travel home, but beyond that, there's nothing I can do."

"There must've been a clerical error or something." I jump to my feet and dial my grandmother's number. It's early in California, but she'll be awake.

Ach, who can sleep late?

I slide the door to the bedroom shut behind me. Much to my surprise, my grandmother sounds sleepy when she picks up the phone. For the first time, it occurs to me that maybe her sleeping habits are different when I'm not there.

I tell her a version of what Dr. Mackenzie told me. There's silence on the other end.

"Please just call the bank, Grandma."

More silence.

"Grandma?"

I hear a rustling sound, and I imagine her sitting up in bed, fumbling for her glasses. Over the years, I've watched the wrinkles in her forehead grow deeper, memorized the crease between her eyebrows that never disappears, not even when she's sleeping. She wears her hair short, just below her ears. It's dark, but not entirely gray. She always said I was lucky I got her hair.

Never dye it, she said. *If your mother had just left her hair alone, she'd have looked so much younger.*

(In family therapy, a counselor said that was terrible advice, implying as it did that I should adhere to patriarchal standards of beauty.)

"I can't call the bank." My grandmother sounds old, tired.

"I'll call, then. Just give me the account numbers." Naomi always said she was the only one who could access the trust until I turn thirty. But she also said there were contingencies for my education and medical emergencies.

"I don't have any account numbers."

"Okay, whatever you do have. Passwords, trust numbers. I don't know what you call it. Whatever you've used for my treatment in the past."

I hear my grandmother take a deep breath, followed by a long exhale.

"The money for your treatment didn't come from a trust."

"Why not? My dad set it up so we could take what we need." That's what she told me.

"He didn't."

I feel something shift beneath my feet, so sudden that my stomach lurches.

I thought I didn't take my privilege for granted, but now the words I said to Dr. Mackenzie echo back to me. I nearly laughed at the notion that I didn't have enough money for something I wanted.

I've never actually seen *documentation* for the trust my father left me, and I never asked to, secure that what I needed would always be there. I try to remember if I ever spoke about it with Georgia, but I only remember

Naomi's voice, assuring me that my father took care of me, that we could afford whatever I needed—school, doctors, therapists. My father wanted to take care of me, she said.

I never doubted it, because I'd read his suicide note, along with the rest of the world. *My daughter will be better off if she doesn't have to worry about her old man's broken brain.* He thought he was helping me, relieving me of what he saw as a terrible burden—himself.

"How did you pay for boarding school, college, my MFA?" I ask.

All my life, *money was no object.* I had no reason to wonder whether we could afford *the best care money could buy.*

"There was some money," Naomi says carefully.

I can still see her face when I told her I wanted to come here. I thought she was shocked I'd chosen this place after what happened with Georgia, but now I wonder whether she was doing the math: If I insisted that only this place could help me, she needed to find a way to send me here.

Grandma Naomi: my rock, the one who kept the house neat and clean, who made sure I got to school on time and brushed my hair and teeth each night; the one I could trust. Georgia: the basketcase who lied like she breathed. All my life, that's what I knew.

"But there wasn't *enough* money," I supply.

Dr. Mackenzie said that Naomi wasn't a healthy role model for me any more than Georgia was.

"No," my grandmother says heavily. It's quiet until she adds, "I mortgaged the house."

Plenty of people have mortgages. Most people do, if they're lucky enough to buy a home in the first place. When I get home, I'll get a job, help with the bills.

Naomi adds, "The bank is talking foreclosure."

"Foreclosure?" I echo. I glance around the bedroom, at the luxury mattress and expensive furnishings. I wonder if the word *foreclosure* has ever been uttered within these four walls.

"I didn't want you to worry," my grandmother says.

"But we might lose the house?"

"Yes."

The house my father bought with the money he made from his music. The house where he died. The house I loved and my mother hated. The house where Georgia got high. The house where I planned to raise the baby I lost. The house I knew I would live in for the rest of my life.

I *knew* it, but like so much of what I knew, it wasn't the truth.

Or more accurately, it isn't the truth anymore.

In her sober diary, Georgia wrote, *My sponsor wants to know why I haven't told Amelia Blue I'm sober. Why I haven't told my mom. She says I can't stay sober without support. She says I can't stay sober if I lie about my sobriety as much as I did about my using.*

Georgia never wrote her sponsor's name. I would've gone through the contacts on her old phone for a clue, but Naomi told the center not to bother sending it back with the rest of Georgia's things. They wiped it clean and donated it to charity.

She doesn't understand that I can't tell them (the word *can't* underlined twice), *not until I'm sure I can keep it up.*

She says sobriety is a promise we make to ourselves, not to other people.

I told her it doesn't matter. They wouldn't believe I'm sober anyhow.

"They say I have to leave here tomorrow," I tell my grandmother.

"I'm sorry." Naomi sounds very tired. "I didn't want to add to your troubles."

My grandmother lied to protect me.

With her final lie, Georgia was trying to protect me, too.

47

Florence

It's time to get the fuck out of Dodge. Where the hell did that expression come from, anyway? What does it mean? My kid would know, smart like that.

I haven't told Andrew my plan. It's a surprise. My kid hates my surprises, my husband, my mom. But my fans *looove* them. Drop an unexpected single, play a secret show, make an unscheduled appearance. That's the kind of thing that keeps fans on their toes, expecting you to give them more, more, more.

I always gave them more.

Until I gave them everything and they stopped asking. Like that book my mom gave my kid, *The Giving Tree*. She said it was a bedtime story, but it gave me fucking nightmares. I hid it away where my kid couldn't find it.

Tonight, I pretend to go to bed early, then get dressed in the dark: my fur coat over a baby-doll white nightgown with a black bra and underwear, almost exactly what I wore the first time I went onstage. My hair is greasy and unwashed, so I pull it into a tight bun on top of my head, dark roots glaring against the platinum tips. I sling my guitar over my shoulder like I'm a one-woman traveling band.

It's so easy to sneak out that I think maybe they want me to leave.

It's fucking cold. Smells like snow, a scent I remember from my childhood in Yonkers, a scent my kid, California born, wouldn't recognize. I should've worn tights. A hat, a scarf. If only I'd had my phone to look up the weather forecast before I left. Not that you need a phone to know it's cold in January, but fuck them for taking my phone anyway. At least I have my coat.

I hum a few bars of my new song as I hold out my thumb, hitchhiking like it's 1967. There aren't many cars on the road, but luckily it's dark. It's easy to spot the headlights that tell me someone's coming.

~

The floor of the Shelter Shack is sticky with spilled beer and sawdust. The lights are turned down low, a single spotlight on a tiny stage in the corner. It's dingier than Andrew made it sound. The crowd isn't big, and mostly old. Everyone's wearing some variation of the same outfit: jeans and work boots, plaid flannel shirt. Mine is the only dress in the place. I don't see anyone drinking anything other than beer.

Whatever. Beggars can't be choosers. No, I'm not a beggar; I'm a beginner. This summer, I'll go on tour in a van, just like in the old days—no tricked-out tour bus and private plane. My kid'll come with me; she's old enough now, she can help with my gear. It'll just be the two of us, a road trip across America with extra guitars in the back seat. I'm not too big for my britches. Anyhow, I'd rather start over on my own terms than work with my ungrateful bandmates ever again.

The locals'll go nuts when I take the stage. They'll record me and release the video, drowning out Callie's terrible statement. This will be so much louder.

They'll remember me, won't they?

Even if they don't, the song is good enough to catch their attention.

Someone's onstage already. The lighting's so shitty I can't see their face. A deep voice says, "This is something new I've been working on."

Whoever's up there is hardly an opening act, but I'll let them sing one song—just one—and then I'll take the stage. I tune everything out to make a mental setlist: "Never Settle" first, to give them a taste of what they know and love. Get them good and warmed up before I shift to the new material. The chorus of dead musicians in my head will cheer me on for once.

Imposter all my life
Never belonged anywhere
Imposter all my life
Wandered round everywhere
Imposter all my life
Someday, I'm gonna get there.

Man, I can't wait. I'm so excited I can already hear it.

I *do* hear it.

I *am* hearing it.

I take a step toward the stage, then another, then another, until I'm close enough to see the face of the person singing, even though there's only one person on the entire planet it can be.

Andrew.

Andrew is singing.

Andrew is singing my fucking song.

48

Amelia Blue

Tonight, Edward doesn't show up at my door, and I don't flash a light at his. I'm not sure we're still on speaking terms. I suppose it doesn't matter. After I leave this place, I'll surely never see him again.

I slip through my bedroom's sliding glass door and make my way along the path between the cottages, toward the gravel driveway. For the first time, I think how absurd it is to call these cottages. They're practically mansions.

According to the weather app on my phone, it's supposed to snow tonight. The sky is violet, nearly as bright as daytime.

I point my flashlight at my feet, keeping my gaze trained on the beam of light, counting each step, each heartbeat, each breath. My hands are so hot that I slide off my fingerless gloves. I wipe my palms on my jeans, then tighten my grip on my phone. There's an electric buzz in the atmosphere, the air itself anticipating snow. For a few steps, all I hear is the crunch of pebbles and leaves beneath my feet, but then there's the sound of someone shouting and the brightness of headlights as a car pulls into the driveway.

"Here!" someone shouts, and at once there are hands on me, gripping me from behind. He—I don't know who it is, but it feels like a *he*—holds me tight, like he'd handcuff me if he could.

"I found her!" the man holding me announces, his shout so loud in my ear that I flinch.

I struggle to shove off the tight grip around my upper arms. A bright light flares in my eyes as someone holding an enormous flashlight comes running toward us.

"Amelia!" I recognize Dr. Mackenzie's voice. She lowers the light. She's wearing a puffy jacket and thick gloves, her voice muffled by the scarf wrapped tightly around her face. She tells the person holding me to let go.

He steps away and I see that it's Maurice, my chef. In the morning, there will be bruises where he gripped me.

"What are you doing outside in the cold?" she asks.

"What do you care?" I answer, knowing I sound like an angsty teenager. "You're sending me home." I reach into my pocket to pull out a cigarette and light it. "Anyway, I'm just having a smoke."

"Have you seen anyone out here?" Dr. Mackenzie sounds frantic.

I'm taken aback. I'd been expecting my former doctor to admonish me for smoking, another bad habit she had no chance to rectify.

"Tall," Dr. Mackenzie adds. "Blond hair."

I recall the girl who crashed into me on the path between our cabins, the one with the bleach-blond bob and the heavily rimmed eyes.

"You mean the patient from the noisy cottage?"

Dr. Mackenzie doesn't ask me to refer to her as a *guest* rather than a *patient*. Instead, she explains, "She's missing. No one's seen her on the property since before dinner."

"I haven't seen anyone," I admit, and Dr. Mackenzie nods, gesturing for Maurice to resume the search. She doesn't tell me to go back to my cottage. Perhaps in an emergency like this, there's no time for that sort of precaution. Or perhaps, now that I'm not a paying customer, my doctor and her colleagues wouldn't hunt for me if I went missing.

The woods fill with the sound of others calling the missing woman's name. Dr. Mackenzie hesitates before adding her voice to the chorus, as though some part of her still thinks she can protect the other patient's anonymity.

Finally, she turns away from me and shouts.

"Sonja! Sonja Carrera!"

49

Lord Edward

After midnight, I pull on my coat and move toward the sliding door in the bedroom, though I don't know exactly why. Surely Amelia doesn't want to see me after last night.

She thinks I don't want to believe this place could be sketchy because I'm scared they'll take my pills if I ask too many questions, but that's not true, at least not entirely. (Anyhow, I don't have any pills left.) But this place is where Harper's parents wanted me to be. I owe it to them—to her—to stay until the doctor says otherwise.

But before I can move across the terrace to the stairs, I'm accosted by light and sound. People shouting, torches blinking beneath me. My heart beats faster, though I'm not technically doing anything wrong. I duck behind the railing, biting my lip to keep from shouting in pain.

Suddenly, I'm back in the headmaster's office at Eton, watching my father's face twist with anger as I'm expelled. There hadn't been many things in his life, including his disastrous first marriage to my mother, that he couldn't throw money at to solve.

My fucked-up leg buckles. I hear the sound of a lighter clicking beneath me as someone lights a cigarette. Voices float up from below.

"You're back in your civvies, I see."

"Civvies?"

"You know, your usual clothes. Not wearing your old man's tweed jackets."

The second man laughs.

"You think the place'll get sued?"

"It didn't last time."

At once, I recognize the second voice—it's Dr. Rush. He sounds different, his words coming out with a hint of a Southern twang he must disguise around me, hidden alongside his *usual clothes*.

"Last time?"

There's a pause, and I realize Dr. Rush is taking a drag on his cigarette before answering. So much for his lectures about healthy coping mechanisms.

"You never heard this story, Maurice? Just after we opened, our first-ever patient flew the coop. Evelyn was still running things then. She was good at keeping the details out of the papers, gotta give her that. 'Bout ten years ago."

"What happened?"

Another pause. It's late, but not terribly dark. I watch a plume of smoke rise as Dr. Rush exhales. "We put in security measures to appease the investors—that's why you need a combination to open the gates instead of motion sensors, why care managers sleep in the cottage with our clients now. Back then, Evelyn stayed in her house across the property. The housekeepers and chefs commuted from wherever they lived."

I blink as snow starts to fall. The flakes are small, dry, the sort that sting one's eyes and accumulate into a light powder.

"Who was the patient? The one who went missing."

Dr. Rush takes another drag, longer this time, like he's weighing whether he ought to share this particular piece of information.

Finally he says, "Some washed-up musician. Remember that wannabe band in the nineties, Shocking Pink? It was their lead singer. You know, Scott Harris's widow."

50

Florence

The rage takes over, same as it did when I threw my guitar at Joni's face, eager to break her plump, dewy skin wide open. I'm on the stage, the spotlight blinding me, so hot it makes me sweat. I slide out of my coat, letting it fall to the ground, and wrench the microphone from Andrew's hand. It falls to the floor with a sickening *thump*.

"What do you think you're doing?" I shout.

"I was doing this for you." Somehow, Andrew's voice is even and calm. "Introducing the world to your new song."

My hands are balled into fists, shaking with rage. "You said it was your song. I heard you." The whole goddamn place heard him.

"It's *our* song."

"Our song?" I echo hotly. I've heard those words before, excuses not to cut me in on royalties for the words I helped write, the choruses and bridges I gave away.

"We've been writing it together." Andrew's voice is gentle, like he's sorry I misunderstood.

He lifts the mic from the floor and turns to the crowd. When he speaks, it's still in that achingly calm voice. "Sorry, folks, my friend here is having a tough time. She needs to get back to Rush's Recovery."

Phones are being whipped out. For a moment, I think they're calling for help, but then I see the way the bar's patrons are holding their screens. They're recording.

No one tells you how strange it is to be famous, how disorienting it is when strangers think they know you, when they believe the lies told by people who've never met you more readily than the words coming out of your own mouth.

This isn't how tonight was supposed to go.

"Why don't we head backstage?" Andrew says to me. Slowly, like he thinks I might pounce if he moves too quickly, he bends to place the mic on the floor, but his other hand snakes up to grab my wrist lightning fast. He smiles at the crowd, but his grip is a vise as he pulls me off the stage.

Backstage turns out to be a storeroom: boxes of napkins and empty glasses, a bare lightbulb overhead. It smells sour, like spilled beer. My Doc Martens stick to the floor.

"'Imposter Syndrome' is *my* song," I hiss.

"That's not how I see it." Andrew's eyes are every bit as unblinking as Evelyn's. I wonder if he learned that from her, part of his training after she hired him.

Maybe someone else would try to reason with him, explain that he didn't write a word, pull out her notebook with the lyrics in her handwriting, no one else's. But my tether—short under the best of circumstances—has snapped.

"Just try to pass it off as yours, Andrew. Once I'm out of here, I'll release a statement—"

"If you come out swinging, it'll only make you look worse." God, I hate how calm he sounds. "They all know you're in rehab for anger issues, an addict who can't control herself."

Fucking Callie.

"Do you even know what you're doing here?" Andrew's voice shifts, an edge taking hold.

"I came to sing *my* song," I begin, but Andrew's laughter cuts me off.

"I don't mean at the Shelter Shack." He speaks slowly like he thinks I'm stupid. "I mean at Rush's Recovery. Your manager cut a deal with Evelyn. Everyone on the staff knows all about it."

My stomach twists.

"Evelyn needed a high-profile client to boost her reputation."

"Aren't places like this supposed to be anonymous?"

Even the regular rehabs I went to before—they never told anyone I was there. And AA meetings, where anyone could come—no one tipped off the paparazzi, no one leaked a story to the press. *There's honor among thieves*, my sponsor said, but now I'm facing a real thief, and there's no honor to be found.

"Callie promised Evelyn she'd leak a story to the press about how Rush's Recovery turned rock's 'baddest bad girl' nice." He uses air quotes, like he's never heard anything so ridiculous. "Callie issuing that apology on your behalf—that was just another step in their plan."

Their *plan*? "What about doctor-patient confidentiality?" I know I'm grasping at straws.

Andrew laughs. "You have to understand the condition Evelyn's in these days. See, she and her husband dreamed up Rush's Recovery together, sold it to their investors—individualized, privileged rehab. But then the old man cheated, and their joint venture turned into a weapon in their divorce. Evelyn needs the investors to pick her to run it, not him."

"How do you know all that?"

"You were so eager for my intel a few days ago. Practically begged me to dig up dirt on Evelyn. What's the matter? You don't like the dirt now that it's getting you messy, too?"

I shake my head, trying to make sense of everything Andrew is saying.

"Evelyn reached out to Callie after you attacked Joni Jewell," Andrew explains, his voice smooth as silk. "She didn't have to promise much to get Callie to turn on you. It's not as though you've been making her a ton of money lately."

Callie said this place was *the best care money could buy*. She had me saying it, too. She convinced my mom and my kid it was different, the answer to their prayers. They were fucking smiling when they sent me away, like they thought I'd come back a new person.

"You're just some poor little rich girl." Andrew's voice shifts again, mocking me as he whines: *"Boo-hoo my daughter hates me, my mom is mean to me."*

"Don't talk about my family," I say through gritted teeth. I've barely mentioned them since I arrived. Andrew doesn't know what he's talking about.

"Boo-hoo," Andrew continues. *"The music industry turned on me, my band hates me, my husband left me."*

Boo-hoo?

I didn't cry when my daughter stopped speaking to me last year, just kept on talking because I figured eventually she'd at least tell me to shut the hell up. I didn't cry a decade ago when it became obvious how much she preferred my mother to me, or a few years before that when it was clear she liked her dad better, too.

Andrew's liquid-brown eyes turn steely. Less than twenty-four hours ago, I thought this man cared for me. "How come you never say your husband is *dead*?"

Because he left me. He left *us*. Despite the heat radiating across my body, I shiver.

"People like you don't need another break. It's people like me who need a leg up, people without industry connections, no inheritance from dead husbands to fall back on."

I came from nothing. My husband didn't leave me a fortune, whatever the tabloids said about it. His bandmates refused to cut me in on the songs I helped write. I had to clear out my savings to keep the house.

God, he loved that house. He talked about growing old there. Losing it would've felt like losing him all over again.

"Everyone knows about you," Andrew spits. "Fucked your way to a music deal. Married yourself famous. Let your husband write your songs."

"No," I manage. I can feel sweat dripping down the back of my neck, pooling between my shoulder blades.

"No one would believe you wrote 'Imposter Syndrome' anyway. Easier to believe it was me."

I hate to admit it, but he isn't wrong. A bad reputation is worse than no reputation at all. Onstage tonight, he made my song sound good. He looked nice onstage, too, at ease with the crowd. Record execs will like him more than they ever liked me. He'll be an easy sell: handsome, young, from a small town. He told me he grew up outside Atlanta.

"You left your daughter to become her own kind of disaster. Evelyn says she's sick."

They've been telling me she's sick for years. Doctors, therapists, my own mother—they all promised they could save her, but I see the truth. My girl wants to disappear.

"What's her name again?"

"Don't say it," I rasp. I hardly let myself say it anymore. I barely even think it.

There's so much power in a name. That's why I changed mine all those years ago, the minute I left home, my mother's sock-drawer money burning a hole in my pocket.

I squeeze my eyes shut. I don't want to be here, in this dingy room that smells like stale beer and Andrew's sour, angry breath. I want to be onstage, under the lights, introducing myself with the name I chose, the name Andrew's never called me, singing the words I wrote.

"Evelyn told the staff not to use your stage name. Who do you think you are, giving yourself a name while the rest of us mere mortals make do with our parents' choices?"

I didn't want to be the girl from Yonkers with the mousy brown hair anymore, the girl whose father left, whose mother never approved.

I loved the name I chose. The first name: strong like a man's, but undeniably feminine. After an artist who could paint skulls as beautifully as she painted flowers, filling her canvases with life and death.

And my last name, my family's *real* name, before they anglicized and bastardized it to *Bloom*, taking away its true meaning. Not that Naomi ever appreciated what I did, bringing our real name back to life. Not even when I gave our name to my daughter.

"You know your phone hasn't rung once since Evelyn had it confiscated? Your family doesn't care about you. They're not even thinking about you."

His breath smells rotten, like something crawled up and died inside him.

"Everyone knows the truth." Andrew's face is so close to mine he could kiss me. I can't believe that just a day ago, I *wanted* him to kiss me. His fingers are still wrapped around my arm. "You're a wannabe hack who only got famous because she married a celebrity."

I shake my head. People forget I released two albums before we got married.

"And then when you'd gotten everything you could from your husband, you threw him away. Bled him dry, then spat him out."

No, I didn't. I loved him. I wanted to keep him forever.

"Is that why you can't stay sober? Can't live with knowing that it was all your fault."

I ball my hands into fists.

"It's all your fault, Georgia Blue."

51

Amelia Blue

*S*onja Carrera. The name is familiar, an itch I can't scratch. I reach my freezing fingers into my pocket, fumbling so that I nearly drop my phone. I open up Instagram and search for @sonjalovesgeorgia. The user who read the police report. The one who was *going dark*.

I dig through her pictures. In her posts, her hair is black and long, not platinum and shaggy—but when I look closely, I can see that it's her. Her clothes are nineties inspired, though not quite as literal as when I saw her the other night: the baby-doll nightgown, the enormous fur coat. I realize now, she was dressed like Georgia, cut and dyed her hair to match my mother's. She wouldn't be the first fan to do so.

Trippy, she said, seeing me here.

No wonder she assumed I'd recognized her.

She'd seemed desperate, almost feral. She never met Georgia, but in so many ways, she's been better to my mother than I've ever been. Sonja's spoken out against the conspiracy theories that Georgia is somehow to blame for my father's death, against Shocking Pink touring without her, against the rock critics who insist that Georgia didn't write her own songs. She shared what she found in the police report from Georgia's last arrest. I barely told my grandmother about Georgia's sober diary, let alone the world.

Sonja said, *It won't be another story.*

She said it would be *the* truth *this time.*

Sonja thinks *this* time—Georgia's tumble off the wagon at Rush's Recovery—was different from all the times she drank and used drugs before. Sonja doesn't know what I know, that Georgia never needed a reason to use, a catalyst, an inciting incident.

As much as I know anything, which is to say, not very much at all anymore.

The snow comes down hard now, and the ground beneath my feet is frozen, cold enough that the flakes don't melt when they land, but I'm sweating beneath my clothes.

This time *was* different. This time, Georgia died.

~

At the edge of the property, I try the door of the Cape Cod–style house.

Locked.

I dig into my pockets, but my kit isn't there. *Crap.* I must have left it in my room.

I fall to my knees, searching beneath the rapidly accumulating snow. All those years with Georgia, I had to get creative sometimes. I try a narrow stick, but it snaps into pieces in the lock.

Tonight is my only chance. I can't let anything stop me.

So I pick up a rock from the ground and throw it at one of the narrow windows on either side of the front door. Luckily, the glass here isn't like the state-of-the-art glass in our cottages—it shatters easily.

I slide my hand through, hardly even noticing when I nick my thumb, then my wrist. I manage to reach the doorknob, turn the lock, twist the knob.

I step inside. There's a long, scratched wooden table and two overstuffed chairs set in front of an unlit fireplace. I pass a worn leather sofa. There's a mess in the kitchen, and distressed rugs rest over the scratched hardwood floors. It doesn't look like a place for hidden files, or difficult patients: There are no padded rooms, no towering cabinets. It looks like a home. Whoever lives here might be the groundskeeper, the one who trims the hedges into perfect circles, who wraps the boxwood in burlap for the winter. Maybe Edward was right, and I didn't see what I thought I saw.

And yet, tonight, the floodlight didn't turn on until I was nearly at the front door, so it must not have been Edward and me activating it from across the woods the other night like we thought. It had to have been someone just outside this house.

I use the flashlight on my phone to light the way as I tiptoe, peeking inside each door. I discover first a bathroom, then a closet. I don't know why I'm bothering to be quiet. If anyone were home, the glass breaking surely would have gotten their attention. Whoever lives here (if anyone lives here) must be out, helping search for Sonja.

I try another doorknob and discover a room lined with bookshelves. There's an enormous wooden desk in the center of the room. Even from the threshold, I can see that it's stained with ink and water rings. There are stacks of papers on top of the desk: everything from bills to used tissues to magazine articles, so disorganized that it reminds me of Georgia.

I step inside. My breath catches in my throat, thick and cold as a milkshake. In the center of the desk is a bulging manila folder with my mother's name on it.

Florence "Georgia Blue" Bloom.

The Driver

Until tonight, the driver has never actually seen a hitchhiker, despite her mother's endless warnings after she got her license six months ago. The way her mother spoke, you'd have thought there was an epidemic of serial killers sticking out their thumbs across Shelter Island, hoping to get a ride from their next unsuspecting victim.

Her mother's warnings about *dangerous strangers* had become only more dire after the recovery center opened.

Who knows what kinds of people that place will attract, she said.

In her mother's stories, the hitchhikers had always been men. They certainly hadn't been women with short bleached hair wearing dresses that looked like nightgowns under voluminous fur coats, guitars slung over their shoulders. *This* woman—the one holding out her thumb on the road ahead—looks more like a ghost than a serial killer.

The driver can always spot summer people—even now, in the dead of winter, the people who own second homes on the island are "summer people." It's not only that they dress differently, drive different cars, carry different bags; their hair is different, their makeup, their skin. They move around the island as though its beaches, roads, shops, restaurants were put there expressly for their entertainment. Even the nice ones—and unlike her mother, the driver does believe there are nice ones—carry themselves differently than the locals, so that she could never confuse one for the other.

The woman in the distance doesn't look like a summer person, but there's no mistaking her for a local, either. As the driver inches closer, she's able to make out the hitchhiker's features: her smeared lipstick, the tattoos peeking out from beneath the hem of her dress, the messy bun. The driver doesn't recognize her, but can tell, somehow, that this woman is famous. She eases off the gas pedal just like her mother taught her, slowing to a stop. She won't take a picture or beg for an autograph. She only wants to be close to someone special, as if glamour might be contagious.

The driver tries to imagine what made this stranger seek help at the recovery center—the only reason a celebrity would be on the island this time of year—but it's impossible. What problems could someone so dazzling actually have?

The hitchhiker grins as she asks for a ride into town, her teeth glowing white in the darkness. Her eyes are set far apart and focused on something in the distance, as though, despite the dark, she can see beyond the reach of the car's headlights. She absently strums her guitar. The melody is sweet, like a lullaby. If this were a fairy story, the driver thinks, the stranger would be some kind of demon, her song meant to lull the driver to sleep before she pounces.

The driver wants to ask the hitchhiker about her life, but something in her gaze—a hunger the driver's never seen before—stops her. She thinks about the story of the wolf in sheep's clothing, pretending to be harmless to slip in among its victims. Or vampires, appearing in the road, waiting for some Good Samaritan to offer them aid.

Later, the police will ask what she saw, and the driver will only remember the sound of the guitar, as though she was under some sort of spell after all. They will ask, did the hitchhiking stranger seem sober, high, drunk, dangerous? They will blink at the driver's answers like she's utterly useless, driving all the way into town without asking her passenger a single question beyond *Where do you want to go?* Her mother will scold her for picking up a stranger, take her keys, and ground her for a month. Briefly, the driver will become a bit of a celebrity herself: Her classmates will want to know every detail of the drive, and the boy who dumped her last month will start texting again.

But for now, the driver knows only that she is in the presence of someone special, so she tries to soak up this stranger's magic by osmosis, breathing in deeply. She offers to turn on the radio, but the stranger says no.

"Don't want anyone else's song in my head right now," she says with a smile. She looks, the driver thinks, happy. She looks peaceful.

52

Georgia Blue

*G*eorgia Blue. Andrew made the name—*my* name, the one *I* chose, the person I created, the woman I made famous—sound like a curse.

He's not the first person to say that what happened was my fault. The press started seeding nasty theories about Scott's death almost as soon as he died.

Why, they said, *would Scott Harris kill himself? He had everything.*

He had everything, until he had me.

They said I killed him because I was jealous, because he was going to tell the world *he* was the one who'd written my songs, because he wanted a divorce and I wanted his money.

Or they said I drove him to suicide, made him so miserable that he chose ending it all over facing one more day tied to me. The industry was rife with stories about how difficult I was to work with; they could only imagine what it must be like to *live* with me. A basket case, they called me. A mess.

There was a time when I would've told them that I wasn't difficult to work with, it was just that I was a perfectionist, determined to get every note exactly right. I singlehandedly wrote two albums, one of which went gold. That kind of thing doesn't happen by accident, no matter the stories people tell about being hit by inspiration. Sure, I showed up to concerts high, but never recording studios. I had *priorities*; there were things I cared about more than drugs.

It's cold out here and I lost my coat. My kid hates it, so good riddance. I don't need it anyway. My skin is hot with rage, so hot that when it starts to snow, the flakes steam when they make contact with my skin. I sit on the curb of a sidewalk and pull my notebook from my guitar case.

For Andrew, I scrawl at the top of a blank page. After a couple weeks here, the notebook is almost full, only a few pages left. There are years' worth of notebooks and journals I left behind in Laurel Canyon. My kid and my mom aren't interested enough in me to snoop, so I never bothered hiding them away.

I can hear the intro to this new song in my head: soft and warm, like a caress. Like Andrew smiling at me behind Evelyn's back. A piano's tinkle-like laughter.

But after the first verse, my voice will scream the chorus:

I thought you cared and you did
Cared for yourself, the self you hid
Thought you helped and you did
Helped yourself, left me for dead
Got what you wanted, picked me dry
Like a vulture, but you can't fly
Away, away, away from me . . .
You'll never
Escape me
This one's for you,
This one's
For Andrew.

The song rushes out of me, verse after verse followed by a roaring bridge. I can't remember the last time I wrote something complete this quickly.

Let Andrew claim he wrote *that*.

I have to get the hell out of here. Stay a minute longer and Callie will turn me into some simpering apologist, ruining any chance of a comeback.

A good mother would be thinking of getting home to her daughter, not to her career. My little girl—not so little anymore, a teenager now.

I close my eyes, hugging my notebook to my chest. When we found out we were having a girl, Scott and I painted her nursery ourselves, all blues and purples, no pink. I was on the outs with the band at the time because I'd refused to play shows while I was pregnant.

And then the delivery, so sick I thought I might die. The doctors said I almost did. Scott holding my hand when I started to hemorrhage, and her tiny face before I passed out, my bright, shining Amelia Blue.

By the time I left the hospital, the rumors were already swirling: It was my fault she'd been premature; Scott paid off CPS so we could take her home; we flew my mom out because I was too high to take care of the baby.

It was Scott's idea to ask my mom to stay. I was too sick to argue. I could barely stand, let alone carry another human being—a tiny, fragile creature who would break if I fell.

Eventually I was well enough that we sent my mother home. Scott and I started writing together. Amelia Blue was growing, happy and strong. I thought everything was going to be all right. For a while, it was, so much that I missed the signs when Scott's depression returned. When I found his note, I managed to stop him from going through with it. I didn't want my daughter growing up with a father who was absent or drugged into oblivion. I know what it is to grow up feeling abandoned, and I didn't want that for her. I thought I could handle it myself. So I didn't call a doctor, didn't get professional help. He told me he changed his mind.

Two days later, he did it after all.

After that, I didn't trust myself with our daughter. Look what happened to the last person I'd taken care of. I was scared to hug her, could barely touch her. Loving her as much as I did hurt; keeping her at arm's length hurt even more. And so Naomi took over, the way she always did, the way I knew she would.

A better mother would have kept herself together for her child. That's what my mom did, when my dad left.

But I took anything to dull the pain. Rock bottom can be where the using starts, not where it ends. They just don't tell those stories.

I don't know what I was on the night I shared his suicide note. Too blocked to write my own music, I thought I could turn it into a song. I certainly didn't consider that the date—two days before he died—would feed the fire of their conspiracy theories.

It took years, but eventually I got sick and tired of being a basket case. There was no dramatic rock bottom, no big *eureka* moment. After a decade blitzed out of my mind, after I'd tried every drug and chased every artificial high, I was curious what sobriety had to offer. I figured I could always go back to getting shitfaced if I didn't like it. So I stumbled into a meeting, found a sponsor, started the steps. Turned out it was more interesting than the alternative.

I thought a good mother would've gotten sober for her daughter, not idle curiosity, but my sponsor told me I was wrong. Getting sober for someone else doesn't work, she said, no matter how much you love them. I had to get sober for myself, because it was what *I* wanted.

And, she pointed out there was nothing *idle* about it. Being sober was something I had to work at every day.

I page back through my notebook, the lyrics I've scribbled and abandoned, so many songs that never got to be.

I know, with certainty, that I can finish them. I'm going to fucking finish them all.

I'll fire Callie, find a new manager. Screw my reputation; they'll all want to work with me once they hear these songs. I'll show Amelia Blue the person I was before Scott died, the force of nature who made a career out of thin air, who wrote half of Scott Harris's songs for him and loved him so much she didn't mind when the world gave him credit.

My girl will be proud to have a mother like that.

As proud as I am to have a daughter like her. She thinks I don't know, but I see everything she does: how neat she keeps her room, the house, picking up after me. How she gets straight A's and goes to bed early without being told. The jokes she makes—usually at my expense—so quick and clever. How sweet she is to my mother, helping when Naomi's back hurts, when she's too tired to make dinner.

When Amelia Blue got sick, I thought it'd have been even worse if I'd kept her close.

But now I wonder—would it have helped if I'd held her tight instead of at arm's length?

I wouldn't have done what I did with Scott, begging him to be well, pleading with him not to leave me.

But maybe I could've shown my daughter what it looks like to be well.

Maybe I still can.

53

Amelia Blue

I pick up the file gently, moving slowly, like it's made of glass. Why is it here, on this desk, away from all the others in the room beside the gym? Inside, there are pages of neatly typed doctor's notes. After all this time, I can hardly believe I'm about to read exactly what Georgia's care manager wrote. Did they call her narcissistic, addicted, emotionally immature? Did Georgia share stories she never told me—why she and Naomi never got along; how she met my father and what it was like when they were in love; her thoughts when she found out she was pregnant?

But my eyes pass over the doctor's words and land on a medium-size spiral notebook beneath the file.

Months ago, when I went through Georgia's things, the sober diary wasn't the only notebook stacked in Naomi's many bins. In fact, there were dozens of them, going back years, some filled with doodles, poems, a couple of the songs from her first albums. My mother was never, not once, without a notebook. Even when she was high, even (according to stories) in the delivery room before I was born—my mother always kept a pad of paper to scribble potential lyrics into. The tattoos that snaked up and down her arms and legs were lyrics she'd etched into her skin for all the world to see.

I went to school for poetry, but I never particularly cared about it. I studied writing because it's what my parents did, like I was going into the family business, the result of a failure to imagine that I might be capable of something else.

I can smell my mother on this notebook now, her particular combination of hair dye and patchouli, sweat and ink. She must have brought this here, began writing in it after filling the one I found. How could I have thought that one was her final notebook? Of *course* she brought another one to rehab.

A lump swells in my throat as I learn something I didn't know, a fact I hadn't been looking for but can no longer deny: I miss my mother.

I lay my phone on the cabinet in front of me, the light facing up. My hands shake as I lean over the pages, eager to see what my mother left behind.

Before I can read a single syllable, a hand lands on my wrist, hot and dry, gripping hard like a handcuff.

54

Georgia Blue

My teeth are chattering by the time I make it back to my "cottage." Only people who were born rich would call these mansions cottages, like they're fucking Marie Antoinette or something, playacting at being poor, pretending to be plain country wives instead of diamond-adorned queens.

Tonight, though, I can see glue poking out where the heavy glass windows meet the sheetrock walls, like whoever put it together was in too much of a hurry to be careful. I see crumbs on the kitchen counter, and a ring left behind by a red wine bottle Andrew set down thoughtlessly. Finally, I see this place for what it is—a shithole, dressed up with shiny glass and gleaming countertops, but a shithole nonetheless. It's all a trick; this place pretends to be indulgent but it actually robs patients of their agency, calling them guests when they're really prisoners.

I have to get out of here as soon as motherfucking possible.

I throw my belongings into my bag, my guitar still slung across my back. I certainly don't bother folding even though the mess is so bad that I have to sit on my suitcase to close it. I pull on a pair of jeans beneath my dress, tucking my notebook into the waistband.

I'm going back to California. I don't want the icy dark Atlantic but the bright blue Pacific. I want the sun to set over the ocean, not rise from it.

Shit, that's a lyric. I pull my notebook from my waistband and start scribbling:

I want the sun to set over the ocean,
I need to get back to my side of the sea,
I can't spend another second
so far from the heart of me.

The words come fast, the chorus rising hard. I sit cross-legged on the floor and write the words to a song from deep inside, every feeling and fear I've had since my daughter was born and my husband died and my mother came to stay; how badly I wanted to be a good mother and how terribly I fucked it up. I scrawl the song's title across the top of the page.

I'm crying. I wipe my eyes, relieved no one can see me like this. Only an asshole would cry at her own lyrics. But the chorus of dead musicians in my head is applauding, Scott most of all.

Great song, babe, he says just like he used to. God, we loved each other so much. And shit did he love Amelia Blue. *AB*, he called her. I bet she doesn't remember that, which means no one on this whole earth knows it but me. I have to tell her so it doesn't get lost.

I hear the sound of heavy footsteps on the floor and then the touch of a hot hand on my bare upper arm, fingers digging into flesh, pulling me up to stand.

"Going somewhere?" Andrew eyes my suitcase, half-zipped, on the floor beside me.

"I'm going *home*." I try to say the word like I mean it, even though I've never felt comfortable calling the house Scott bought, the one he didn't leave me in his will, my home. My mom is Amelia Blue's power of attorney, not me—I signed those rights away a long time ago—so she's the one who controls the house. She could kick me out anytime. I guess I should be grateful she never did.

"You can't leave."

"Oh no?" I laugh, but it comes out sounding desperate, weak.

"'Imposter Syndrome' is just as much mine as it is yours."

"What are you talking about?"

"We wrote it together."

"No." I shake my head. Scott and I wrote together; I know how writing as a team works. "I wrote it, and you were in the room. That doesn't make you my coauthor. It makes you my audience."

Andrew's face hardens.

"Andrew," I try to sound reasonable. My kid says it's the best way to win an argument. "It's a personal, feminist song. It doesn't make sense coming from you." I lift my suitcase onto its side. "But thank you for being there. I'll mention you in the liner notes."

I won't, not anymore, but I need to throw him a bone. I step toward the door. Andrew blocks the way.

I shove the suitcase in front of me, trying to force him to move, but he stands strong.

I throw myself at him, my fists pounding against his rock-hard chest.

I don't see the syringe, but I feel the needle pierce my skin.

Almost immediately, my body feels like it weighs a million pounds. I slump against Andrew, and he lifts me, carrying me to the bed. He's not gentle, not kind. He drops me like I'm nothing. It's hard to remember that just a day ago I held him willingly.

He must've dosed me with a sedative, just like Evelyn threatened when I first got here. I try to say something, but my tongue is thick in my mouth. It feels like there's a bear sitting on my chest, pressing against every breath.

That first day, I was so panicked that they might drug me, that being here would throw my months of sobriety out the window. It nearly happened again when Andrew showed up with Evelyn's wine, but he didn't seem to notice when I only pretended to drink it. It was tempting; if I'd had my phone, I would've called my sponsor, but I wasn't about to give Evelyn the satisfaction of asking for it.

I concentrate on my heart. Each beat takes effort, as though my blood has turned from liquid to sludge. I beg my lungs to fill with air.

"Shit!" Andrew says at the sound of my wheezing. "It's not supposed to—shit!"

I hear him shuffling around the room.

"You have to get here, *now*," he says frantically. He must be on the phone.

I don't know how much time goes by before I hear another set of footsteps, lighter than Andrew's.

"What did you do?" Evelyn's voice sounds frantic and out of breath. There's something else in her voice that takes me a moment to recognize: disappointment.

She must have run from her house. Andrew told me it's on the edge of the property, the one structure they didn't tear down or renovate after Evelyn and her husband bought the land for the recovery center. *They wanted a place of their own*, Andrew said, then scoffed, adding that Evelyn's husband only lived there for a few months before Evelyn kicked him out.

I wait for Andrew to explain, to spew a lie about how I attacked him and he had to restrain me, but instead I hear him hiccup and cough. His voice is octaves higher than when he spoke to me, so that he sounds like a little boy.

"I'm sorry, Mama."

Mama? Again, I try to speak, but my tongue is made of cotton.

Evelyn is Andrew's *mother?*

Of course. He said it was *a long story*, how he got the job here. Turns out, it was a very short story: plain old nepotism.

How could I have missed it? It's not only that Andrew knew so many details of Evelyn's personal life—and she's not the sort who would've shared all that with a mere employee—but the disgust when he spoke about her drinking, like it offended him somehow. He was pissed that his mother couldn't keep her shit together. I've seen that same disgust on my kid's face a thousand times.

"You said you could handle this." Evelyn's disappointed-mom voice is undercut by the fact that she's slurring her words slightly, obviously a few glasses in. "Your father was right, for once. I never should've given you this job."

"This was an *accident!*"

I can hear echoes of my own voice, whining every time Naomi scolded me. I'd called a lot of things accidents, trying to get out of trouble, but Naomi always saw through me.

"This isn't tinkering with your guitar in your room. My job—your job—involves people's *lives*—"

"It's not tinkering!" Andrew sounds *shrill*, I think, though no one ever uses that word to describe a man's voice. "And music can touch people's lives just as much as you can."

I can practically hear Evelyn rolling her eyes. If I were able, I'd roll mine, too. "Not this nonsense again."

"If you'd just supported me to begin with, I wouldn't have had to move here with you."

"You begged me to help you meet *Georgia Blue*. You said you had something useful to offer."

"I *did*! I still can!"

"We can't afford this." There's desperation in Evelyn's voice. "She's supposed to be our success story! Callie already started leaking items to the press."

Despite the drugs coursing through my body, rage bubbles up at the sound of Callie's name. All the drugs in the world couldn't dull that anger.

"What do we do?" Andrew sounds panicked. "I could get sent to jail!"

"We'll say she was trying to hurt you." I can tell Evelyn's trying to sound rational, but she's too drunk to pull it off. "No one would trust her word over ours."

What's more believable than a woman with anger issues losing her temper?

"No." Andrew's voice cracks. "I gave her too much. Her breathing—"

At once, I understand: Andrew thinks he killed me. He's not worried that I'll tell my side of the story. He's worried that I'll never tell anyone anything ever again.

"Don't worry," Evelyn says. "I'll take care of it."

For maybe the first time, I feel something like a *connection* with Evelyn.

In fact, this is the least I've ever hated her.

She's willing to do anything to protect her child.

55

Lord Edward

Once I'm certain Dr. Rush and his colleague are gone, I limp toward the stairs, my leg aching horribly. I think about everything I vomited up a few nights ago, and I'm tempted to go back to my room, see if any detritus remains in the toilet.

Good lord, I'm considering licking the fucking toilet bowl.

I hold the railing and hop down the stairs on my right leg. Before he stamped out his cigarette, Dr. Rush said they were looking for a patient named Sonja Carrera, here for digital detox. I cross the courtyard and make my way to Amelia's room. As I suspected, she's already gone.

I think I know where she went: the house on the edge of the property. I start walking toward it, avoiding the beams of searching flashlights, trying to breathe through the pain like they say in PT, but my mouth fills with wind and snowflakes, the cold as sharp as a knife.

And then, I lose my footing. I fall to the ground, on my back like a turtle that's been flipped over.

At once, I'm back in the hospital, lying flat on a gurney. I'm shouting Harper's name, or maybe I'm just thinking it because I'm too weak to shout. Around me, the doctors are frantic. They say I've lost too much blood. They don't tell me how Harper is. Later, I learned that they drove us in separate ambulances—me first—and I don't know if I was first because my situation was more dire or because the EMTs recognized me.

All I know, at the time, is that something is wound around my left thigh, so tight that I can't feel my foot, can't feel my knee. God, it hurts. I manage to reach down, try to undo what they've done, trying to free my leg. Someone shouts, and then they're sticking me with needles, holding me down, securing me with restraints. Later, I'll be told that I tried to untie the tourniquet on my left leg. If I'd succeeded, I would've bled out in a matter of moments.

When I woke after surgery, I asked to see Harper. They said I wasn't family; therefore I wasn't allowed into the ICU. I said she was my fiancée. Someone lifted my body onto a wheelchair, covered me with blankets.

At first, I didn't recognize her: There were tubes in her mouth, her nose, an IV dripping something into her arm. They told me she was in a coma. I didn't know if she would want me there, and part of me was relieved she couldn't ask me to go away. I was selfish enough to stay because *I* wanted to be there.

I was still beside her when her parents arrived. They told the nurses we weren't engaged. We would never be engaged. Their daughter wouldn't marry me, the man who'd nearly killed her.

Someone wheeled me out of the ICU. It was only when I was back in my room, when they lifted me out of my chair and into the bed, that I realized my leg, just below the knee, was gone. Maybe someone had already told me, but I didn't remember. All I remembered was needing to get to Harper, to see that she was all right, and then the agony of knowing she wasn't.

It's cold on the ground. The snowflakes are fat and wet now, the sort of heavy snow that turns to sludge. My jeans are damp. I read once that hypothermia feels like falling asleep. The worse it gets, the less cold one feels. Apparently, it's quite comfortable to freeze to death.

I close my eyes. It's peaceful here.

56

Amelia Blue

I turn, coming face-to-face with an older woman, wild white hair tumbling over her shoulders, hanging down almost to her waist. Her grip is tight on my wrist, and in the dim light coming from my phone, I can see veins protruding on the back of her hand.

"Florence," she says, "can you ever forgive me?"

"Florence?" I echo. My heart thumps in my chest. I try to remember the last time I heard my mother's name—her real name—spoken aloud. Naomi never says it. If she must mention Georgia, she refers to her only as *your mother*, as though anything else she ever was no longer matters.

"Georgia. I know. You wanted us to call you Georgia, and we refused. We said it was part of your therapy. Like taking your phone, when really we just needed to keep you quiet. What if you'd made a statement that contradicted ours? No, no—we had to take it, even you can understand that. And who's to say it didn't benefit your therapy?"

This woman participated in my mother's *therapy?* I compare her to Dr. Mackenzie, to what Edward has told me about his doctor. I can't imagine her sitting on one of the cottages' white couches, crossing her legs and asking Georgia, *And how did that make you feel?*

"It was a good deal for you, too, you know. You got to benefit from our facility almost for free, the best care money could buy."

I look down and notice that the woman's bare feet are bleeding. She must have walked through the shattered glass I left by the front door.

Again, she says, "Georgia."

"I'm not Georgia," I murmur, unsure whether this will calm or agitate her. The woman simply shakes her head. I try to pull my arm away, but her grip holds fast.

The truth is, I look like my mother. Not just the nose I wasn't supposed to inherit, the pale skin. I didn't see it until after she was gone: the way my upper lip thins when I smile, the way my hair frames my face.

"My husband wanted to take the business for himself," she says. "You know, Georgia, what it's like to have a husband like that. He gets the credit while you do all the hard work."

The woman wears a stained nightgown beneath a too-big flannel robe with frayed cuffs. Her mouth hangs open, slack, her teeth blotchy and stained. I smell alcohol on her breath.

"He only wanted to calm you down. He didn't know what he was doing. He gave you too much."

Blood drips from the cut on my arm onto her pale skin, snaking between her fingers.

"I was trying to save my son. You understand, don't you? You're a mother, too."

The woman squeezes my wrist so tight that I think I may never be free of her.

"Your body was so heavy," she says.

57

Georgia Blue

My mind is racing. I wonder what kind of sedative Andrew gave me, blunting my body but not my brain. Then I think maybe it's that my brain knows something is wrong, knows I'm not safe, so despite the drug fighting to put it to sleep, it's wide awake, trying to work out how to get away from these awful people.

Andrew slides his hands beneath my armpits, and Evelyn holds my ankles, her skin smooth and soft against mine. I bet she uses expensive lotion that smells like roses made by some company that's been around for a hundred years. The sort of scent that would smell rotten if I tried it, clearly not meant for someone like me.

Andrew heaves like I'm an enormous burden he can't wait to unload. I want to beg him to put me down, let me go, but he holds firm. Unlike Evelyn, his hands are rough and his grip hurts.

I feel the chill when we move outside. Through my barely open eyes, I see plumes of steam coming from their mouths, the stars overhead, snow flurries in the moonlight. My head lolls to one side and I see dead leaves crunching beneath Andrew's feet, his brown boots, his long steps.

"This way," Evelyn says firmly. She sounds sober now, determined. She has a plan, though she's yet to say it aloud. *Share it with the class, Evelyn.*

I can feel Andrew resisting. He tries to pull me in the opposite direction, and it feels like they're pulling me apart, wrenching my body in two.

"Andy," Evelyn says, and for a moment, I hear how she must have sounded when he was a little kid. The nickname should be a sign of affection, but her tone is exasperated, impatient, weary. I can still hear my mother calling me *Flo* in exactly the same tone. "*This* way."

What must it have been like to be raised by Evelyn, her unblinking eyes assessing every bad grade or broken curfew? Did she and her husband therapize their son at the dinner table? Or were they too busy with their patients to notice the little boy who wanted to be a star?

The air is getting saltier now. I can feel my hair growing knotty in the breeze, having long since fallen out of the messy bun I tied it in hours ago. I was going to sing. I was going to put on such a show.

"Now what?" Andrew asks, out of breath. His hands are growing slick with sweat despite the cold. He squeezes me tighter, like he thinks he might lose his grip.

Please, I think, *lose your grip.*

I imagine myself running away, then remember I can't. Besides, Evelyn's hands are still dry, her hold firm. I should've guessed she'd be the strong one between the two of them.

"Now we're going home." Evelyn lets go suddenly, and my legs hit the ground hard.

"Just like that?" Andrew asks. He sounds impressed.

"Just like that," Evelyn says, and I can hear her smacking her hands together, like she's brushing away all traces of me.

Andrew sets me down. He pulls my notebook from the waistband of my jeans.

I feel their absence when they leave me, the cold snaking its way to the places where their hot hands held me so tight.

58

Amelia Blue

There's the sound of a switch flipping, and the room is flooded with light. I crane my neck (the older woman is still holding me so I can't quite turn entirely) and see a tall man standing in the doorway. He's holding a baseball bat.

"What the hell are you doing in my house?"

"Your house?" I repeat.

I review the facts that I (sort of) know: This building is on the grounds of Rush's Recovery. This place looks like a private home. This room seems more a helter-skelter home office than any sort of official records room.

I blink as my eyes adjust to the light. The man looks familiar: dark hair, brown eyes, evening stubble. Jeans with a nondescript thick sweater beneath a wool coat, beat-up boots. He would be handsome if he didn't look so menacing.

"Do you work here?" I ask, groping for an explanation.

The man coughs. "I'm Andrew Rush."

At once, the article I swiped from the records room appears in my mind's eye. He was in the picture, younger then, but it's definitely him—the Rushes' son, the one who went into the family business.

But that's not why I recognize him. Now that there's a name with the face, I remember that Andrew Rush is (was?) a musician. He released a one-hit wonder years ago. The song was praised for its vulnerable take on navigating the world as an imperfect person, always hungry for more. Even now, clips from the music video pop up on social media alongside covers of fans doing different takes—setting it to piano or mashing it up with club music. His brown hair is graying at the temples, and there's a bit of a paunch spilling over his waistband, but it's definitely him. I even recognize his voice, inescapable when his song was blowing up the charts.

"Why aren't you looking for Sonja with everyone else?'"

He narrows his eyes. "I was. But then my alarm went off."

"Your alarm?"

He shakes his head as though he can't believe he's explaining all this to the woman who broke into his house. "My phone alerts me if the windows or doors open when I'm not home. In case my mom gets out. She's"—he pauses—"not well. Had to retire a few years back, so I took over the business."

That makes him the center's owner, the one who's sending me home because I ran out of money. I shift my gaze back to the woman gripping my arm, realizing she was locked inside, just like Edward a few nights ago.

"Wait," she begs as her son begins to cross the room. Her words are slurred but insistent. "I have to tell Amelia Blue."

It's the first time she's referred to me by my own name, not my mother's.

"The coroner had a daughter to send to college. All I had to do was call—"

"Come on, Evelyn," Andrew says. He's trying to sound gentle, coaxing, but there's an edge to his voice. He stands over her, so much taller than either of us, and I'm seeing a version of what I saw the other night: the woman outside the house, the man restraining her.

"Evelyn," I repeat. Ten years ago, a woman who introduced herself as Dr. Evelyn Rush called the landline in Laurel Canyon early on a Sunday morning. I was home for a long weekend from school. (With Georgia out of town, I didn't have to stay away.) Evelyn Rush said that she'd been Georgia's care manager, and calmly explained that my mother had checked herself out. There was nothing they could've done to stop her, she added. Georgia was of age, and her stay at the recovery center was voluntary.

"We worked it all out with Callie," she says now.

"You knew Callie?" I ask. I haven't heard from my mother's manager since she died.

"Like I said," Andrew explains. "She's sick. Gets confused."

"I've kept the secret for too long," Evelyn says, wringing her hands. "I've had enough of it."

"I better get her back to bed before she gets more agitated." Andrew's trying to sound like a dutiful son, but I still hear that edge in his voice. He glances at Georgia's open file on the desk. It's obvious he doesn't like the idea of leaving me alone, but his mother is writhing in his arms.

"I'll be right back."

When he's gone, I page through Evelyn's notes. Is there something inside Andrew didn't want me to see?

Florence is reluctant to open up to me, she wrote.

Florence appears to be sober, she wrote. *No signs of withdrawal since her arrival.*

Further proof: My mother was sober when she arrived.

Despite her reputation for anger, Florence strikes me as terribly sad.

The notes are neat and concise, but hardly revelatory. Georgia was a widow whose career had soured and whose sick daughter barely spoke to her. You don't need to be an expert to notice she was sad. (Then again, I never noticed at the time.)

I set Evelyn's notes aside and open my mother's notebook instead, turning to the last page first. Adrenaline flutters through me at the sight of Georgia's nearly illegible but unmistakable scrawl. Across the top of the page is the title "The Good Mother." The preceding page is labeled, "For Andrew."

These aren't diary entries like the notebook I found, but songs. I recall the nonsense phrases in between entries of her sober diary—they were, I realize now, snippets of lyrics.

I'd thought she stopped that kind of writing. By the time she'd died, it'd been years since she'd recorded a single song, let alone an album.

I turn another page and see a song titled "Imposter Syndrome." I find myself humming along with the lyrics. The words in the notebook are slightly different from the ones I know by heart.

Was the tower his prison, or the wide world outside?
Was he looking for a rescue
Or another place to crawl inside?
Would he always be searching for somewhere that felt like home?
Some place he could be himself, unafraid to be alone?
No longer afflicted with Imposter Syndrome.

Andrew Rush's one-hit wonder.

59

Lord Edward

My phone is vibrating in my pocket.
I open my eyes.

That unknown number again. Some intrepid journalist—if you can call them journalists—digging for dirt. Haven't they learned yet that I know better than to pick up? The snow continues to accumulate around me, but now I'm wide awake, cold and restless.

I push myself up to sit. The ground is wet, soaking my jeans and gloves as I shift onto all fours. I take a deep breath, concentrating on the pressure where my prosthesis meets what remains of my leg as I stand.

I resume my limping hike toward the structure at the edge of the property. I follow the path Amelia and I took days ago until I make out cedar shingles and a slate roof.

The front door is open, giving the house the look of a mouth that's missing a tooth. I recall the story of Hansel and Gretel, the charming cottage in the woods where wandering children met their doom.

But this house doesn't smell like ginger and sweets. As I cross the threshold, I smell rot: There's dirty food strewn across the kitchen counter alongside open bottles of wine left to turn sour. If there is a witch here, she isn't interested in luring children close with promises of lollipops and cookies. My winter boots crunch over broken glass scattered with drops of blood.

What the hell am I walking into?

60

Amelia Blue

I hear Andrew's footsteps, heavy on the hardwood floors like an alarm signaling his return, so I tuck my mother's notebook into the waistband of my leggings, hiding it beneath my bulky sweater.

There were always rumors that my father wrote Georgia's biggest hits for her. It wasn't hard to believe. After he died, she didn't release any more albums.

But I know my mother's handwriting as well as I know my own. I spent months studying her sober diary, almost identical to this notebook—spiral bound, college ruled, black cover. I know that she dashes, rather than dots, her *I*'s. That even in the middle of sentences, her *B*'s are written like upper-case letters, and even when she's writing my name, the *A*'s look lowercase.

My whole life, I thought Georgia had the opposite of the Midas touch, turning things that had been worth so much to trash. By the time I was old enough to listen, the rest of the world had declared her music all but worthless. When Shocking Pink tours later this year, they'll fill only small theaters, nothing like the stadiums where they once performed. Her clothes (that god-awful fur coat)—she ripped them to shreds, spilled red wine on them, stained them with lipstick and blush, left them crumpled in piles on the floor. Even her body, her face—my grandmother's shown me pictures, and the truth is, she was beautiful before she turned to plastic surgery and hair dye.

Her husband, the hottest bass player on the planet when she married him—now a faded memory.

Her daughter, born, like all human beings, with all the potential in the world—now a body that's failing. A body that failed.

"You stole my mother's song," I say as Andrew steps into the room.

"It was my song, too." His voice is eerily calm, as though I'd asked about the snow outside, not accused him of theft.

The lyrics scream through my brain, the melody so catchy it's like a spell. The song doesn't sound like the man standing in front of me. I imagine *her* voice singing the words, her hands moving over a guitar the way I've seen in videos on the internet from her heyday, the way I never saw in real life.

"Why did you let me come to Rush's Recovery?"

Surely, Andrew knew full well what I might find here. Perhaps, after so many years treating wealthy patients, he absorbed their false sense of security, their certainty that privilege is protection. Or maybe he'd simply thought I was the sort of patient who would never venture outside my cottage.

Andrew cocks his head to the side, leaning against the doorjamb. "I was curious."

"Curious?"

"Yes. Would Florence's daughter be as fucked-up as her mom?" He sounds cold, as if his curiosity is clinical, not personal.

"Georgia." My correction makes Andrew smile, as though calling my mother by her chosen name is a joke.

"Unfortunately, the way things worked out, I couldn't be your care manager. The family of another guest paid extra to ensure that I would be treating him, you know how people can be about that sort of thing. But not to worry, I've been reading Dr. Mackenzie's notes, comparing them to the notes my mother took years ago." He steps closer to the desk, absentmindedly lifts a paper and sets it back down. "I have to admit, I was disappointed. Mommy issues are so obvious." He heaves a sigh. "Your mother, at least, was never dull."

My toes curl in my boots. This place may not have hidden cameras, but someone was spying on me all the same. The spiral of my mother's notebook presses against my belly, so hot it feels alive.

"Unfortunately, I didn't anticipate how much your presence would upset my mother. She hasn't been the same since everything that happened with Florence, you know."

I shake my head. Of course, I didn't know.

"Alcohol abuse can cause dementia, but you try convincing an alcoholic it's not worth the risk. Course, you're already familiar with the pitfalls of trying to reason with an addict, aren't you?"

Is this eerily calm man the reason Georgia used one last time? Is he the reason that time was different?

I consider what I know (what I thought I knew) about the night my mother died: Georgia hitchhiked to a bar in town. The driver, just a teen, was interviewed by *People* magazine for their brief "in memoriam" article, not even a full page. Patrons posted videos of Georgia at the bar, her hair greasy and her makeup smeared. She looked agitated and erratic, arguing with a man out of frame who (Evelyn told us) worked at the center, who was trying to help. (I wonder now: Was Andrew that man?) Georgia ran off without her coat. Evelyn said she must've scored some drugs and made her way to the beach, passed out, and simply never woke up, the elements getting the better of her. An *accident*, Evelyn said. No note, no intent, unlike my father, though the result was the same.

But tonight, Evelyn said *he* wanted to calm her down, *he* didn't know what he was doing.

The pieces are clicking into place, but the puzzle's not complete, not yet.

Andrew continues. "Evelyn tried to get out the other night. I had a hell of a time getting her back inside. Had to sprint back to my guest's cottage so I could be there if he needed me."

The struggle I saw from across the woods. Not a hallucination, a trick of the light.

I should be frightened, but instead I concentrate on working out the puzzle, as focused as if I were taking my SATs all over again. Just a few more questions to work out, a few more possibilities to eliminate, before I land on the correct answer.

"I couldn't chance it happening again, so I had to start locking her inside. For her own safety, of course. She could freeze to death out there." Andrew gestures absently at a window. Outside, the snow is accumulating rapidly.

"And you were worried about what she might tell me," I supply.

"Not at all," he replies, almost shrugging. "True, this isn't quite how I saw things playing out. I thought Sonja being here, playing your mom's old music so loud you'd be able to hear it in your cottage, might provoke more of a reaction, but according to Dr. Mack's notes, you never so much as mentioned it."

"You arranged for Sonja and me to be here at the same time?"

"She wanted to be here for the anniversary of Florence's death," Andrew says. "A fan on some macabre pilgrimage. You know, she requested your mom's old cottage?"

He sounds disdainful, as though he can't imagine why anyone would still be so devoted to Georgia.

They took her phone so she wouldn't be able to communicate with her fans directly. Evelyn said, *What if you'd made a statement that contradicted ours?* I recall a press release issued by Callie a few days before Georgia died, explaining that she'd checked herself into rehab. Georgia's months of sobriety wouldn't have fit with their story.

"Your mother's notes say that Georgia was doing well when she was here."

Evelyn showed up to Mom's funeral in a tailored suit, not a single hair out of place. She shook my hand and said she was sorry for my loss. It's no wonder I didn't recognize her tonight. She hardly looks like the same person.

He gave you too much, she said. *The coroner had a daughter to send to college.*

I was trying to save my son, she said.

"My mother's notes are protected by doctor-patient confidentiality," Andrew says, then adds, "Plenty of addicts fall off the wagon after rehab."

I wonder if he knows, like I do, that *fall off the wagon* has origins in the temperance movement, when individuals who pledged to abstain from alcohol were said to be *on the water wagon,* from the image of horse-drawn water wagons that were used to dampen dusty roads each summer. Surely no one but the child of an addict bothers looking up that sort of trivia.

You understand, Evelyn said. *You're a mother, too.*

The final piece of the puzzle clicks into place.

61

Lord Edward

I limp into what looks like a disorganized study and see Amelia standing on one side of an enormous desk. Leaning against the desk is a man, his back to me. Amelia is bleeding.

"It's time for you to go back to your room," the man says. The room smells like cigarettes. There's a baseball bat leaning against the door; I pick it up and run my fingers over it.

"Dr. Rush?" I ask.

The man—my therapist—turns to face me. It's the first time I've seen him without his blazer and pressed slacks. He looks smaller.

Amelia shakes her head. "He's really a wannabe musician."

She seems to think this will shock me, but I already know Dr. Rush used to be some kind of rock star. Anne read me his bio aloud when she decided to send me here. Andrew Rush earned a PhD in psychology after his own brush with fame, the experience rendering him uniquely suited to work with high-profile clients. *He's perfect for you,* Anne had said. I knew she meant not only that he had personal experience with celebrity but that he'd had his own youthful dalliance—with music—before falling in line and pursuing the family business.

"Edward, thank goodness you're here," Dr. Rush breathes. "As you can see, one of our patients is a bit confused. She broke into my house, and I'm afraid she's become a danger to herself and others."

At once, he lunges across the desk and wraps his arms around Amelia like a straitjacket.

"Amelia isn't dangerous," I say, but even as the words come out of my mouth, I question them. I knew how much she wanted to access her mother's file. I recall the broken glass I stepped over to get here and take in the pile of papers on the desk in front of her.

Dr. Rush gestures for me to take his place restraining Amelia. "I need you to hold her while I get something to calm her."

He sounds nearly as reasonable as he does during our therapy sessions, though only half his words are accented with the Northeastern drawl I'm used to hearing from him; the other half are punctuated with the Southern twang I heard earlier. Somehow, with Amelia squirming beneath his grip, his calm voice is more unsettling than if he were screaming, like a doctor listing clinical statistics after delivering a fatal diagnosis.

"Of course, it's highly unusual to ask one of our guests to assist with something like this, but as you can see, special measures must be taken."

Something to calm her means he wants to sedate her. Well, why wouldn't he? She broke into his house. She's twisting beneath his arms. She's become, Dr. Rush said, *a danger*. I take a single step forward.

"Edward." My name sounds like a plea coming from Amelia's mouth. She looks so small beneath Dr. Rush, but I know how strong she is. She supported my weight more than once. "Please. He killed my mother."

I stumble backward, bumping into the doorway behind me.

"Lord Edward." Dr. Rush has never called me that, his voice solicitous. "As you can see, this patient is suffering from paranoic delusions."

Amelia thought she saw something in the woods the other night. I told her it was a trick of the light, but could she have been hallucinating?

"My mother wasn't really here for rehab. I'll tell the police. They'll question Evelyn. That's why she was trying to get out the other night, right? To tell me what really happened?"

"You think the word of Florence's grieving, mentally ill daughter or my demented mother will convince anyone of anything, Amelia Blue?" Dr. Rush smiles cruelly, and for a moment he looks nothing like the calm therapist who's been speaking with me all this time. He even *sounds* different, emphasizing Amelia's full name like it's the punchline to a joke.

My doctor turns to me, his calm demeanor back in place, as though he's slipped behind a mask. "You've been doing so well, Lord Edward. Your sister will be so pleased to hear that you're ready to go home."

"I'm ready to go home?" I echo.

"I was going to call your family with the news tomorrow."

I imagine myself in the apartment in Tribeca, waking early to watch the dog walkers and runners out my window overlooking the Hudson River, their brisk steps along the West Side Highway.

Dr. Rush adds, "Of course, I might have to change my assessment if you're backsliding."

"Backsliding?" The word makes me think of falling backward, of brakes that fail.

"Aiding an out-of-control patient is hardly a sign of progress."

I catch his meaning. If I help Dr. Rush now, then he'll tell Anne I've been a model patient, I'm cured. Back home, my doctors will refill my prescriptions.

"Will you tell them to send me back to Manhattan, instead of London?"

"I can tell them it would be healthier for you to return to your old life."

This is almost exactly what Amelia thought she saw in the woods days ago. A man restraining a woman. Seeing it right here, in front of me, I can't recall why I ever doubted her. How can I doubt a word she's saying now?

At once, Amelia brings her foot down, hard, on Dr. Rush's instep. He howls in pain, loosening his hold enough for Amelia to break free.

When my doctor dives toward my friend, I don't hesitate.

I bring the bat down hard and hear a terrible *crack* as it makes contact with my doctor's skull.

He falls to the ground. The adrenaline coursing through my veins dulls the ache in my fucked-up leg.

Amelia bends over him. "He's still breathing," she says. "Edward? Did you hear me?"

"I heard you." I look around the room, taking note of the mess.

"We gotta get out of here," she says.

"What about your mother's file?" I gesture to the pile of papers on the desk. After all Amelia went through to get it, I can't imagine she's willing to leave it.

Amelia shakes her head, her eyes very bright. "Let's go."

62

Amelia Blue

The snow flickers around us as we stumble between the trees, along the path and up the stairs to Edward's cottage. I feel drunk, my feet unsteady. I lean on Edward, counting on him to get me where we're going. My heart taps wildly in my chest. There's no discernible rhythm, no steady hum. I feel like someone who is very, very sick.

For most of my life, *weak* was my mother's insatiable hunger and her inability to curb it. It was other patients in treatment with me, the ones who gave in to the therapy and got better. *Weak* was crying over the pictures of me on the internet, the so-called friends who sold me out.

Tonight, all at once, *weak* is the inability to put one foot in front of the other without someone else supporting me.

"Come on," Edward coaxes, guiding me toward the sliding glass door.

I don't want to step into the warmth of Edward's room. It feels like a trap, a cage.

Oh god, they killed her. I can't catch my breath.

This place. It—*they*—*him*—Andrew Rush killed my mother.

The best care money can buy, that's what Evelyn said, what Callie said, what Mom echoed, the trill in her voice, the way she made everything sound like a song. It used to annoy me—couldn't she ever simply *talk*?

I'm shaking, but I manage to hold myself upright so I can back away from the door.

"Amelia?" Edward holds his arm out to me, but I shake my head.

The cause of death listed on the death certificate was *exposure*. We believed she'd passed out on the beach and slept through her own death, too careless to save her own life.

But she wasn't careless. *We* were. We didn't insist on a toxicology report, ask for a more thorough investigation into what had happened. We didn't question that Georgia would be cavalier with her life, so we were cavalier with her death.

We should've been suspicious the instant her suitcase arrived without a spiral notebook inside.

I look down at the wide cedar planks below, slippery with snow, then at the floor-to-ceiling windows in front of me, flakes clinging to the frame. If I were in California, I'd think I was trying to stand during an earthquake but it's *me* setting everything off-kilter, not the ground beneath my feet.

The snow turns to ice in my hair and sticks to my leggings like dust. I'm crying so hard I can't stop.

All this time, I thought her death didn't matter. Months before she died, I'd already made up my mind never to speak to her again, so what difference did it make whether she was alive or dead? I hated her. I *knew* that I hated her.

Suddenly (there it is, the word my professor told me never to use), I know why I destroyed the tattoo beneath my breast, why I slashed my mother's initials into nothing but scar tissue. Deep down, I had already decided to name my child after Georgia, imbuing them with all the history my mother gave me when she named me.

I always loved my mother.

63

Lord Edward

My leg hurts and my hands are trembling. Is this withdrawal? Or perhaps it's merely adrenaline leaving my body. I want to crouch beside Amelia, but I can't; my body literally cannot make that shape.

"Amelia!" A striking woman emerges onto the terrace from below. She's wearing a parka zipped to her neck, and her hair is twisted into braids, gathered into a bun on top of her head. She's taller than Amelia, but still several inches shorter than I am. Her walk is rushed but even; she's wearing insulated duck boots, perfectly appropriate for the weather. She's slightly out of breath as she says, "What are you doing here?"

When Amelia doesn't answer, the woman turns to me and briskly introduces herself as Dr. Mackenzie, Amelia's care manager, then pulls her phone from her pocket.

"Just letting my colleagues know you're here," she explains as she moves her fingers over the screen.

"What about Sonja?" Amelia asks hoarsely. I look at her in surprise. I'd all but forgotten the missing patient.

"Sonja's okay, thank goodness. She hitchhiked into town, but she's all right."

"To the Shelter Shack?" Amelia asks.

Dr. Mackenzie looks at her quizzically, but nods, then crouches beside my friend. Glancing up at me, the doctor says, "You should go inside, Lord Edward. Unfortunately, we have to send both of you home tomorrow."

"I was already leaving," Amelia says.

"You were?" I ask dumbly.

Amelia doesn't answer.

Dr. Mackenzie explains, "We're closing the facility until more effective security measures can be put in place," she says. "Sonja's underage, so matters are a bit complicated."

"Dr. Rush will just lock patients on the property," Amelia says, her eyes bloodshot.

Dr. Mackenzie looks tired. "I don't know exactly what we're going to do." She pulls Amelia to her feet. "But you don't have to worry about that. For now, let me walk you to your cottage."

"I can't go back there," Amelia says.

"I understand you don't want to be here, Amelia, but we're on an island in the middle of the night. Everything is closed, and the ferry doesn't run at this hour. And with the weather . . . " She gestures at the snow, though it's coming down more lightly than it was an hour ago.

Amelia shudders. "I can't spend another night on this property." She sounds desperate.

Dr. Mackenzie must recognize something in Amelia's tone, because she doesn't argue. "Okay." She nods. "We're leaving."

Amelia follows her doctor off the terrace. She doesn't pause to say goodbye. I open my mouth to apologize—I should have believed her, I should have helped her sooner—but she's gone before I can make the words.

When Harper's parents kicked me out of her hospital room, I protested with apologies. Her parents looked as though they couldn't believe I had the nerve to offer a simple *I'm sorry* after what I'd done.

All my life, I've had this feeling that there's a way I'm supposed to be, a role I'm meant to play. Not the upstanding citizen Anne and my father claim to want me to be. In fact, I think, they *want* me to be the family fuckup; they *need* me to be, a distraction from their own shortcomings.

But I took it too far, played my part too well: I was meant to do poorly at Eton so the press could call me the *Dunderhead Duke*, not get kicked out. Meant to get a reputation for partying just a tad too hard so the press could label me *Overeager Eddie*, not for falling down drunk. Meant to casually date inappropriate girls (*Lord Lays-A-Lot*), not fall deeply in love with one of them. Meant to damage expensive cars (*Fender-Bender Eddie*), not destroy them. I'm supposed to be a laugh, a lark, a clown rather than a cautionary tale.

Instead, I've done such terrible things that *I'm sorry*, no matter how well-intentioned, isn't nearly enough.

64

Lord Edward

I limp from one side of my room to the other, inhaling deeply. All I smell is my own animal sweat.

Is Dr. Rush awake by now? Amelia said he killed her mother, and something in the way he held her, the way he said her name, even, at times, the way he spoke to me, hiding his accent and dressing like he was playing a part, makes it easy to believe.

Perhaps he'll tell Anne that I assaulted him. Perhaps I'll be arrested or sent to some other facility like this one. Anne will scramble to secure *another* cover-up.

I dig through my sock drawer, reach into the pockets of my coat, my jeans, my pajamas, desperate to find a forgotten pill, an overlooked crumb.

Nothing.

Fuck.

I wish I'd searched Dr. Rush's pockets before we left his cottage, rooted around until I found my medication.

How could Amelia leave me here alone, without even saying goodbye? I chose her over freedom.

I have no right to be angry. With all that happened, of course she wasn't thinking about me. *Selfish*, just like Anne always said I was. Putting my needs before the family—moving to the wrong country, loving the wrong girl.

It's not selfish to want a life of your own, Harper once told me. She said, *Anne and your father are the greedy ones, asking you to put their needs first, to build your life around them.*

I direct some of my anger toward Dr. Mackenzie, for the way she said *Lord Edward,* for the way she was able to crouch beside Amelia when I couldn't. I send some to Dr. Rush, not only because of what he did to Amelia, but also because he locked me in my cottage, because he was pleased with the *progress* I was making, because, even now, he has the power to send me home to Anne with full marks or a failing grade.

My phone is ringing. I look at the screen, my hands slick with sweat, expecting to see Anne's name, ready to be scolded for embroiling myself in yet another problem for her to solve.

It's not Anne, but that bloody unknown number again.

I've had enough of this.

"Hello?" I answer roughly. I decide that this time, I will answer every question the journalist on the other end asks. They deserve some reward for their persistence.

A familiar voice, one I thought I'd never hear again, says my name softly.

65

Amelia Blue

Dr. Mackenzie stops abruptly at a narrow gap in the trees on either side of the driveway. Carefully tucked between evergreen foliage, perfectly hidden year-round, is a small parking lot. There are three black Range Rovers with tinted windows (one of them, I suppose, is the car that drove Edward and me here), but Dr. Mackenzie walks past them to open the door of a dark-green Suburu. She helps me heft my duffel bag into the back seat alongside a child's car seat. I see a handful of Cheerios scattered on the floor. Real Cheerios, I bet, not whatever organic alternative Dr. Mackenzie tried to feed me.

I sink into the passenger seat and close my eyes, running my fingers over the rough tan upholstery. It's so cold that I can see my breath. Dr. Mackenzie puts the car in drive, pausing to type a combination into a keypad at the gate so that it swings open.

"How did Sonja get out?" I ask.

"Apparently she bribed her housekeeper to give her the combination," Dr. Mackenzie explains. "They had some kind of arrangement."

Got someone looking for me, if you know what I mean.

I close my eyes. Should I go to the police with what I know? Andrew said that my word, his mother's word, would be worthless. Evelyn's notes might be useful; Andrew said they were protected, but medical records can be subpoenaed. There's also the police report Sonja found, further proof of Georgia's sobriety.

But all that proves is that she was sober for one night before she came to Rush's Recovery and appeared sober during treatment. Like Andrew said, plenty of addicts fall off the wagon after rehab.

"You can stay on my couch tonight." Dr. Mackenzie's offer shakes me from my thoughts, and I blink my eyes open. "It's not exactly professional, but technically you're not my patient anymore." She shifts her gaze from the road long enough to smile at me.

By the time my mother died, she hadn't put out an album or had a successful tour in years. She popped up on celebrity worst-dressed lists, was included in only the D-list nineties tribute events. Nonetheless, her funeral was packed. Strangers I'd never met hugged me, murmuring about her magnetism like they assumed I'd recognized it, apologizing for my loss like they knew what I'd be missing without her.

I can't imagine who would come to my funeral had Andrew hurt me the way he hurt her. It occurs to me that Andrew wasn't putting me in any more danger than I've been putting myself in for years, so startling I almost jump from my seat. I could just as easily become another statistic, a victim of the second most deadly mental-health issue.

The streets are quiet, dusted with salt, the snowfall not much more than a flurry now. Most of the houses we pass are closed up for winter, forgotten nine months of the year. I try to imagine summertime, bright skies and long days, crowded streets and the smell of barbeque in the air, but I can't see past the cold and dark.

As the car warms, the snow in my hair melts to water, dripping onto my shoulders, soaking through my sweater. The car's wipers move back and forth with a steady hum. The first time I saw snow was from the window of Georgia's hotel room at a tour stop in Michigan when I was eight. I left the room, made my way downstairs, and built a snowman in the courtyard of the hotel. I didn't have a proper coat then, either. One of the hotel's employees brought me inside, soaked and shivering, and gave me watery hot chocolate from a machine meant to serve bad coffee to business travelers. I closed my eyes when I sipped it, imagining my mother had made it, along with homemade whipped cream. But when I opened my eyes, there was only the concerned stranger sitting across from me in the hotel lobby and the certainty that my mother was passed out somewhere in the rooms above us.

When I got back to LA, Naomi bought me a coat. I realize now that Georgia must've told her I needed one. Had she been watching me, after all?

Dr. Mackenzie pulls into a short driveway. In the glow from her head-lights, I see a white clapboard house. There's a red plastic sled in front of the garage door, small footprints in the snow, and a shovel leaning against the front porch. Someone let the child who lives here stay up late for the snowfall, then shoveled the driveway so Dr. Mackenzie could pull in. The front porch light is on.

I wonder how long it's been since Dr. Mackenzie came home. Surely, not since I arrived at the center. I imagine her texting someone earlier, ex-plaining that she was finally coming home.

Dr. Mackenzie holds a hand to her lips as she leads the way inside. "My wife and son are sleeping," she whispers. For the first time, I notice a slim gold ring on her left finger.

"What's your son's name?" I don't think I've asked Dr. Mackenzie a question about her life before.

"Milo."

"Is Mackenzie your first or last name?" I ask.

"My last name. My married name, more precisely. My first name's An-nisa," she answers.

Dr. Mackenzie spreads a sheet and blanket over a beat-up brown couch in the center of the living room. The house smells like burning wood and the remnants of whatever was made for dinner, hints of garlic and onion. It doesn't smell rotten or cloying, but inviting. After my grandmother cooks, the kitchen smells like cleaning supplies.

Dr. Mackenzie brings out a first aid kit and rubs alcohol over the cuts from the shattered window on my fingers and wrist. It stings but I can see now that they're just scratches, barely bleeding anymore.

"We'll talk in the morning," Dr. Mackenzie says. She doesn't offer to stay up all night if I want to speak now, like she would at the center. Here, in her home, she's no longer at my beck and call.

I lie on the couch, my mind racing. They killed my mother. They cov-ered it up. They stole her song. I wait for the hunger to kick in, to lead me to the kitchen to binge on Annisa Mackenzie's food.

Much to my surprise, my eyelids grow heavy, and I sink into a deep, dreamless sleep, my mother's notebook still tucked into my waistband.

66

Lord Edward

"Hello," I say again. It isn't a question this time. And yet, I've never been less certain of myself. Maybe I ought to hang up. I promised not to communicate with her again.

And yet—can it really be her?

I wait, hoping she'll repeat my name.

Good lord, I want to hear her say my name.

"Edward."

There's tenderness in her voice.

How can that be?

"Edward, it's me. It's Harper."

There's a lump in my throat that suddenly hurts as much as my leg. I try to swallow, but I can't.

Why is she calling at this hour?

She must think I'm in London. Anne's plan to get me here without the paparazzi catching wind of it was effective, after all.

"Edward, can you hear me?"

She sounds healthy. She sounds strong.

I nod, though of course she can't see me. It's all I can manage.

"Edward, I've been trying to reach you for over a month."

She's been *awake* for over a *month*?

"They told me—my parents said—that you didn't want to hear from me. They said you changed your number. They changed *my* number."

She thinks *I* don't want to talk to *her*?

"I know you must be furious with me. I understand if you don't want to talk to me. The other night, you hung up as soon as you heard my voice."

The other night? The night I almost OD'd. Before Amelia got to me, I picked up the phone. But at the sound of Harper's voice, all I heard was screaming, crying, sounds from the moment the car spun out of control and there was nothing I could do to stop it.

"Please give me a few minutes. Let me apologize, and then you can go back to hating me for the rest of your life."

The shock of her words shakes the lump from my throat. *She* wants to apologize to *me*? I feel as though she's speaking a language I don't understand.

"Why did you take the fall for me?" she asks. "Why didn't you tell them the truth?"

The truth?

The truth.

I can see it, hear it, feel it: our argument over my family; my weight in the driver's seat; Harper yelling that she wouldn't get in the car with me, I wasn't okay to drive; my slamming the car door shut and stomping to the passenger side, my final steps on two feet; later, reaching for the steering wheel and slamming on the brake only to find that there was no wheel in front of me, no pedals beneath me.

Relief makes my entire body shake.

"My parents assumed you were the one driving," she explains. "After I told them what really happened—I thought the police would question me, but they never did. I waited for your family to launch a lawsuit or something. Eventually, my mom let something slip about a deal they'd made. She said it was better this way, insisted your family had resources to protect you that we didn't have. I couldn't reach you, but I finally spoke to Anne. She said cutting off contact was your idea."

Anne knew I wasn't the one driving.

Instead of telling me, she sent me here.

"You saved my life," Harper says. "Dragging me from the car. How did you do that with your leg injured like it was?"

It had to have been Anne who told Harper about my leg.

"I needed to talk to you one last time, to tell you how sorry I am."

I sink onto the bed. I feel like a little kid who's run around in circles and abruptly stopped. It's as though, for months, the world has been spinning and now it's finally set itself to right.

"I don't hate you," I manage finally.

"You don't?"

I look at my hands. I can still feel the silkiness of Harper's blond hair between my fingers. I can see her dancing in her underwear across the kitchen of my Tribeca apartment, her bare feet slapping against the hardwood.

"Would you let me visit you?" Harper asks. It sounds like she's crying. "I'll fly to London, Scotland, wherever you are. I need to see for myself that you're okay."

I pause. "I'm not in the UK."

"Where are you?"

I could lie. Let her think we're thousands of miles apart. That's certainly what Anne would want me to do.

"New York."

"New York?" Harper echoes. "Where? I'll get in a cab now."

The idea that I could see her in a few hours sends a rush of joy through me. Harper would come if I asked.

My hands tremble such that I nearly drop the phone. I prop myself upright against the bed's headboard. I imagine Harper's head on my shoulder, just like it used to be, but so much is different now. I reach down and undo the fastening that secures my prosthetic.

I hear Anne's voice, loud and clear: *You wouldn't have wanted Harper to be a caretaker for the rest of her life, would you?*

She made a *caretaker* sound like a terrible word. Certainly, she made it sound like I'd never be able to take care of myself again. What reason had I to disbelieve her? I'd never taken care of myself *before*.

I hang up.

67

Amelia Blue

"Wake up, missus." The words sound thick, far away. "It's breakfast time."

I open my eyes groggily and find myself face-to-face with a pair of thick-rimmed wraparound yellow glasses.

I blink until I'm able to focus on the little boy behind the lenses. He looks about three or four, and when he smiles, I can see some of his chewed-up breakfast in his mouth. He holds out a piece of dry cereal from a plastic bowl in his hands, his face open and expectant. I part my lips, and he slides the cereal into my mouth.

He feeds me another piece, humming along to a made-up tune, "Breakfast time."

"Sorry 'bout that," Dr. Mackenzie says. I stand and see her in the kitchen. She's dressed in sweats, her braids loose down her back. The crisp white blouses and cashmere wraps she wore at the center, I understand now, were a uniform, just like the black scrubs Maurice and Izabella wore. "My wife left for work a while ago, but our day-care center's closed because of the weather. I wanted to let you sleep in, but Milo had other ideas."

"Milo's a smart kid," I say. Before I can fold the blanket and sheets on the couch, Milo climbs into the warm space my body left behind. He turns on the TV and expertly finds *Sesame Street*. The sound of sweet, silly music fills the room. He leaves his cereal bowl, its contents half-eaten, on the coffee table, as though he's forgotten about it completely.

I recall what Dr. Mackenzie said, that children of narcissists don't know there's a place in between, a middle ground between selfishness and self-erasure. I never understood that hunger, too, has a middle ground.

My former doctor gestures for me to sit at the kitchen table across from her. "How'd you sleep?"

"Better than I expected."

"Do you want to tell me what happened last night?"

I'm filled with gratitude that she didn't ask me hours ago, simply brought me here without insisting on an explanation.

"You're not my therapist anymore, you know."

Dr. Mackenzie takes a sip of coffee and smiles. "Old habits."

I press my hands against my empty belly, no food, no baby to fill it. I begin to wrap two fingers from my left hand around my right wrist, noticing the scratches from shattered glass turning into scabs. I drop my hands abruptly.

"Can I tell you something?" I ask. Dr. Mackenzie nods. "I always blamed my mother for my eating disorder. I thought anorexia was a reaction to her, like I was trying to make order out of her chaos."

Mommy issues, Andrew said last night.

"You don't think that now?"

"Now I think—if that's true, then why didn't it get better after she died?"

"Some ED researchers believe people with anorexia long to stay small because they're phobic not about fat but about adulthood."

Hasn't that theory been debunked by now? "You think my anorexia is just a bad case of Peter Pan syndrome?" I ask drily. "My childhood wasn't exactly easy. I hardly think I would've tried to prolong it."

"Maybe not. Or maybe you were desperate to be parented, and part of you believed you could give your mother infinite chances to try again. Maybe you even imagined that if you made yourself small enough, you could become the little girl who'd had both her parents."

"That'd be quite a feat of magical thinking—believing that if I could transcend the fact that both my parents are dead."

"One could argue that believing you could live without nutrients is quite a feat of magical thinking."

I think of the lullaby on my dad's last album, the song Georgia insisted they wrote together. I never believed her, because it was about a desperately desired child, the words of a parent who had so many plans.

Was I trying to be the perfect little girl they wrote about, longing for the fantasy of parenthood they portrayed? Did I want it as badly as they did?

"I really hated that place," I say finally. "Other treatment centers don't pretend to be anything other than what they are. But it's like Rush's Recovery wants you to forget why you're really there."

"I know what you mean." Dr. Mackenzie smiles.

For a moment, the only sound is Milo's show in the background. I take in the dishes crowding the sink, the scribbled drawings on the refrigerator door.

"How'd you end up working there anyway?"

"Honestly?" Dr. Mackenzie asks, and I nod. "They offered more money than anyplace else, and I have a pile of student loans up to here." She holds her hand just beneath her chin. "And I thought, what does it matter whether the people I'm helping are rich or poor, as long as I'm helping them? Not that it has to be one or the other, but I got certified by working in a women's prison."

"Rush's Recovery must've been a culture shock."

"In some respects." She smiles wryly.

"Do you think you'll keep working there? When it opens again?"

Dr. Mackenzie moves her gaze from my face to the little boy in the living room. "My family and I live here, and it's not like there are a ton of places on this small island in need of therapists. But—Rush's Recovery never quite felt like the right fit for me. Andrew—Dr. Rush—his approach isn't quite conventional."

"No," I agree. My mouth tastes sour. "It's not."

Dr. Mackenzie puts her hands on her lap, pressing herself to stand. "We better get going if we're going to get you to the ferry in time to make your flight back home."

Home. To the house my grandmother mortgaged to the hilt.

Dr. Mackenzie, Milo, and I pile into my former doctor's Subaru. The snow on the sides of the road has melted to gray sludge.

Milo stays in the car as we dig my bags from the back, my mother's notebook now tucked neatly alongside my gum wrappers and cigarettes. Dr. Mackenzie hesitates like she's not sure whether to hug me goodbye, so I move to embrace her. Can't be more unprofessional than letting me sleep on her couch, letting her son feed me Cheerios. She holds me tight, the way only Naomi has ever held me. I feel a lump rise in my throat, homesick for my grandmother's touch, my house in the hills.

"I hope, I truly hope, that you find what you're looking for," Dr. Mackenzie says. "I'm sorry that Rush's Recovery couldn't give you what you needed."

I feel the weight of my mother's notebook in my bag. Maybe I'm leaving this island with exactly what I need.

68

Lord Edward

My sister picks up on the third ring.

"Yes?" she says, instead of hello.

"Why did you send me here?" I ask. After the call with Harper, I didn't fall asleep, but lay awake staring at the ceiling as the sun rose.

"You know why. It was to keep you out of trouble after you'd nearly killed a girl."

She lies so easily I can almost believe she's forgotten the truth. Perhaps that's what happens when you grow up in a family like ours.

"I wasn't the one driving that night." For once, I sound as reasonable, as in control, as she does. "Now tell me, why did you send me *here*? There are a million rehabs closer to home." She could've easily convinced Harper's parents that any of those places was better.

Anne doesn't hesitate before answering, doesn't weigh her options. When she speaks, her voice is clear, certain, and unapologetic.

"I thought if that place didn't jog your memory, nothing would."

I close my eyes. I can see Anne's assured gait: never rushed or harried, her shoulders back. She doesn't swing her arms or wave her hips. She moves precisely the way a woman like her is meant to, as though she's balancing a book on her head.

"So sending me here was some kind of test?"

"One you failed, apparently."

"Actually, Harper told me the truth."

Dad's gait is shorter, brisker. When he's angry, he hunches his shoulders, a man on a mission, walking with his eyes tilted toward the ground. When he's smiling in front of a crowd, he rolls his shoulders down.

"She contacted you?"

"Yes," I answer.

"Well then, she is officially in breach of contract."

Breach of contract? I practically hear Anne's smile. Harper's family will have to return whatever money Anne offered them.

"What's more," she continues, "we're under no obligation to conceal the fact that Harper was the one driving. I'll have the story leaked to one of the more reputable papers. Really, it's better this way. An American social climber to blame will garner more sympathy. We can get ahead of it if we manage it right."

"I'm not pressing charges."

Anne laughs. "It's not entirely up to you. I don't think the police will care that you don't want your ex-fling to get into trouble."

"She wasn't a fling."

"Edward, not this nonsense again."

She says it as though I'm a child begging to stay up past his bedtime.

"How could you let me believe I was the one driving?"

"You didn't want the world to know about your leg. This was the best way I could think to delay the story."

She makes it sound as though she did this entirely for my benefit, because I asked her to.

Of course, I want to be like those Invictus athletes, unashamed of my injury. Harper would say I've fallen for an ableist narrative about how our bodies are supposed to look, how they're supposed to function.

Perhaps I wanted to hide my injury because I still hoped I might become the man my father and sister want me to be; as though, if I managed myself just right, I could finally gain their approval.

But the man they want me to be wouldn't have fallen in love with Harper in the first place.

And I don't want to be someone who doesn't love Harper.

The Thief

He slings his guitar over his shoulder. It's been a while since he's performed at the open mic in town, and it's the dead of winter, so no one who matters will be there, but he has a plan, and this is its next step.

He's been patient, watching her work for weeks now, coaxing every lyric out of her mouth and onto the page.

After the incident with Joni Jewell—splashed across every tabloid cover, impossible to miss—he told his mother that *she* was their chance. Rehabilitate the baddest bitch in rock and roll, and the whole world—well, the right people within the world—would flock to Rush's Recovery.

He doesn't care—he's never cared—which of his parents get the center in the divorce. They've been at each other's throat for months, like the center is their baby, like King fucking Solomon needs to come along and cut it in half. He wonders—if he were under eighteen, would they fight for custody of him with quite the same fervor?

He doubts it. He's always been a disappointment: didn't get into the college they wanted, didn't pursue the career they approved of, in trouble through elementary school and high school. They'd been too distracted he thinks, all his life, by their own ambitions and their patients' struggles—complaints, really—to pay much attention to their son's.

None of it matters now that he's turned their precious center into a means to an end. He just had to stay on Evelyn's good side, persuade her to let him have the most menial of jobs—a cook for a woman who doesn't eat anything but candy, a fucking chipmunk could do it. He got the tattoo—*Never Settle*—as soon as he was certain she was coming. He pushed up his sleeve that first day to make sure she would see it.

It was his idea for his mom and the rest of the staff to call her Florence. Take her down a notch from the moment she arrived, make her vulnerable by calling her the name she'd probably barely heard since she was a child.

His parents went to school for years to get their degrees, but he understood what all their training never taught them: Baby someone enough, flirt with them so they feel important, praise them until they feel talented, and they'll give you anything you want. Give an addict alcohol while she's in rehab, and she'll love you forever, too grateful (and too loaded) to be suspicious.

He'd been planning to hit her up for connections and contacts, but it quickly became apparent she wasn't well-connected anymore, if she ever had been. So he shifted course—he's nothing if not adaptable—and now it's worked out better than he'd imagined. The song is more valuable than a handful of phone numbers and email addresses could ever be.

He knows the words by heart, better even than she does. Months from now, if she tries to release the song as her own, he'll have a roomful of witnesses who saw him perform it first. No one will believe her—even her own manager was quick to turn on her for a few bucks—and if there's a scandal, it will only help his rising star. Joni Jewell's simpering "Get Her Back" never would've hit number one if people didn't know it was about Georgia Blue. And now look at Joni: touring the world, sold-out shows, riding the wave of Georgia's infamy for all it's worth.

Later, the police will ask about the altercation at the bar, but no one will accuse him of wrongdoing. *She's* the crazy one, everyone knows, even people like his parents who disapprove of the word *crazy*.

In the months to come, he'll wonder if it might have been better if she'd lived. Without a scandal over who really wrote the song, he won't get the boost Joni Jewell got. His mother will know the truth, but she'll never tell. And if she does . . . well, he'll cross that bridge when he comes to it.

He'll keep the notebook, but its contents will be useless to him: songs about motherhood and daughterhood; songs about him; unfinished snippets of songs he can't pretend he wrote. He'll reread the pages sometimes, hoping inspiration might strike, but it never does. The record execs who embraced him for "Imposter Syndrome" will be quick to drop him when his sophomore efforts fall flat.

One-hit wonder, they'll say, *happens all the time.* He'll have to adapt all over again.

But right now, tonight, none of that has come to pass. He knows only that he's about to hit the stage with a surefire hit. And who can blame him for taking what he needs? He's not like the no-talent brats who spend their summers on the island, born with connections and silver spoons. They can barely drive the hundred-thousand-dollar cars they were given on their sixteenth birthdays, and they have the sort of parents who would finance a move to LA or Nashville if they asked, pay to put them in rooms with vocal coaches and stylists. They'd pick up their Grammys with tears in their eyes, thanking their mommies and daddies for so much support.

When he wins, he's not gonna thank anyone.

He has the syringe in his pocket. Gotta be prepared. Whatever it takes. *Georgia who?* they'll say. *Play that Andrew Rush song again.*

69

Georgia Blue

It's hard to stay awake, but even with my eyes closed, I can sense the light coming over the horizon when dawn arrives. I feel sand beneath me, rough and dirty. I smell the ocean. I hear the waves.

I should be angry. Angry that Andrew stole my song, shot me up with drugs, carried me out into the cold, left me here alone. He took my notebook, all the fragments I haven't finished. "Imposter Syndrome" and the song I wrote for him. The song I wrote for my little girl, the one that spilled out of me before Andrew shot me up with whatever is coursing through my system now.

But for once in my desperately angry life, I'm serene. Instead of thinking about Andrew and how much I want to punish him for what he did to me, I'm thinking about Amelia Blue.

Would she listen, if I sang to her? Maybe not. She's sick and tired of the sound of my voice. She thinks I talk too much, but there's so much I never told her.

Tonight, I tried to put everything I never said into that song. But now my brain is fuzzy and my notebook is gone. I struggle to remember the lyrics.

I want the sun to set over the ocean,
I need to get back to my side of the sea,
I can't spend another second
so far from the heart of me.

I'll write it all over again if I have to. I found the words once, I can find them a second time. I'll find them as many times as I need to, until Amelia Blue gets my message. Maybe every song I'll ever write for the rest of my life will be *that* song, over and over again. In my head, the chorus rises.

But I'm a Bad Mother,
They don't make 'em like me
No more
You deserve better than a
Bad Mother,
Baby Girl.

The second verse will tell her how deeply she was wanted, how much we'd hoped to protect her.

I want to walk the sand with your feet next to mine,
Want to tell you 'bout all the times,
Your daddy and I dreamed of you,
We wanted to give you such a sheltered life,
we were gonna do it right, us two.

I can hear my fears and apologies, my ache to be a good mother.

Sweet Girl,
Darling Pearl.
You see I hid the truth,
I didn't want you to know—
Why your good father had to go.
So I ran away,
Thought at least that way
I could be a
Good Mother.

In the state I'm in, I can't write or sing aloud, but somehow I can see the words of the bridge dancing across my brain.

I wanted so much, and I can't be sorry
for wanting so much,
that need came from inside me.

I wanted to be a star, shining bright,
wanted a man who lit up the night,
I wanted fame,
to win the game,
And I wanted to give you my own name.
I wanted it all, but never more
than I wanted to be your Good Mother,
Baby Girl.

The song won't have a catchy chorus or a bouncing melody. It will never be a hit like the singles Joni Jewell drops for her fans. But it's something true, and that's all I care about now.

Now I only want to tell you why I lied,
Why I didn't turn the tide.
I'm so sorry, Little Girl,
So sorry, Precious Pearl,
But I believe there's still time
Gonna do it right, gonna walk the line.

Like magic, I can *hear* my girl singing along. It's been so long since she's spoken to me, but I know her voice as well as my own. It's my favorite sound. I can still hear her begging me to take her to the beach like she did when she was very young.

I'll take you tomorrow, I said, confident that I had time for the right tomorrow to arrive.

I fight to stay awake. I don't want to miss a single syllable she has to say ever again.

Another voice, deep and thick with emotion, asks me, *Will she be all right?*

Scott sounds so close, so real, that if I could lift my hands, I would reach for him, across the veil that's separated us since he left. I thought my love could save him. I was wrong.

But it's not too late for our girl.

Gonna walk on the beach with your feet next to mine
My baby girl at my side
I'll tell you true, won't ever lie
Not a Bad Mother
But a good mother,
A good mother,
I'm a good mother.

Finally, I let myself sleep, the sound of my daughter's voice in my head like a lullaby.

70

Lord Edward

The world is sharper this morning. My leg aches, though to my surprise, it's not actually that much worse than when I was taking every pill I could get my hands on.

It's other things that feel different. My hands, shaking in my pockets. My eyes, sleep-deprived but clear. My sense of smell somehow more acute. Hunger in my belly, making me realize that for months now I've been eating simply because someone put a plate in front of me, not because I wanted food.

I drag my luggage into JFK, another weary traveler on his way. Around me are businesspeople walking determinedly toward their gates. Harried-looking parents clinging to their children's hands, worried they might lose them in the crowd. No private plane today. On short notice, Anne was unable to arrange it.

Just thinking my sister's name makes my stomach twist. I imagine Anne and my father, their heads bent close in the drawing room as they discuss their reasons not to tell me I wasn't the one driving.

It's for his own good.

Is it? How would they know what's good for me when they've never, not once, asked me what I want?

He'd never have gone to rehab if not for this arrangement.

Do they really care if I'm sober? I think Anne wouldn't mind if I woke up each day sloshed as long as I woke up on time.

This is the only way he'll come back home, marry an appropriate girl.

There's the truth. They wanted to control me.

I feel a rush of anger, but it's no longer directed at Amelia or Dr. Mackenzie or Dr. Rush.

I should, I suppose, be angry at Harper's parents, for keeping their end of Anne's arrangement even after they knew the truth of what happened that night. They would have let me live with terrible guilt for hurting their daughter, the woman I loved. But they thought they were protecting her.

Maybe it wasn't even *me* they were protecting Harper from—I always thought they liked me fine—or even prosecution for the accident she caused. Instead, maybe once they met Anne and saw what she was willing to do to keep up appearances, they wanted to keep their daughter as far from my family as humanly possible.

I don't suppose I can blame them for that.

Before Harper, I didn't think I had the right to be unhappy. Not only because of the privilege I was born into—though certainly that was part of it—but also because of the narratives woven around my family. Dad and Anne acted as though I ought to have been grateful that my mother left, like I had no right to miss a woman they found dreadful. Everyone I met respected my father, and it seemed my entire country adored my elegant, charitable sister. If they were disappointed in me, it was because I was failing to meet the high standards they set. If I didn't fit in, it was due to shortcomings on my part, not theirs.

I roll my shoulders down my back, sensing eyes on me. Across the terminal, a young woman is holding up her phone, pretending to take a selfie when really she's sneaking a picture of me. I imagine I can hear the whirring snaps of paparazzi cameras.

But I'm not angry at the fan, or the phantom paps, either. Today, my anger is directed only at two people.

I walk toward the first-class security line, fingering my passport, proof of my British citizenship, my family name. Lord Edward of Exeter, son of a duke, brother of a future duchess.

Son *of*, brother *of*; who am I alone?

Someone taps me on the back, shaking me from my mental fog. I think back to last night, lying in the snow, when Harper's phone call roused me. I might have gone on lying there forever had the phone not rung.

I turn, expecting to meet a stranger who's recognized me. Perhaps the girl taking fake selfies crossed the terminal to meet me. But an older man in a wrinkled suit simply asks, "Excuse me, but are you in line?"

I look at the security line in front of me, metal detectors and bored TSA agents. Beyond that, shops with row after row of magazines, tabloids filled with stories about people like me.

I imagine my face splashed across a cover, the headline reading: *Lord Edward's Untold Story*.

Much to my surprise, the idea doesn't fill me with shame. At once, I understand that I wanted to conceal the truth not because of my actual injury, but because of how it happened. I was ashamed of what I'd done.

But it turns out I didn't do it at all.

"Excuse me," the businessman prompts.

I move out of the man's way and pull my phone from my pocket, my fingers hovering over Harper's new number. I may not have been the one driving that night, but that doesn't mean I'm blameless.

Before I can make a call, my phone buzzes in my hand, once, twice, three times. I brace myself for a series of texts from Anne outlining her latest strategy to handle the press.

But the texts aren't from Anne. They're from Amelia.

I need some fresh air, so I pocket my phone and walk with my new lopsided gait toward the sliding glass door into the cold. There's so much noise: cab drivers vying for space, families saying hello or goodbye to their loved ones. Amelia told me once that she loves the airport because everyone there has somewhere they need to be, some mission they're undertaking.

I take a long breath. I've waited long enough. It's time for me to go home.

71

Amelia Blue

Somewhere over Middle America, I hold my mother's notebook tightly. My muscles are sore, my body aching, as though I ran a marathon last night. I gaze out the window, studying the cloud cover like I'm going to be tested on it later.

My mother's file is probably already back in place alongside the others in the cabinets beside the gym like it's nothing special, as if she's no different from any of the center's other patients. For all Andrew knows, I went straight to the local police station this morning. He surely realized that a misplaced file would be suspicious. Easier to say (should the police come asking questions) what he said last night: Plenty of addicts lose their sobriety after rehab. He is, after all, an expert in the subject.

Perhaps he spent the night on the floor in his office, woke up bleary-eyed, his head sore where Edward hit it with a bat. Maybe his mother offered him an ice pack, but he shoved it away because he didn't want Evelyn taking care of him, her teeth stained with red wine, her eyes bloodshot with a hangover.

I agree with Andrew about one thing: The word of his impaired mother and Georgia's mentally ill daughter probably isn't enough to make the police open an investigation after all these years. At least leaving Andrew and Evelyn together on that island feels like some kind of punishment, though it's certainly not the justice Georgia deserves.

I shift in my narrow seat, twisting one leg over the other. I don't wish I'd taken Georgia's file. Edward was right. There was nothing for me in Evelyn's notes. They didn't have miraculous answers, only a flawed woman's rather mundane observations.

Moreover, I'm through listening to what other people said about my mother. The press claimed to be experts, and they lied. That place, that was supposed to save her, killed her. I want, for the first time in my life, to hear what *she* had to say.

So I open Georgia's notebook, focusing on the familiar quirks in her handwriting. For years, I thought (*I knew*) she was too messed up to concentrate on anything beyond her next high, but she never stopped songwriting.

There is so much I don't know.

I reach into my bag, digging past the packs of gum and cigarettes, and pull out my phone, log on to the plane's Wi-Fi, and pull up Sonja's profile. I want to learn about the Georgia *she* knows.

Sonja's most recent post is dated last night. After she read the police report showing that Georgia was sober when she attacked Joni Jewell, sick of the rumors and lies that had dogged my mother's career and determined to remind fans that Georgia was the reason Shocking Pink had any success to begin with, Sonja pretended to be in need of a digital detox and booked a stay at Rush's Recovery. She dyed her hair blond and had a fur coat custom made to look nearly identical to the one Georgia had been wearing the night she disappeared. Last night, Sonja hitchhiked to the Shelter Shack, the last place the public saw Georgia. At the time, witnesses said Georgia had her guitar with her, like she'd been planning to perform.

Sonja interviewed the bartender. She tracked down the woman, a teenager at the time, who picked up my hitchhiking mother and her guitar.

Andrew thought Sonja wanted to experience what my mother did, a *macabre pilgrimage*: stay in Georgia's cottage, have her rooms cleaned by the same housekeeper, hitchhike into town just like Georgia had years before. He thought Sonja was no different from people who lay flowers outside the Dakota to honor John Lennon, or who visit Jim Morrison's grave at Père-Lachaise.

But Sonja wasn't simply following in my mother's footsteps. In the face of Shocking Pink's so-called reunion tour, Sonja wanted to remind the world that Georgia Blue ached to perform for her fans right up until the moment she died. She risked her life for it, Sonja says, sneaking out of rehab for one more chance to sing.

The truth this time.

I never knew (or more accurately, never cared to know) how much my mother loved being onstage, singing for strangers, listening to them sing her own words back to her. I finally understand why she was constantly writing, singing, marking her body with words for strangers to read. Maybe I'd have known it sooner if I hadn't been so determined not to hear what her fans had to say.

I bite my thumbnail, guilt twisting in my stomach. *I* should've been the one asking questions, not last night, but immediately after Georgia died, when everyone's memories were fresh and clear. Naomi and I should've insisted on an autopsy, rather than take the coroner at his word, then cremating Georgia's remains. (What Georgia wanted, Naomi said, even though it's against Jewish tradition.) If the police refused to investigate, I should've tracked down not only the bartender and the driver but also the local police chief who got the call that she was dead, the housekeeper who cleaned her cottage—*anyone* who might have come into contact with her during her stay on the island. Who knows what they might have seen, what their stories, woven together, might have revealed?

Instead, I came to the island and searched only for answers about my mother's disease, as though nothing else about her mattered. Did I forget—or did I never know to begin with (yet another gap in the things I thought I knew)—that there was more to her than her illness?

Maybe I forgot there's more to me than mine, too.

The flight attendant walks down the aisle, handing out breakfast. I place my hand over my heart, feeling its beat. It wasn't Georgia but *me* who was cavalier with the rules of life and death, neglecting the responsibility of having a body.

When the attendant gets to my row, I don't pretend to sleep. I accept the tray she offers. Airplane food isn't exactly appetizing. No one would blame me if I shoved the tray away, refused to eat, spat each morsel from my mouth. I think of Milo and the cereal he slipped between my lips this morning.

I open my phone's texts, scroll to the name I've been avoiding.

I'm sick, Jonah. Maybe you knew that already, but I never actually told you.

I steady my hands, then type, *When I get home, I'm entering treatment.*

Slowly, I open a shiny foil packet of butter, spread it over a slice of crumbly bread, so stale it practically dissolves in my mouth. The butter is the texture of glue. A day ago, Maurice would have cooked me anything I asked for with a smile, but today my arms ache where he gripped them. I take three bites. I feel the calories enter my bloodstream, consider rushing to the bathroom. I tighten my seat belt, stare at my phone, and start a new text thread.

I'm sorry I left without saying goodbye, I write to Edward. *I have so much to tell you.*

I return to Sonja's profile, balancing my phone on top of Georgia's notebook. After a childhood growing up in magazines and blogs, I kept my social media accounts private, anonymous, using them for ED tips and not much else. I don't have a legion of devoted followers.

But Sonja does. More than one hundred thousand people follow her.

Maybe the truth about what happened to Georgia won't be proven with subpoenaed records and testimony under oath. And maybe Sonja, even with her many followers, can't keep Shocking Pink from going on tour without Georgia. But, I think as I clutch the notebook tight, there's another way to get justice for my mother.

It won't be another story.

Before I can send a DM, my phone vibrates in my hand. It's a text from Edward, two small words.

Me too, he says.

I turn back to Mom's notebook. By the time I land, I'll know every song inside by heart.

Let me tell you what I know now.

She was singing to me all along.

@ dismoi • August 16, 2025

Spotted: Lord Eddie in NYC with Stunning Blonde—again!

Our favorite British export was spotted in New York's West Village Wednesday. Edward braved the August heat, looking cool and casual in shorts and a collared-tee while he tried to block the paps from taking a picture of the stunning blonde on his arm, wearing a slinky slip dress (looked vintage to us) accessorized with a messy ponytail.

THE
SHELTER ISLAND
REPORTER

JANUARY 7, 2026

RENOWNED REHAB SHUTTERED

DESPITE A COURT RULING THERE'S INSUFFICIENT PROOF THAT HE STOLE FROM ONE OF THE CENTER'S FIRST PATIENTS, OWNER LOSES IN THE COURT OF PUBLIC OPINION.

ENTERTAINMENT
EXTRA

FROM BEYOND THE GRAVE, ROCK'S BAD GIRL KEEPS DRAMA ALIVE

Despite months of negotiations, the remaining members of Shocking Pink will not perform at the Georgia Blue tribute concert next month. In other news, Georgia's never-before-heard final song, "The Good Mother," will be performed by Joni Jewell, causing some fans to call for a boycott while others cheer the new material. Will the Georgia-drama ever end? Amelia Blue says, "Mom wouldn't have it any other way."

Acknowledgments

Thank you to Pete Knapp, Stuti Telidevara, Danielle Barthel, Abigail Koons, Angela Lee, and all of the wizards at Park, Fine & Brower. I'm grateful every day to have your brilliant team in my corner.

Thank you to my wonderful editor Sarah Grill, and to everyone at Emily Bestler Books and Atria who helped make this book a reality: Emily Bestler, Abel Berriz, Maudee Genao, Jimmy Iacobelli, Lara Jones, Laura Levatino, Paige Lytle, Debbie Norflus, Laura Petrella, Shelby Pumphrey, Vanessa Silverio. I'm so glad this story found its home with all of you.

Thank you Berni Barta and Austin Denesuk at CAA. Thanks also to Chlöe Berlin, Rachel Feld, Olivia Griffiths, Danielle Rollins, Haley Scull, Jenny Wikoff.

And once again, thank you JP Gravitt, for everything.